THINKWAVE

THINKWAVE

BOOK III: Draw of the Narciss Glass

R. DUNCAN WILLIAMS

ISBN: 9781081152130 (paperback)

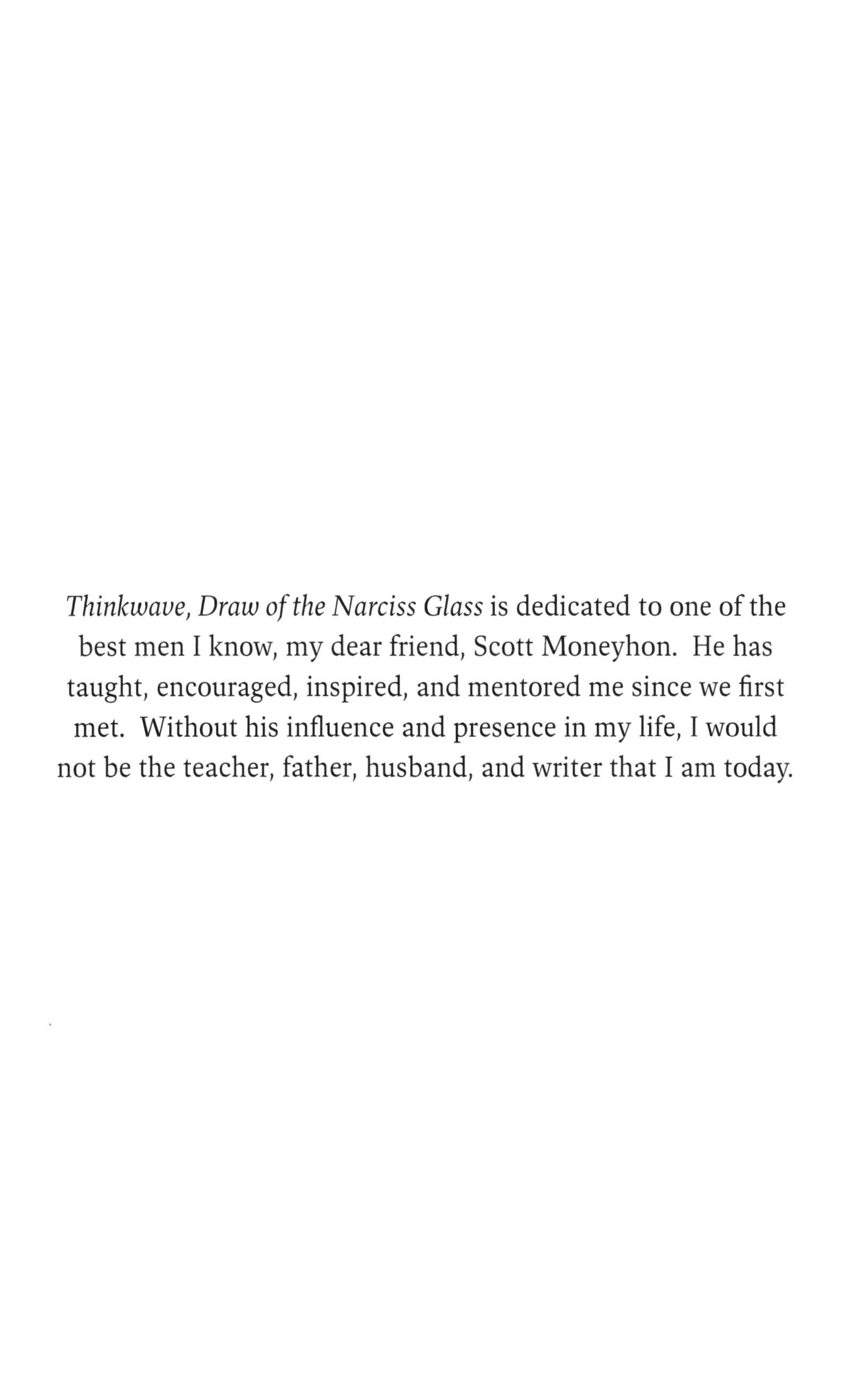

Thinkwave, Draw of the Narciss Glass is dedicated to one of the best men I know, my dear friend, Scott Moneyhon. He has taught, encouraged, inspired, and mentored me since we first met. Without his influence and presence in my life, I would not be the teacher, father, husband, and writer that I am today.

PROLOGUE

Fromp and Akeila were already atop the reflection. Each latched on to a piece of it with their teeth, and with a strong yank, flipped the image over like a manhole cover. Underneath was a deep black hole, and at its very bottom was what appeared to be a small blue and green marble.

Madora was already running to the opening. "EVERYONE, NOW! BEFORE IT CLOSES!" she yelled as she jumped through, falling down and back, to a planet below and before

Harvey was the last to jump. As he descended through, he wondered if this mad-capped adventure to save Ecclon and all worlds could possibly get any more bizarre. Moments later, he entered the atmosphere of 1930's earth, freefalling toward a small town in southern California, where he would soon learn the answer to his question.

INNOCENCE

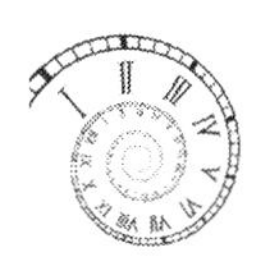

1

Rapidly approaching terminal velocity, the group freefell toward earth without any means of braking its descent. The soon-to-be-felt impact would end both the group and a quest that had only just begun

Moments prior, Harvey, Sheef, Madora, Gwen, and the two dogs, Fromp and Akeila, had narrowly escaped the Phantasian alive, and surprisingly, still in one piece. They had avoided death by machine gun bullet, geometric rearrangement, man-eating shark, and pirate sword blade.

But now, after all of their hair-raising death dodges, after Grauncrock and his Vapid Lord were submerged under billions of gallons of seawater and the group had dropped through a portal on the back of a Harvey-imagined blue whale in order to travel back to 1930's Hollywood to destroy the Narciss Glass, it seemed that the force of gravity would be their final undoing.

Sheef shook his wind-whipped head back and forth, unwilling to accept this as their fate. It was inconceivable to him that the Unseen would allow them to make it this far, only to die by impact.

Harvey had a very similar thought only seconds before, but unlike Sheef's, his thought wasn't left wondering. Yet again, Harvey had an idea. While in the Phantasian, he was able to manipulate matter and create new realities. "Perhaps," he thought to himself, "some of that Phantasian 'magic' is still with me."

Harvey looked over to Sheef, who was about thirty feet away and below him, and attempted to scream that he had an idea to stop their fall. But due to the fact that his face and body were lying flat and parallel to the earth below, as soon as he opened his mouth, hurricane-force winds rushed in, expanding his cheeks like a puffer fish.

Sheef had been watching Harvey, and it appeared to him that Harvey was about to yell something when his cheeks suddenly bulged to chipmunk proportions. His own body was perpendicular to the ground below, so that when he opened his mouth to shout "what", the words were viciously grabbed by the streaking winds and hurled high into the stratosphere. There would be no verbal communication between the two.

If they hadn't lost their backpacks with the Kreen nectar when their rowboat sank in the last Phantasian movie world, then with only one quick swig they would be able to communicate telepathically. Even so, with less than a minute before their fall dead-ended, there probably wouldn't have been time to hatch any type of plan.

Fortunately for everyone, Harvey already had a plan of his own, and it involved the fluff and puff of a large cumulus cloud quickly rising up to meet him.

"Soft as cotton and flexible as Silly Putty," Harvey thought to himself as he began to desperately imagine.

The group hit the cloud, continuing their lightning-fast descent. And just when Harvey despairingly concluded that no Phantasian magic had traveled back with him, his descent dramatically slowed.

The deceleration was jolting, and very soon the entire group had come to a full and complete stop. When Harvey looked down, he saw that they had not exited the cloud, but were still in a portion of it that had stretched downward like a trampoline mat, one hundred feet below the base.

With befuddlement coloring her face, Madora made brief eye contact with Sheef and Harvey. Gwen wore an expression of profound joy and wonder, while Fromp and Akeila tilted their puzzled heads in opposite directions.

The suspension of motion only lasted a second or two before everyone was violently flung heavenward. Like a crazed, out-of-control elevator rocketing toward the top of a skyscraper, the group soared back through the cloud, flying clear hundreds of feet above the fluff and the puff.

When gravity once again reasserted itself, they fell back into the cloud. This time, though, they didn't stretch below its base, but only sank down twenty feet before being gently tossed back into the air.

Fromp spread his legs wide and excitedly "woofed" to Akeila, who performed a graceful back flip before replying with a bark of her own. There were five lesser and lower bounces before the group came to a rest.

Sheef landed flat on his back and was attempting to sit up,

which was proving to be a very difficult feat to accomplish on such a cushiony surface, when he shouted to Harvey, “Don’t know exactly what you did to this cloud, but once again, quick and nice thinking!”

“I quite agree, Harvey. Great thinking, which has momentarily saved us,” said Madora as she attempted to locate her breath.

“Momentarily?” asked Sheef.

“Yes,” replied Madora, panic edging its way in, “Harvey’s rewriting of the cloud into something substantial enough to break our fall and support our weight is only temporary. Unfortunately, the influence of the Phantasian fades within minutes of one’s return to earth.”

“But that would mean . . .” Harvey said as the density of the cloud suddenly lessened and everyone dropped down a few feet, so that only their upper bodies were visible.

“Exactly,” said Madora, finishing Harvey’s thought. “Once the cloud returns to nothing but minuscule water droplets, our freefall to earth will resume.”

“Then there’s only one way out of here” said Sheef. “Fromp has to open a warp hole to Millud’s office where we saw the little weasel working before we jumped through the portal. And fast!”

Sheef called to Fromp, who responded by clumsily lumbering toward him through a substance that was quickly changing. The cloud had begun to liquefy, so that moving through it was like moving through an enormous bowl of vanilla pudding. When Fromp had slogged close enough to make eye contact with Sheef, the warp-hound received an image of

Millud's office, and he immediately attempted to open a warp hole by turning a speedy tight circle, but try as he might, he couldn't find enough traction on the gooey cloud to complete even one rotation, and like being in quicksand, the more he moved, the deeper into the pudding-like substance he sank.

"Fromp can't get any traction!" shouted Sheef. "We'll have to create a solid surface for him. Everyone gather around me. Lie down on your stomachs next to each other. We'll make a human platform for Fromp to turn on."

Even though no one was more than ten feet away from Sheef, moving through the cloud, which now offered the support and resistance of a milkshake, was time-consuming, for the only way to move through it was by swimming motion.

The effect of Harvey's Phantasian-induced thought upon the cloud was waning much too rapidly, and Sheef knew that at any given moment, the cloud would revert to its original non-supportive state, which is why he ordered Fromp to begin rotating even before everyone was in position.

Grunts and moans were forcefully expelled from both men and women under the unrelenting thumps of Fromp's two hundred-pound-plus frame. As the warp-hound picked up rotational speed, the rhythm of heavy-pounding paw upon human back and leg became a rolling blur of sound.

And just when Harvey felt that his back would snap if the abuse continued, the thumping pressure vanished. Relief from the tortuous weight upon flesh was evident on everyone's face.

"Where's Fromp? What happened?" asked Gwen, who still viewed everything through an innocent lens, experiencing whatever came to her as an innocuous game devoid of any injurious or deadly peril.

Madora tilted her head upward. Five feet above their prostrate bodies was a swirling vortex of indigo.

"It looks like Fromp spun so rapidly in creating the warp hole that the entire swirling mass lifted into the air like a helicopter," answered Sheef.

Breathless from Fromp's back trampling, Madora replied, "I'm glad he's not pouncing on me any longer, but how are supposed to get up and into the warp hole? If we try to stand up, we'll only sink down in the cloud."

Harvey was just about to reply when something walloped him on the side of his head. He turned to determine the wallop's origin but observed nothing but cloud and sky. However, when he looked in the opposite direction, he clearly saw a large indigo tail swinging like a jungle vine away from him.

Reaching its motion apex, the tail slowed and then briefly hesitated, pausing in midair as if to consider its next directional move before gliding backward. Harvey realized that an escape from the impending fall would literally soon be within his reach.

He shouted to the others to hold on tightly to one another.

Madora was in the process of forming the "w" of the word "why" with her lips when Harvey grabbed hold of the tail, roughly pulling him and three other humans off the cloud.

As Harvey clung like a barnacle to the furry swinging vine, he was afraid that Fromp would be pulled down by the combined weight of the four humans, but when he looked up, he realized that there was no need to fear. Fromp was no longer spinning circles. Once the warp hole had opened, he had anchored his front paws over the top edge and let his tail drop down. Akeila had somehow made it up also and was hanging in like manner next to him.

Harvey, as it turned out, had taken hold of the tail not a moment too soon, because seconds after, the effects of the Phantasian vanished, and the cloud reverted to water vapor.

Fromp's tail stretched and dangled wildly thousands of feet above the trees and grass below. Unfortunately, Harvey's grip began to slip. The warp-hound must've felt the slippage because he immediately hooked the end of his tail, allowing Harvey to lock his arms around it and to provide his hands with a much-needed rest.

But even this securer hold wouldn't last very long under the weight of the group and the erratic motions of the tail. Harvey's forearms were throbbing and pleading for release. Beads of sweated stress surfaced and wobbled about his arms and hands, further weakening his tail-hold.

Fromp let loose a piercing howl, and somehow Harvey understood that it was the warp-hound's way of telling him to summon all of his remaining strength for one final, solid and secure hold. Harvey squeezed his arms tightly together, locking his fingers around his biceps.

It was fortunate that Fromp had given a warning yelp, for his upward tail yank was sudden and jolting. The warp-hound, though, didn't need to yank Harvey very high. After rising only three feet, he was caught in the warp hole's pull, and he and the others were vacuumed up and away.

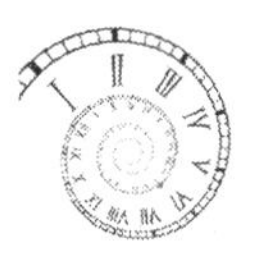

2

Harvey wished that for just once, he might exit a warp hole smoothly and gently land — perhaps feet first — upon a surface soft enough to welcomingly absorb and gracefully accent his arrival. Such an exit and landing, however, would have to wait.

The warp hole opened up about four feet off the floor in a large, wood-paneled office. A ponderous desk heavily reposed on the far side of the office. Affixed to the flanking walls were shelves holding hundreds of metal canisters of film, and on the wall opposite the desk, hung an eight-foot framed painting. It was a gaudily done portrait of Millud, the thief who had stolen the Narciss Glass and the man the group had traveled back in time to find. He was also the one presently seated at the desk.

The group exited the warp hole directly above Millud's head. Four humans and two dogs shot out of the portal like B.B.'s from a shotgun barrel, scattering in different directions.

Sheef and Madora were the first ones out, angling away from

one another and directly into the two shelves. Upon impact, the four shelves on both walls came crashing down, the metal canisters loudly clanging together like dropped trash can lids.

Harvey flew out next. His flight was higher, with a trajectory straight across the room. Unfortunately, the height of his flight path put him on a collision course with a large ceiling fan in the middle of the office.

The impact violently dislodged the fan and a fair chunk of ceiling plaster. Harvey's forward momentum was redirected downward, landing him atop a small coffee table. The legs of the table snapped like toothpicks with the tabletop splitting in half.

Gwen was the only one who wasn't bruised or cut during her exit. She emerged at a slight angle, which allowed her to fall upon the cushions of a teal-colored couch adjacent to the now-destroyed coffee table.

Fromp and Akeila's path was similar to that of Harvey's, but with no fan to obstruct their flight, they made it to the other side of the room, hitting the dead center of Millud's portrait. Their crash was so forceful that they broke through the canvas, paneling, and plaster of the wall.

A few more chunks of ceiling fell onto the carpet, and the sides of the picture frame collapsed inward upon one another before tumbling to the floor. The sound of metal shuffling upon metal echoed throughout the office as Sheef and Madora attempted to unbury themselves from piles of broken shelving and canisters.

Harvey lay in the crevice of the cracked coffee table, moaning and surveying his body for any broken bones, while Fromp and Akeila climbed out of the wall crater they had created.

Millud, meanwhile, was cowering under his desk, which he had ducked under when the chaos in his office first erupted. And though he could clearly see the effects of the group's calamitous arrival, he was unable to perceive the true cause.

Prior to the group warping to the Phantasian, Madora had said that if they accessed the past through a character Millud had portrayed in one of the Phantasian movie worlds, then they would be undetectable to Millud when they traveled to earth's past.

Madora had explained how humans are all moving through time at set speeds, but that no two humans are ever moving at exactly the same speed. The speed difference, though infinitesimally small, allows humans to see and hear one another. However, if one human, Harvey for example, was to increase or slow his speed to match that of someone else, something interesting would occur. Harvey would be able to see and hear the other person while remaining invisible and silent to him or her. She then informed everyone that it was for this very reason that they needed to travel back to 1930's earth from the Phantasian, via a portal opened by Millud while acting in one of his movies. Were this to occur, as it did, they would drop into his life traveling at exactly the same speed, resulting in Millud being completely blind and deaf to their presence, even when occupying the very same room. This is why Millud only saw collapsing shelves and falling ceiling fans, not flailing and flying human and animal.

When Millud tentatively poked his head out from under the desk like a spooked turtle reemerging from its shell, there was only one reasonable assumption for him to make: Once again, Hollywood, California, had been struck by a substantial earthquake.

Once Millud was certain that the shaking was over, he slowly stood up and walked to the middle of his office. He stopped a foot or two away from Harvey's feet. To his right and left, Sheef and Madora were still sitting amongst piles of broken shelving.

Harvey and Sheef were frozen in exposed fear. At that moment they failed to remember what Madora had taught them about Millud not being able to detect their presence. They believed that they were clearly visible and thus remained silent and motionless.

Just then, Gwen, who was sitting upright on the couch, stood up, walked over to Millud, and warmly introduced herself. Millud failed to react with even the slightest blink. When Gwen introduced herself a second time, he suddenly jumped backward, but not in response to Gwen's greeting. A piece of ceiling plaster the size of a pizza had fallen off, landing directly in between Millud and Gwen. Before Gwen could make a third introduction, Madora interjected with an explanation.

"Gwen, he can't hear or see you. You're invisible to him."

Gwen, whose unscripted life had only recently begun, looked at Madora with the brimming wonderment that a five-year-old might express when told that people have actually been to the moon.

Without a wisp of disbelief, she replied, "Really? I'm actually invisible to this man right in front of me? How amazing!" And with these worlds, she waved her right hand in front of

Millud's face and then leaned in close and shouted loudly, "Hello there!"

The shout was followed by her repeatedly clapping her hands inches from his nose, her antics resembling an exuberant seal anticipating the tossing of a herring.

Looking over at Gwen happily clapping away, Sheef called out, "Gwen honey, I think that's enough for now. Like Madora said, he can't hear anything, but let me assure you that the rest of us certainly can."

Oh, I'm sorry, Daddy, I guess I just got a little carried away," Gwen said with a soft, endearing giggle. "I've never been invisible to anyone before. This is so much fun."

"Would someone remind me why Millud can't hear or see us?" asked Harvey.

"Remember what I said before we warped to the Phantasian," replied Madora while standing up from the debris pile, "how all humans are traveling at slightly different speeds, but if—"

"A human such as myself," interrupted Harvey, "were to match the exact speed of another human, he or she wouldn't be able to detect my presence."

"Precisely," said Madora. "It's good to see that your crash landing on the coffee table didn't damage your memory."

Harvey smiled at Madora while rubbing the back of his head.

The office door, with the letters "H.B. Millud, Producer and Director" stenciled on the opaque, foggy glass window, was suddenly thrown wide. Filling the doorway was a tall, uniformed security guard.

With startled expression and short of breath, he shouted, "Mr. Millud, sir, are you okay?" Who are these people and what've they done to your office?"

Millud turned toward the guard and said in a sniveling voice, which was iced with a fear-flustered irritation and condescension, "As you can clearly see for yourself, Arnold, I am quite fine; as for my office, well, that's another story, but I'm confident that the rest of the building is in the same condition after the earthquake. But what was it you asked about people in my office? There's no one here but me," said Millud, holding his hands in front of him. "I've been working by myself all morning. Perhaps you took a hit to the head during the quake. Might want to have that looked at, Arnold."

Arnold was momentarily baffled.

"But, sir, right there," he said, pointing to where Harvey was lying. "In the middle of the room, don't you see? It's a—"

The guard abruptly stopped speaking.

"What's that, Arnold?" asked Millud. When Arnold failed to reply to his question, Millud said in a snarky tone, "If you have nothing more to add, then I would appreciate your help in putting my office back together. I have a meeting with Dexter Harris in thirty minutes, and I would like him to be able to walk into my office without twisting an ankle."

The something that had gotten a hold of Arnold's tongue and fragmented his sentence was what he saw when he looked to where the portrait of Millud had hung only minutes ago. He saw exactly the same destruction as did Millud, but with the unhindered ability to also see everything in the room in striking three dimensions and arresting color, he observed the real cause of the chaos: four humans and two dogs. But it wasn't the sight of the humans that had snatched words from his mouth, but that of a giant, shimmering indigo hound. Like a wind altering the contours of lake water, Arnold's expression quickly changed from surprise and shock to puzzlement and then understanding.

He glanced over at Madora with a smidge of a smirk and then turned to Millud. In the most composed voice he could conjure up, he replied, "Of course, Mr. Millud, I will assist you in putting your office back in order, but I must first check the rest of the building. You know . . . to look for any damage from the quake."

"Well, be quick about it then," responded Millud, clearly annoyed that he had to take a back seat to the security guard's job priorities.

"I'll be back to help as quickly as I can, sir."

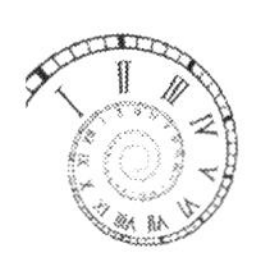

3

Millud returned to his desk, whereupon he sat down and began shuffling through papers. Apparently, he had no intention whatsoever of doing any of the office cleaning himself. When he asked Arnold to help him, what he actually meant was for Arnold to do it all.

As soon as the guard's footsteps had faded out of earshot, Harvey addressed the others. "What was all that about? Why didn't that guy say anything else about us being in the room, and for that matter, why did he stop mid-sentence while speaking to Millud?"

"I don't know," replied Sheef as he walked over to Harvey to help him up and out of the coffee table. "Strange the way he dropped the issue of us being in the room and then pretended that he couldn't see us."

Sheef glanced nervously over at Millud. Though logic was doing its best to convince him that he was imperceptible to the man seated behind the desk, experience and the presence of a living human with two fully functional eyes was resisting its best efforts.

"Do you think the guard will say anything to Millud?" asked Harvey

"I don't think so," replied Madora in a tone that suggested she knew more than the others and was withholding information. Walking over to Millud's desk, she studied the weasel that was oblivious to her existence and scrutinizing stares. "If he had any intention of telling Millud what he saw, he would've brought it back up."

"I actually think he was about to argue the point with Millud when something caught his attention and stopped him dead in his tracks," said Sheef.

"Like what?" asked Harvey.

"I'm not sure, but I suspect that our friend Arnold is more than just your everyday security guard."

"What do you think—"

Harvey's question was interrupted by the shrill clanging bell of a 1930's telephone.

"Yes, what is it?" snapped Millud.

"Sorry to disturb you, Mr. Millud," answered a pleasant female voice on the other end, "but there's someone here to see you — a Mr. Dexter Harris"

"Oh," replied Millud, shifting his emotions to a less agitated gear. "Well, he's early, which I find hard to believe considering what's happened. By the way, Clara, what's the damage like down there?"

"Damage, Mr. Millud? I'm not quite sure I follow, sir."

"Damage! Damage to the reception area! How difficult is it to answer a simple question?" asked Millud as he shifted back up to high gear.

"My apologies, sir, but there's no damage down here."

"You're telling me that the earthquake that shook my office to pieces didn't do any damage down there?"

"Earthquake? I'm sorry, but I'm not aware of any earthquake."

"Not aware! Are you sleeping on the job, Clara! How could you possibly . . . Oh, never mind. Just go ahead and send him up. And for goodness sake, Clara, stay awake!"

Millud slammed down the receiver. On the other end, Clara's warm and sweet voice cooled sour as she seethed, "That skinny, slimy little ferret. He's the last one who should've been given even an ounce of power. He was nasty before he had any, and now . . . now he's simply intolerable. Clara girl, you can't take this abuse any longer. Tomorrow you hit the pavement and find yourself a new gig."

"Sounds like we're about to have some company," said Madora, "and we won't be invisible to whomever it is."

"Everyone, quickly, through the door next to the portrait," whispered Sheef urgently. "Must be a storage closet or something."

The group hustled to the back of the office and through the door. Sheef was right. It was a storage closet filled with the odds and ends of film production: old projectors, film canisters, cue cards, and various props.

Everyone took a seat on the cold concrete floor. Sheef kept the door cracked enough to hear the conversation in the office. Madora's eyes suddenly widened in alarm.

"Where's Gwen?" she asked in a whispered panic.

"I thought she was behind you," said Sheef.

“She was, and I know she followed me into the closet.”

“She did,” offered Harvey. “She was in front of me.”

“Then where’d she go?” asked Sheef in an accusatory tone, as if Harvey was actually responsible for her disappearance.

“How am I supposed to know?” asked Harvey defensively. “I’m sorry; I wasn’t paying attention to her after we entered the closet.”

“There’s a door at the back of the storage room,” said Madora who had slipped away during Sheef and Harvey’s exchange in order to look for Gwen. “It opens to an alleyway. It’s the only place she could’ve gone.”

“What do we do? Shouldn’t someone go after her?” asked Harvey.

“Too late for that,” replied Sheef. “Sounds like the company has arrived.”

A light tapping on the door was followed by a shrill command, similar to the yipping yowl of a poodle that’s had its tail stepped on.

“Yes, yes, I hear you! Come in, Harris! I haven’t got all day!”

The door creaked on its hinges as it inched open. Once it was open enough for a human to slip through, a tall, athletic man with a square jaw and a lion’s mane of blonde hair stepped into the office.

The man was dressed as if he were about to climb aboard a private yacht for an afternoon’s jaunt around the harbor: white cotton pants, a light blue knit shirt, a navy sweater, and brown canvas boat shoes.

“Watch your step, Dexter, there’s debris everywhere, and

please take a seat," said Millud, clearly irritated by the visitation. "Then tell me what you want. I'm a very busy man, and I don't have time to waste on meaningless prattle."

Stepping around a broken piece of shelving, the man asked in a soft, undulating baritone, "What happened here? Was your office robbed? Are you okay, Mr. Millud?"

"Of course I'm okay," Millud snapped in a squeaky voice. "Can't you see that for yourself? And why is everyone acting so shocked? It was the earthquake you idiot!"

"The what?" asked Dexter Harris

"Oh never mind. Now, Harris, why are you wasting my valuable time? I certainly hope that you came here to tell me the only thing I want to hear from you."

The voice of Dexter Harris suddenly pitched higher as his pupils grew abnormally large, threatening to overflow and blacken his irises.

"I know you told me not to come back until I was cleared to take the role, but please, Mr. Millud, let me have just one more quick peek at that mirror of yours."

Dexter Harris, the usually cool and collected Hollywood heartthrob of the silver screen, began to sweat profusely. He wrapped his hands tightly together to try and subdue their shaking.

Millud grinned fiendishly and then said in an annoyingly pleasant voice, "Why, Dexter my friend, are you going back on our agreement? The terms were very straightforward. You obtain a release from World Wide Pictures to act in my production of *The Tempest's Fury*. Once you complete this simple task, you can gaze in the mirror to your heart's content."

"Sheef," Harvey whispered, "the mirror, Millud must be referring to the Narciss Glass. And *The Tempest's Fury*, that's the movie where it all began. It doesn't sound like they've begun filming yet. We're in time."

"I think so, but it seems that our friend Millud has already begun using it on actors like this poor Harris character."

"Boys, please, I can't hear what they're saying," Madora said, shushing them silent.

With Harvey and Sheef no longer whispering, everyone could once again hear the conversation. By this time, Dexter Harris had worked himself into a frenzy, continuing to plead with Millud.

"Please, Mr. Millud, just one more look; that's all I'm asking for. No more than a second or two. I need a glance. One glance is all I need to make it through the day. I promise afterward to get you what you want. I'll star in your picture, rob a bank, heck, I'll even rub someone out for you! Do you hear me! I'll do anything! JUST GIVE ME ANOTHER LOOK IN THAT MIRROR!"

Millud folded his hands together, making a pyramid with his index fingers. He smiled satisfactorily, reveling in the suffering of the famous actor, for he alone had the only thing in the world that the man wanted. Dexter Harris – the man with the looks, fame, and wealth – would gladly give it all away for just one more look at his reflection.

The Narciss Glass provided H.B. Millud with power and leverage. What it was doing to Dexter Harris, had already been done to dozens of unsuspecting victims. It was the means by which an insignificant Ecclonian thief was able to go from an obscure set worker, to a "B" movie actor, and finally to a Hollywood director.

"Oh, I suppose one little glance is permissible," said Millud while standing up, "though it was certainly not part of our original deal."

"Sheef," Harvey whispered again, "this guy's a goner if he looks into the Narciss Glass again."

"I think he's well down the road of being a goner, kid," Sheef replied with a defeated look upon his face.

Millud stepped behind his desk and knelt in front of a medium-sized safe that was built into the space that the drawers on the left side of the desk had once occupied. Clicks to the left, right, and to the left again freed the safe's handle to drop downward with a metallic clunk. The heavy door slowly swung open, revealing a small leather attaché case securely fastened by a sturdy brass lock.

Millud pulled the case from the safe and placed it upon his desk. He unfastened his gold wristwatch and turned the small side knob to adjust the time.

Counterclockwise to 4:45, clockwise to 10:15, and again counterclockwise again to 7:01. The back of the watch popped off and landed in his other hand. A small brass key was cradled in the middle of the back.

"Can't be too careful, now can we," Millud said with an oily smile.

He opened the lock on the attaché case and flipped back the leather flap, revealing a black velvet bag. After removing the bag and untying the drawstring, he unsheathed the mirror.

The mirror was face down. Even so, the light of the room darkened. Millud moved the Narciss Glass in front of Dexter Harris.

The actor greedily reached out with both hands to receive the object, only to have Millud pull it back and say, "Remember the rules, Dexter. You may only look. I'm the only one who can handle the mirror."

"Right, sorry, Mr. Millud, sir," the actor replied, shaking. Beads of sweat dotted his forehead.

Harvey peered through the crack. The heads of Sheef and Madora were stacked above his. Seen from the other side of the door, it was a totem pole of wide-eyed, shocked faces.

As Dexter Harris peered intently into the Narciss Glass, the color and contour of his face began to change. Harvey had assumed that staring into the mirror would pull one downward, toward the mirror. The reality, though, was just the opposite.

Rather than Dexter being pulled into the glass, all the energy and light in the room was drawn into his eyes: tiny black holes with an irresistible gravity, strong enough to compress and crater his face.

His expression was a contradiction of crazed, partial satiation and ravenous hunger. Everything his selfish nature was gorging itself on only served to hollow out his hunger, making him deliriously rabid for more.

The skin of his facial divot erratically danced as he drew more energy from the office into himself. Age spots blotched and spread through his yellowing and thinning skin.

Though Harvey was more than twenty feet away, he could feel life being drawn from him, caught in Dexter Harris's imploding undertow. Millud turned his head away from the actor, knowing what would happen if he were to catch sight of his own reflection.

Sheef noticed this and whispered to Harvey, "Millud's clever and shrewd; I'll give him that. He's smart enough not to fall victim to the Narciss Glass himself, only using it to clear his own ambitious trail."

"While destroying lives along the way," remarked Harvey with a sigh.

Sheef nodded as Millud flipped the mirror back over and deftly slipped it back into its bag.

"I believe that's quite enough for now, Dexter," said Millud with a fiendish grin.

A hard, snarling anger momentarily furrowed Dexter's brow. He then snapped, "How dare you remove me from myself! It's mine! I'm mine! All of it! EVERYTHING IS ABOUT ME AND FOR ME!"

"My, my, my, a tad touchy today, aren't we? Millud asked pleasantly. But I must tell you, that's no way to behave if you ever want to look into the mirror again."

As the warped reality of the Narciss Glass dissipated, the contours and colors of Dexter Harris's face softened and returned to normal. His mind cleared, and he realized the potential consequence of his words. Sniveling but demanding, he apologized pathetically but pleaded ruthlessly.

"Oh no, Millud, I didn't mean to . . . it's just . . . the mirror . . . sorry, sir, please forgive me. You can't refuse me! I must have one more look! Please, I beg you. I'm so sorry. It won't happen again; I swear it. I'll do anything you want! Let me look again!"

"He's pathetic," whispered Madora to the others, "willing to hand over anything and everything to peer at himself again."

"I see now why its use as a punishment back on Ecclon was banned," commented Sheef.

"That's a much more appropriate attitude," said Millud sneering. "And back to our original agreement, Mr. Harris. Once again, all I need you to do is obtain contractual release from World Wide Pictures to star in my film. Then, and only then, will you be free to gaze upon yourself all day long. Now, you must excuse me. I have to prepare for the first *Tempest Fury* cast party at my home tomorrow evening. And, Dexter, I expect to see you in attendance as both my guest and employee."

With these words, Millud placed the bag containing the Narciss Glass back into the attaché case and placed this into a larger steel briefcase, fastening its heavy metal combination lock. After Millud and Dexter exited the office, the hidden group emerged from the closet.

"I guess that takes care of our evening plans tomorrow," said Sheef, stretching tall after remaining still for so long.

"And just how do you propose we get into the party?" asked Madora with raised eyebrows.

"It sounds like a casual affair. The party's at his house. It's the first casting party. I seriously doubt that anyone will be checking names at the door. But if so, we'll find a way in. Don't forget, we're invisible to Millud."

"But not to everyone else," replied Madora.

"True, but all we need to do is get into the house and grab the briefcase."

"But what about the lock?" asked Harvey.

"Doesn't matter," said Madora, "we don't need to the get the briefcase open, and to tell you the truth, I'd be perfectly happy never to see that thing again. All we have to do is get the mirror away from Millud so he can't use it in *The Tempest's Fury*. But before worrying anymore about tomorrow night, there's a member of our own party that we need to locate."

"Gwen . . ." said Harvey, rubbing his forehead, "I completely forgot.

"No telling how far she's wandered away by now. Let's go out the back door the way she left and put Fromp and Akeila's noses to the trail," said Sheef, leading the way to the rear exit.

In less than a minute, the dogs had their noses to the pavement, vacuuming up Gwen's lingering scent.

4

Once Fromp and Akeila had picked up Gwen's scent, their gaits shifted from searching saunters to determined dashes, speedy enough that the two-legged humans found it difficult to keep them within eyesight. The group chased the dogs five blocks south of Millud's office, and the only reason that they were able to catch up to them is because the dogs came to a halt at a major intersection.

Madora, who was in the best shape of the three due to her physical training and weekly excursions to the Phantasian, was the first to arrive at the spot where Fromp and Akeila had ended their pursuit. Seconds later, Harvey joined Madora, followed by a heaving Sheef who stumbled to a stop.

"What's wrong?" Sheef sputtered as he bent over, resting his hands on his thighs. "Don't get me wrong . . . my lungs and legs are grateful . . . but why'd the dogs stop? Lose the scent?"

"Seems so," Madora replied, "but Gwen definitely made it this far. It's a busy intersection. Her scent might've been overpowered or masked by a stronger odor, diesel exhaust or something."

"Hot dog vendor," Sheef said, pointing to his right.

"What?" asked Madora judgmentally. "Really, Sheef? Gwen is missing and all you can think about is your stomach?"

"Actually, now that you mention it, I am famished, but that's not why I pointed to the vendor. He likely saw Gwen and might be able to tell us which way she went."

"My apologies, Sheef. Good thinking," Madora said, with an accompanying expression of appreciation that reflected her words.

The group walked over to a heavyset vendor with curly black hair and a bushy mustache. He had just finished handing a customer a steaming hotdog. Wiping his hands on a blue apron with the words "Hanks Deli Dogs" stitched in fire-engine red across the top, the man smiled widely at three potential customers.

"What can I get you fine folks on this glorious California day? Won't find a special like what I'm serving up anywhere in the city: two of my famous chilidogs and a bottle of soda for just a quarter."

"Actually, sir, we would just like to know if you happened to see a very striking woman, perhaps looking lost, in the last thirty minutes or so," said Madora.

"Lady," responded Hank with a chuckle, "this is Hollywood. It practically rains striking ladies around here. Now... I might've seen someone like that, but it'll cost you."

"Wonderful, a hotdog extortionist, exactly what I needed today," said Madora sarcastically. "Alright then, I'll take three of your chili-thing specials."

"You mean chilidogs?" Hank asked rhetorically with

another chuckle. "Say, where you from lady? Your accent ain't from around here. Probably never had yourself a hotdog."

"Can't say that I've ever had the culinary pleasure," Madora said with a forced smile.

"Well, my dogs are the place to start. Ain't nothing better for hundreds of miles."

Madora nodded before realizing that she didn't have any money. She sheepishly leaned over to Sheef and asked him to pay for the food. He fished out three quarters from his front pocket and gave them to Hank in exchange for six chili-dogs filled to the bun-brim with a meat sauce that looked like steaming lava.

"There's cheddar and onions if you want 'em," said Hank, pointing down to two small metal containers. "And now that I've made a sale, I seem to recall a certain striking lady who fits the bill of your little lost lamb. About twenty-five minutes ago, this drop-dead platinum blonde comes walking down the street from the direction you just come from. I'll tell you this; she looked like a little girl going to the carnival for the first time. She was smiling earlobe to earlobe, like it was her birthday or something. Anyways, she stopped at the curb right over there, and just when I was about to offer her a dog, the city bus stopped and away she went."

"She got on a bus?" Sheef asked, clearly concerned. Do you know where it was headed?"

"Yeah, I believe it was the Number 30 — the WCC route."

"WCC?" asked Madora.

"Oh I forgot, you ain't from around here. Western Coast College is about two miles from here. The route is a loop from this part of the city to the college campus. Goes all day long. Should be back in five minutes or so."

"Looks like I'm headed back to college for the day," remarked Sheef after thanking Hank and turning back toward the street. There's a bench over there. Must be the bus stop. Let's rest there and eat our lunch before the bus arrives. Hopefully, the driver will be as helpful as Hank was."

Harvey and Sheef inhaled their chilidogs with a pattering of slurps and smacks, much to the disgust of Madora. She pantomimed to Sheef to wipe away his chili goatee before taking an exploratory bite of her own dog and then giving the rest to Fromp and Akeila.

When the bus arrived and the doors opened, Fromp and Akeila bolted up the steps, only to be greeted by the bellowing command of a portly bus driver dressed in a navy blue jumpsuit, white shirt, and tie.

"No, no, absolutely not! Read the sign, folks. No pets allowed on the bus!"

"But, sir, Harvey said, it's extremely important that we get to the college. Kind of an emergency. I've lost my sister, and we need the dogs to help find her."

"Listen, son, that's real a heartbreaker, but I don't care if you was the president himself and the Ruskies was about to attack. No dogs are allowed no matter what the reason."

Harvey, realizing that the longer they were delayed, the farther away Gwen was prone to wander, had to act quickly. He called to Fromp who was standing on the landing above the top step. The warp hound turned around and was met with a purposeful, concentrated stare from Harvey.

"Okay, sir, guess we'll just have to walk," Harvey said with the slightest mischievous twinkle in his eye. "Come on, Fromp; let's leave the nice bus driver alone."

Rather than complying, Fromp hopped into the driver's lap. The bus driver immediately began shrieking in panic and screamed, "GET THIS STUPID MUTT OFF OF ME! I SWEAR, IF IT'S NOT OFF WITHIN—"

The driver's last words were smothered into silence by Fromp's large tongue laying a wet lick on his lips.

"Ugh! Disgusting! You gotta be kidding me! "said the driver, vigorously rubbing his lips with a handkerchief. "Get this lump of fur off of me before he crushes my legs!"

"Sir," Harvey replied, doing his best to keep his composure, "he seems to like you, and obviously really wants to go for a ride, and I'm sorry to say, but when Fromp gets a notion in his head, he can be pretty stubborn until he gets his way."

"I told you, no pets allowed, especially gigantic ones!"

"Okay, but good luck in persuading my dog," said Harvey, the cracks in his composure spreading.

As Fromp moved in for a second smack on the lips, the bus driver finally relented. "Alright, I'll let them ride this one time. Just don't let this fleabag lick me again, and get him off my legs!"

Harvey climbed the steps and lightly tapped Fromp on the head. He immediately responded by jumping down from the driver's lap and followed Harvey to the rear of the bus where he and Akeila hopped into seats across the aisle from Harvey.

As Madora and Sheef stepped up the stairs, they both avoided direct eye contact with the driver, knowing that it would release inner snickers and culminate into full-fledged hysterics.

When Sheef sat down, Madora observed him wiping a couple of tears from his cheeks. Before anyone had much of a chance to relax their minds and bodies, the bus made its first stop at the WCC campus. The group agreed that this stop was as good as any to begin their search for Gwen.

The stop was next to an enormous grassy common area. Immediately to the right of the bus was a large blue pond, polka-dotted with bright green lily pads. Surrounding its banks were towering trees, their upper trunks gently swaying to the breezes rolling off the nearby foothills, and beyond and to the left of the pond stood the school's library.

Seconds after the bus's airbrakes exhaled their compressed air, Fromp blasted through the rear door before it had time to open. The closed door was no match for the bounding inertia of indigo fur and rippling muscle and was easily ripped from its hinges.

Fromp was soon at the base of a large tree, circling and barking wildly. The bark was a high-pitched yelp: a dog's cry of frustration, used when a quarry has proven elusive. The sound ascended the tree trunk, following a brown streak that had fled upward only seconds before. The streak ended near the top of the tree, where a petrified squirrel, with its heart in its mouth, chattered angrily at the circling dog below.

Harvey and the others stepped off the bus. Sheef immediately called to Fromp multiple times to stop barking and come over. The scent of the squirrel, however, was like a powerful anesthesia, putting the warp-hound under and rendering him unconscious to all else but his prey.

All at once, Fromp stopped moving and barking. He turned and stared at Akeila, who had exited the bus behind Madora and was now sitting princess-like just outside his circle.

"Uh oh," Sheef said with a stuttering laugh. "This can't be good."

"What do you mean?" Madora asked suspiciously as she pulled up next to him.

"Fromp's looking intently into Akeila's eyes, and that can mean only one thing: he's sending her a thought."

"He's recruiting her for help, isn't he?" Harvey asked, grinning.

"You two boys," Madora said sternly. "Do not let that hound of yours corrupt my sweet girl."

"Sorry, Madora, but it's too late for that. It seems the thought has already been sent and accepted."

Fromp began to rapidly spin, and before long, a warp hole had opened.

"That rascal of ours has opened a portal for his girlfriend to leap through," Sheef said laughing. "And I've a pretty good idea as to where."

Madora looked at Sheef. Her head tilted in confused curiosity like that of Fromp. But not for long, for when she looked to the top of the tree, she was not pleased to see the warp hole's exit.

"Squirrel in the middle," Harvey said with a laugh.

Madora was just about to scold both of the boys for laughing at Fromp's ploy of trapping the treed squirrel and to call Akeila to her side to keep her from leaping through the warp hole, when the lumbering sounds of the bus driver bumbling down the steps interrupted her intentions.

His face was an overly ripened tomato, high-pressure anger stretching skin thin. It appeared as if his entire head might explode at any second. He was so upset at what Fromp had done to the rear doors of the bus that he couldn't find words to express his anger. Instead, he vented fiery sighs like a puffing locomotive.

His rage at the warp-hound was so intense that his previous cowardice toward the animal momentarily dissipated as he menacingly chugged and spewed toward Fromp, who was now sitting next to the rotating warp hole. Although he was tired and heavily panting from his rotational exertions, the warp-hound's eyes sparkled with excitement. Akeila stood only a few feet away, readying herself for a leap through the warp hole and to the top of the tree.

If the bus driver had been walking at a leisurely pace and his eyes had not been murderously fixed upon Fromp, he likely would've seen the exposed root of the tall tree lying directly in his path. But he didn't. So rather than Akeila leaping through the portal, the heavyset driver tripped and took her place.

One second the driver was preparing to put a stranglehold on the animal that had destroyed his bus, and the next he was desperately clinging to a narrow tree trunk eighty feet above the ground.

Whereas Akeila's light weight wouldn't have over taxed the thin branches at the top of the tree, and her nimble alacrity would have enabled her to gracefully negotiate the branches as if descending a spiral staircase, the bus driver's two hundred eighty pound clumsy frame could do nothing but hug the trunk. Beads of nervous perspiration covered his face as he listened to the loud cracking of branches below his feet.

The humans, dogs, and even the squirrel perched on a branch in the middle of the tree, all looked up at the uniformed man madly embracing the skinny trunk, which, overburdened by the unfamiliar weight, had begun to sway back and forth. To Harvey, it appeared as if a doodlebug was riding the end of a swinging metronome.

The angle created between the bus driver's left and right leaning was growing larger with each sway cycle. At first it was small and acute, but soon grew obtuse, and it wasn't long until it flattened into supplementary — the bus driver and the tree trunk inscribing a massive half circle in the sky.

Though no one said it, everyone was thinking the same thought: either the driver's grip or the slim tree trunk would soon reach its breaking point. Even the squirrel seemed to know.

It turned out that the trunk had a bit more strength than the driver, for on his eleventh sway to the left, he was flung free, sixty feet above the pond and a regatta of drifting swans.

When he hit the pond, his two hundred eighty pounds displaced a fountain of water, interspersed with feathers and punctuated with trumpeting honks. The impact knocked so much wind from him that he was unable to mount much of a swim and sank under, only stopping when he came to rest in the muck on the bottom.

Fromp bounded into the pond, his high-powered four-stroke dog paddle propelling him to the sink zone in mere seconds. After making a few surface circles, accompanied by water snaps characteristic of most swimming dogs, he blew his ballast tanks and sunk under. The indigo submersible was soon twelve feet below the surface, leveling off with neutral buoyancy directly in front of the driver's face. His black hair wispily drifted in the current as a small trickle of bubbles escaped from his mouth and scrambled to the surface.

Fromp swam behind the driver and bit into the collar of his uniform. A thrust of hind feet against the bottom of the pond and five power strokes sent the warp-hound and the unconscious man to the surface. He dragged the driver through a bed of lily pads and onto a sandy bank. Still unconscious, the portly man lay prostrate on the warm sand like a beached whale.

Fromp and Akeila hopped atop his back, and after a dozen or so bounces, quarts of murky pond water were coughed free from his lungs. Sheef and Madora helped the bewildered driver to his feet. The trauma of being warped to the top of the tree and nearly drowning had drained away all of his anger, and he now wore the expression of a lost and confused little boy. Madora apologized for everything that had transpired and placed an object into the man's right hand, bending his own fingers around it.

"This should more than pay for the damage to your bus and enable you to take a well-deserved vacation."

The driver, drenched and heavily dripping, nodded slightly and mumbled something indecipherable.

"Why don't we get you back to your bus," Madora said in a kind, motherly tone, "where you can gather yourself together before returning to your depot."

Taking a firm hold of both of the driver's arms, Madora guided him back to the bus, not releasing him until he was seated safely in the driver's seat.

"You'll be just fine now," she said with a reassuring smile.

When she returned to the others, Sheef asked what she had slipped into the driver's hand.

"An ancient Egyptian jeweled bracelet," she responded. "If he sells that thing, he'll be able to buy his own bus company. Now, Sheef, if your dog is done corrupting my girl, perhaps we can resume our search for Gwen."

"By all means," Sheef replied, both of his hands raised in a posture of surrender.

"Good. Well then," Madora said with a slight sigh, "this being the first bus stop, it's likely that she got off here, but if she did, she probably didn't remain stationary very long. Remember, her mind, personality, and perception of the world are still being formed. We can't forget that she's really no more than a few days old. When we took her from her Phantasian movie world, she left behind the person that her writer and his script created her to be. In a sense, she was erased and became a blank page. Everything she's experienced, everything we've said and done to her is shaping her into the woman she will be for the remainder of her new life. And our kind and gentle treatment of her thus far has clearly had a very positive effect on her personality, disposition, and even her appearance."

"And if this keeps up, she'll soon be the most beautiful woman in Hollywood,"

Harvey remarked.

"Which could easily lead to all sorts of other problems that we could do without," Sheef replied.

"What do you mean?" Harvey asked.

"Boys," interrupted Madora rather curtly, "can we stay focused on the matter at hand — finding Gwen? The other discussion can wait. Now, back to what I was saying. Gwen's mind and personality are still very young, and as such, she's excited and curious about everything. Considering the fact that this appears to be the college library stop—"

"Then we should begin our search here," Sheef finished. "No better place for an inquiring mind."

Fromp and Akeila sat down on the grass in front of the library while Harvey and the others walked through the entrance and into a cavernous, silent space. The enormous interior was packed with hundreds of large wooden bookcases.

"There's a lot of square footage to cover," said Madora, "probably best if each of us takes a different section. I'll search through science and technology. Sheef, focus on history, and, Harvey, why don't you take fiction."

They nodded in agreement, and after looking at a map of the library, they went to their designated areas. It took Harvey a few minutes to locate the literature section, and he had hardly begun his search for Gwen when Madora stole up from behind and whispered, "Harvey, I found her, but she didn't see me. We need to find Sheef. You're not going to believe it. Wait until you see what she's doing."

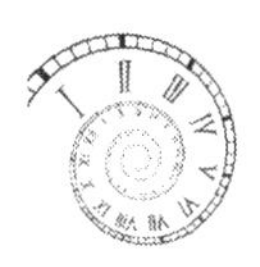

5

Harvey and Sheef followed Madora, who was quickly winding through the maze of bookshelves. She stopped just before the Natural Science aisle and motioned to the Harvey and Sheef to stop and stay quiet. Cautiously, she craned her neck around the bookshelf and invited them to do the same.

Before Harvey peered around the corner, he observed the play of color dancing upon Madora's cheek, evidence of a powerful, multi-colored light shining somewhere between the shelves.

When his neck finally stretched and curved enough to get a clear view at what was occurring, Harvey couldn't believe what he saw. There, on the left side of the aisle was Gwen, the light's source. She was walking very slowly in his direction, her right arm bent slightly backward, with fingers lightly trolling over the spines of books on the third shelf.

Her fingers feathered upon a book no more than a few seconds before brushing over to the next. Each touch of a new book created a soft burst of colored light that lingered momentarily in the air before drifting to her head, where it gently parted her hair and disappeared.

"What in the . . ." Sheef said under his breath.

Madora quickly retracted her head back around the bookshelf and motioned for Harvey and Sheef to do the same.

"It must be . . ." whispered Madora excitedly. "I don't know how, but it must be related to her still being so young — impressionable, malleable."

"Malleable?" asked Sheef.

"Shapeable. You know, moldable."

"I know what the word means," Sheef replied, "but what's your point?"

"Well, remember what I just reminded you of? What happened to Gwen when we removed her from the Phantasian movie world she had been scripted for?"

"Her personality, her disposition, basically everything about her was erased. She became an empty page, and everything we've done and said, everything she's experienced in the last days, is rapidly filling up that empty page," Sheef whispered back.

Madora nodded, paused for a minute, and then said, "But apparently there's another way to write upon that page of hers."

"You think that Gwen's somehow able to absorb the information in those books just by touching them?" asked Harvey.

"Makes sense, doesn't it," whispered Madora excitedly. "Since she left the Phantasian, she's been behaving like a wrung-out sponge, absorbing everything around her: our words, our actions, and as it now appears, whatever's in these books. Go ahead, take another look and observe her face."

Harvey and Sheef did so and witnessed her touch another book. A whirlwind of expressions — wonderment, puzzlement, comprehension, delight, curiosity, perplexity, and satisfaction — reshaped her face, and then she was on to the next book, which initiated another round of expressions. With each book, it was as if she was listening intently to a professor teach an entire semester's worth of material in a matter of seconds and comprehending every word of it.

"You really believe that she's absorbing all the information in each book she touches?" Sheef asked.

"I guess there's only one way to find out," Madora replied, abruptly standing up and stepping into the aisle. As soon as she did, Gwen, whose head was oriented at a slight angle to the ceiling, looked down, meeting Madora's gaze. She smiled ear to ear, and with bursting exuberance, ran to Madora and embraced her. The excitement emanating from her body was palpable, only surpassed by the enthused, machinegun-like discharge of her words.

"Madora, you're here! Isn't this wonderful?" Did you know that a place like this existed? It's marvelous! So much to learn! Dragonflies, they're amazing! Did you know that they can fly close to forty miles per hour, and each of their four wings moves independently, allowing them to fly in all directions, including backward? Or the human cell! We humans have trillions of these, and each one is as complicated as a modern factory, with a variety of machine-like systems that build new proteins to repair and maintain proper functioning throughout the body! It's unbelievable and . . ."

The rapid-firing of Gwen's worlds suddenly decelerated and

then stopped. When they restarted, they came out slower and deeper. "Madora, how did all of this amazing beauty and engineering come about? Whoever created all of this must be . . ."

"My lack of words exactly," Madora said with a smile. "You can find the answer to that question in another section of the library."

"Where would that be?" asked Gwen enthusiastically before her thought was blundered into by another captivating scientific nugget. The rapid-fire began again.

"Oooo, Madora, did you know that our sun is basically one massive continual nuclear reaction. An enormous atomic explosion, but it's far enough away that we are safe from the radiation, but the precise amount of heat energy reaches Earth, fueling the process of photosynthesis in the plants and trees, which forms the glucose that provides energy for all animal life on earth, including we humans, and—"

"Gwen," Madora interrupted when Gwen paused to catch a breath, "Why don't you tell us what's in this book." Madora then handed her a book that she had grabbed off the shelf.

Gwen eagerly reached out for the book, entitled *Advanced Physics and the Quantum World.* Upon touching the book, an aquamarine light burst like pollen into the surrounding air where it lingered momentarily before traveling to Gwen's head and disappearing.

Gwen closed her eyes. The skin of her eyelids bubbled as if a rolling boil was occurring underneath. It was no more than twenty seconds when the bubbling stopped and Gwen opened her eyes. A rapturous expression stole across her face.

"Madora," she said exuberantly, as if she had just taken

her very first bite of a warm chocolate chip cookie, "who would've ever believed that the laws of the quantum world are so entirely different from those of Newtonian Physics and that these two understandings of reality somehow coexist! But it makes perfect sense; the mathematical equations clearly prove them both to be true!"

"So you understand the equations in the book?" asked Madora.

"Not until I read through it."

"What do you mean?"

"Don't be silly, Madora, just what I said. I didn't understand everything, including the math, until I had read the entire book. Don't you read, too?"

"Yes . . . but not like that."

"Are you saying," Sheef asked in disbelief as he approached from behind Madora, "that you read everything in that book in less than half a minute?"

"Is that too slow?" Gwen asked, sounding disappointed. "You probably read much faster, don't you?"

"No, no, trust me, honey, not even close. But how much of what you read did you actually understand? I mean, quantum physics is a very new branch of science and one of the most difficult subjects to comprehend. Few people even know about it, much less understand it."

"Really?" Gwen asked, clearly astonished by what Sheef had said. "Well, to answer your question, I . . . suppose I understand all of it. It's really not that difficult. It actually makes perfect sense," she continued without the least trace of arrogance. "Don't you think so, too?"

"To tell you the truth," Sheef said while looking down at his shoes and feeling slightly embarrassed, "I was never all that great at science."

Sheef had actually flunked physics in high school and remembered how the concepts of the quantum world had completely overwhelmed and sunk his understanding.

"Gwen," Madora said, while reaching out and gesturing for the physics book, "can you recall everything you just . . . read?"

"Of course, what page?"

"Page . . . yes, page," Madora replied, not immediately registering what Gwen was referring to. Madora opened the book and randomly flipped to a page. "How about page fifty-two."

And with that, Gwen recited verbatim every word on the page. When she finished, she looked up adoringly at Sheef and said, "Do you want me to explain it do you?"

"No, that's quite alright. Maybe later. I'll tell you what, why don't you finish reading all the science books in this section. I can see how excited you are to learn about how everything works, and I don't want you to miss anything. You finish up here, and I'll go grab coffee for everyone. When we got off the bus, I noticed a small café nearby. I'll get everyone something to drink, and then we can sit down at one of the picnic tables and enjoy the beautiful weather while you tell us all about everything you've learned."

"Really!" Gwen squealed as she performed a stationary skip. "Thank you so much! I can't wait to tell you everything! It's all so fascinating."

"Uh, Madora, why don't you and Harvey help me with the

coffees, and let Gwen finish her reading," Sheef said as he motioned them back down the aisle and toward the exit. Before leaving the library, Sheef glanced back at the science section. Above the bookcases, various colored lights circled about on the ceiling.

What Sheef said to Harvey and Madora was just an excuse to get them alone in order to assess the situation and decide what to do next. Nevertheless, he did walk over to the café and purchase four coffees. When he returned, he joined Harvey and Madora who were seated at the picnic table where they had left the dogs.

Shafts of sunlight filled the gaps between the tall trees surrounding the library, creating dapples of yellow on the lush grass. Fromp was stretched out on one of the dapples, belly up and drying. Akeila lay more dignified close by.

"That was definitely the most interesting experience I've ever had in a library," Harvey remarked. He placed five cubes of sugar into his coffee and continued, "If I could read like that, school would be a breeze."

"There's nothing 'reading' about what Gwen's doing," Sheef said. "And if you could do whatever it is she's doing, you wouldn't need to ever enter a classroom again."

Harvey nodded as he took a sip of his coffee. "You know, if she stays in there much longer, she'll be the most intelligent person in the world."

"You're likely right," Madora said, "but it may not be something to get too excited about."

"Why not?" asked Harvey.

Madora placed a cube of sugar into her coffee and stirred

it in before replying. "Acquiring so much knowledge so quickly could prove to be very dangerous." Madora paused for a sip and to organize her thoughts before continuing. "When knowledge is absorbed over weeks and years, and especially when the acquisition is the result of diligent study and perseverance, a healthy amount of wisdom is usually mixed in to help a person handle the knowledge. But the rate at which Gwen is learning . . . I just don't know, but I think it's safe to say that no human mind was designed for what she's doing."

"True," Sheef agreed with a sip of his coffee, "but then again, she's not exactly human."

Madora and Harvey stared at Sheef in disbelief at the insensitivity of his words.

"What?" Sheef replied in a defensive tone. "Come on, you both know that it's true. She's a fictional character from a movie who we should've never taken out of the Phantasian in the first place."

"That's fine for you to say now," Madora said shortly, "but don't forget that you were the one responsible for taking her out, which, if you recall, I strongly warned against."

"I know; you don't need to remind me. It was my fault, but—"

"Why are you two even discussing this," Harvey interrupted. "It doesn't matter how she got here or whether or not Sheef should've taken her with us in the first place. The only thing that matters is that she's with us now, and for all intents and purposes, she's my sister, and from everything I've observed so far, she's just as human as the three of us."

Sheef silently nodded, but when Harvey glanced over to Madora to gauge her response, it appeared as if she hadn't listened to a word he'd said.

"Madora." Harvey said, lightly tapping his spoon on the picnic table. Madora ignored Harvey for a few seconds, gazing intently at something near the pond before averting her attention to his words and look.

"Sorry, Harvey, I was listening, and I agree. All that matters is that she's here with us now and is our responsibility, but changing the subject, I think we're being watched.

"Watched? Are you kidding? By whom?" Sheef asked while turning around. Harvey, who was seated next to Madora, stood up to see over Sheef's head.

Peering around the trunk of a medium-sized sycamore tree was the security guard from Millud's office who had clearly seen them after they crash landed, but for some inexplicable reason, had ignored them and played along with Millud's belief that the damage was due to an earthquake.

"It's Millud's security guard. Arnold's his name, right?" asked Sheef.

"I believe it is," Madora replied, staring once again in the direction of Arnold, pursing her lips together and nodding knowingly. She then stood up unexpectedly and walked to the security guard.

"Madora, are you crazy? What do you think you're doing?" asked Sheef in a loud whisper.

"I think it's time we got to know this guard a little better and see what he has to say. Just sit tight while I go over and invite 'Arnold' to join us."

Harvey and Sheef looked at each other and shrugged their shoulders.

When Arnold saw Madora marching over to him, he no longer made any attempt at concealing himself but stepped out from behind the tree trunk.

"Interesting and talented dog you have there. Never seen an animal able to ascend a tree so quickly. Not on this planet anyway," the guard said with a twinkle in his eye.

"Talents you're no stranger to, considering the fact that you used Akeila's sister to travel back in time," Madora said in a business-like tone. "I knew you looked familiar, but it's been quite a number of years since I last saw you. Time and that uniform of yours clouded my memory. But when I noticed you poking around the tree, and the fact that you obviously ignored us back in Millud's office, the clouds cleared. I thought there was the possibility of our paths crossing, though I certainly didn't foresee us literally crashing into yours, Arrick, or should I call you Arnold?"

Better stick with my alias for now. Madora, you are, without a doubt, the last person I ever expected to happen upon in earth's past, especially in light of how you received me back in Egypt, or have you forgotten your initial opposition to my mission?"

My opposition was warranted then and still is. Traveling through the Phantasian and going back to earth's past are fraught with perils of every color and shape. It's a fool's gamble, to put it mildly, and I wouldn't have done it myself if the situation in the present wasn't so bad."

"Bad? What do you mean? I've hardly been gone. What could've happened in that short amount of time?"

Madora turned and looked back at Harvey and Sheef before resuming their conversation. "Listen, Arrick, the others must already be wondering why two supposed strangers are so engrossed in a conversation. They don't know who you are or that we've ever met, and I wish we could keep it that way, but whatever happens, we can't talk here by ourselves much longer."

"What? Madora, you're making no sense. Tell me what's gotten so bad in the present," Arrick said worriedly. "Is my family alright? Madora, tell me what's wrong!"

"Arrick," Madora said in a calm voice, "I need you to maintain your composure. I'll explain what I can, but it needs to be done quickly. Your son, Harvey, is more than fine, but your wife hasn't much time left. The clouds of Ecclon have gone dark, and the planet has been overrun by Nezraut and his Vapid. Bellock and many of the Flurn elders are—"

"It can't be. You're talking nonsense. It's not possible that the situation could've worsened so much in only a month!"

Madora looked at him queerly. "Arrick, you're the one who's making no sense. You've been gone for over twelve years.

"Twelve years!" Arrick shouted. "Are you out of your mind? I traveled through the Phantasian four weeks ago and met with you in Egypt just before that."

"Arrick, lower your voice please." Madora paused to look down at her boots as she whispered to herself. "The Phantasian . . . it's the only explanation that makes any sense, for what else could place us here at roughly the same point in time."

"Sorry to interrupt," Arrick said shortly, "but would you mind sharing with me what you're mumbling on about?"

Madora looked back up at Arrick and said, "Sorry, I was sorting it out myself. Okay, stay with me. We traveled through the Phantasian twelve years after you did, and I assume we both exited through the opening created by Millud's character in that horrendous pirate movie, *The Barnacle Buccaneers*."

Arrick nodded. "That's the one I used, but I came through another actor in the movie. It's why Millud can see me. I thought by working for him I would be able to locate the Narciss Glass more quickly."

"Don't you get it then? Since we both entered the 1930s through the same movie, we also entered at relatively the same time. The movie acted like a time doorway. The departure time to the past is irrelevant if the destination time is the same. We could've left five hundred years after you did and still only a month or so would have transpired between your arrival time and ours."

"Okay, I think I understand, but that would mean Harvey's now a teenager."

Dots connected. Mixed expressions of loss and hope. Arrick carefully peered around Madora's body to get a good look without being caught in the act.

"That's him, isn't it? My son's with you!" Arrick said excitedly

"He is, Arrick, but he doesn't know who you are. He's never seen you before, not even a photo. In fact, until recently, he thought Thurngood was his real father."

"Thurngood, the captain of the royal guard?" Arrick asked in disbelief.

Madora nodded.

"My son . . . that's really him over there, the teenager at the table? But I've missed so much. Where do I even begin? What do I say?"

"I don't know," Madora replied in a soft, empathetic tone before turning all business again, "but that might have to wait. We have more pressing matters to deal with. As I said, Ecclon has fallen, which is why your wife hasn't much life left in her body. Her fate is somehow tied to that of the planet. And your theory proved to be correct. Millud's use of the Narciss Glass in his movies has, over the decades, turned millions of humans away from the thoughts of the Unseen, which led directly to Nezraut's books being created and the clouds of Ecclon going dark."

"Books? Bellock believed that there was just one," said Arrick.

"No time to explain and it doesn't matter now. What's important is that it all began with Millud's reckless use of the Narciss Glass. It was the first domino that caused everything else to fall. Arrick, we have to keep Millud from using it, destroy it if need be. This is why we've risked our lives to come back. We didn't know if you were even still alive. I don't know when or how you should tell Harvey the truth, but I'm afraid that when you do tell him, it could very well complicate matters more. And believe me when I tell you, they're complicated enough already."

"I don't understand what Harvey has to do with any of

this," Arrick replied, clearly growing frustrated. "What does he even know about Ecclon and Nezraut?"

"Arrick, he's been there. Bellock warped him to Ecclon not even a month ago."

"What?" You've got to be kidding! What could a thirteen year old from another planet do to help?"

"That was my thought when I first met your son, but trust me, there's much more to Harvey than meets the eye. His thoughts, well they're . . ."

"They're what? Tell me, Madora!"

"Well, for one, he used them to defeat Nezraut in battle, and for another, we would've all died in the Phantasian if not for his quick thinking. As hard as it may be for you to believe, your son is a warrior of the Unseen, unlike any I've ever encountered. And he's the key to stopping Nezraut."

Arrick looked around Madora and over to Harvey once again.

"This is insane. You're telling me that the baby I left month ago grew up and became a warrior capable of defeating the most powerful Vapid Lord? I'm sorry, but this is a little difficult to take in all at once."

"I can only imagine. Look, there'll be more time for absorption and explanation later, but for now, we have to get hold of the Narciss Glass and keep another problem from developing."

Arrick gave Madora a questioning look.

"You'll find out soon enough, but I need to get back and join the others. I don't know what you're going to say when we get over there, but you have at least a full minute to figure it out."

Madora did an about face and led Arrick over to the picnic table. As she reseated herself at the table, she gestured to him. "Harvey and Sheef, let me introduce you to our not so inconspicuous security guard who would like to explain why he's been tailing us. Isn't that right, Arnold?"

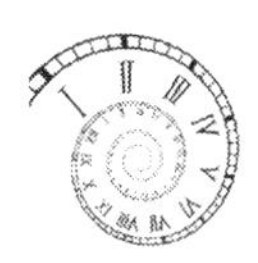

6

All eyes focused on Arrick who shifted uncomfortably. Though it seemed like many minutes, it was, in fact, only a few seconds before Arrick launched into his cover story, one that he hoped would create enough breathing room for him to determine the place and time to tell his son the truth.

"Well, your friend Madora here," Arrick began haltingly, "easily surmised that I'm not really a security guard. Unlike the thousands of actors in this town who have the ability to impersonate others, I seem to lack that particular talent. The truth is, I work for a certain government agency, and H.B. Millud's recent activities have caught its attention, specifically his meteoric rise from a stagehand grunt to director in a very short span of time. Our suspicions were particularly aroused when—"

Arrick's false narrative was interrupted by the library's front doors violently swinging open. Loose paper and a fair number of catalog cards were carried on the back of an artificial wind. Madora, Harvey, and Sheef exchanged worried looks. Saying nothing to Arrick, all three stood up and ran through the entrance and back to the section where they had left Gwen to continue her 'reading' of science.

When they reached the section, the group saw that the adjacent bookshelves had fallen into one another, forming an A-frame roof over the aisle. Below was a pile of books and underneath these were Gwen's protruding feet, the only part of her body visible. Though Arrick had trailed behind, he soon joined the others under the shelf roof. Everyone began shoveling books off of Gwen. Their collective but unspoken fear that she might've been hurt by the cascade of falling books was alleviated when they heard smothered giggles from underneath the pile, and when Harvey removed a rather large tome entitled *A History of Scientific Thought and Discovery from Archimedes to the Atom,* Gwen's ecstatic, child-like face beamed up at him.

"Harvey," Gwen said while still giggling, "the bookshelves fell."

"I can see that," he replied smiling. "Can you tell us what happened?"

"I don't know exactly. I was reading a most fascinating book about meteorology — you know, weather — all about high and low air pressure and how their interaction creates much of the observable weather on the planet. Well, I began to imagine what an area of very low air pressure must be like. I thought about such an area floating right in the middle of the aisle, and only seconds later, I heard a tremendous whooshing sound and then a very powerful wind blew from all parts of the library and knocked down the bookshelves!"

Sheef bent down and helped Gwen to her feet. A dozen or so books, still atop her body, fell away as she emerged from the pile like a butterfly from a cocoon.

"Gwen, did I hear you say that you imagined an area of very low pressure and then winds began blowing?" asked Sheef.

"Yes, but I didn't think winds blew inside buildings, but then again, everything is so new to me."

"No, you're correct, winds don't normally blow inside buildings, especially ones strong enough to knock over heavy bookshelves."

As he said this, Sheef glanced over at Harvey. They both knew that the mission was becoming more complicated and challenging by the minute, and the faster they found the Narciss Glass and warped out of the past, the better it would be for everyone.

A library clerk tore around the corner and scurried to where Gwen was just standing to her feet. "Is everyone okay? I don't know what just happened! Earthquake or something!" the clerk frantically blurted.

"I don't believe it could've been an earthquake," Gwen began cheerily, "it was the extreme wind which—"

"Oh, Gwen, I think we should go and have you examined at the infirmary to make sure there's no broken bones or anything," interrupted Sheef.

"But I feel absolutely fine; I've no broken bones."

"That's good to hear, but why don't we head outside anyway and get out of the way, so that this mess can be cleaned up."

"Okay, but you have to let me tell you about Einstein's prediction of gravitational waves. I absolutely agree with him!" She shouted joyfully. "Why, they must exist; the equations are irrefutable!"

"That's wonderful, Gwen, you can tell us all about it once we leave the library, but first, why don't you go and see Akeila and Fromp. They're outside lying next to a picnic table," said Sheef.

And with that, Gwen merrily skipped around the scattered books, through the library, and out into the afternoon sun.

"This is not a good development," Madora said as she walked down the aisle with the others. But before saying anything else, she turned to Arrick and said, "Arnold, would you mind following Gwen out to the picnic table. I know she said that she is physically fine, but I would feel better if someone kept an eye on her. I need to have a few words with these two if you don't mind. We'll join you in a minute."

Arrick nodded and quickly left the scene, happy to have additional time to figure out if he was going to continue the charade he'd only just begun, or be done with it and come clean with the truth.

Once Arrick was out of hearing, Sheef was the first to speak as they walked slowly to the front of the library. "Am I crazy or did Gwen just do what I hope she didn't?"

"Would be that she didn't, but we all saw the results, and I don't think Gwen is incapable of lying, not that there was a reason to do so," said Madora. "And the science works. Higher air pressure always moves in the direction of lower pressure. It's why we have wind. Apparently, Gwen created an area of very low pressure, which acted like an opened drain, but instead of water, air rushed in to fill it."

"But that means that Gwen was able to manipulate matter with her thoughts," Harvey said, "like what I was able to do in the Phantasian when I levitated the whale."

"Yeah, but we're not in the Phantasian anymore," said Sheef.

"So do you think she brought some of that world with her?"

"I think it has little to do with the Phantasian and more to do with who she's becoming," said Madora.

"You've got to give us more than that," said Sheef.

"I was planning on it before you jumped in ahead of me."

"Sorry. Please continue."

"Scientists have speculated for decades that humans only use a small percentage of their brain's actual capacity, which I believe is a safeguard put into place by the Unseen."

"But why would he limit humans?" asked Harvey.

"Consider human nature. The primary, underlying motivation for humans is fear. They fear not having enough to survive, not being accepted by others, not having what it takes to succeed. They also fear sickness, aloneness, and most especially, death. So what do they do to alleviate or ward off these fears? They try and protect or insulate themselves. They do anything and everything to amass whatever will provide them with a sense of security."

"So all these fears cause people to be very selfish," Harvey summarized.

"Exactly, and think about all the destruction, suffering, and even loss of life that has occurred because of such selfishness.

Most fights, large and small, and most crimes, minor and major, are manifestations of this selfishness. Now imagine if humans could use their full brain capacity to fulfill their selfish ambitions. Though there would be the potential for incredible good, I believe that man would, intentionally or unintentionally, use his enhanced mind to unleash all manner of evil upon the world."

"That's a pretty bleak assessment of mankind," Sheef commented.

"If you'd lived as long as I have, you'd agree."

Sheef raised his eyebrows and nodded. Okay, but let's get back to why you brought up the topic in the first place. I think that you were about to tell us that if humans could access more of their brain's potential, they might be able to manipulate physical objects by nothing but their thoughts."

"Think about it," said Madora. "What is the basis of all matter? Isn't it just organized moving energy? When you break matter down into its tiniest subatomic particles, you discover that these particles are composed of nothing but energy, which means energy and matter are really just two sides of the same coin. And aren't thoughts energy as well? Is it really much of a stretch to imagine that energy in one place could affect energy in another?"

Sheef turned to Harvey and jokingly said, "In light of what you did with your thoughts in the Phantasian and to Nezraut, I'm beginning to think that maybe you and Gwen are actually brother and sister."

Harvey smiled.

"Well, there's definitely one thing we all can be grateful for," Sheef continued. "If Gwen really does have such an ability, it doesn't appear that she's aware of it, and her being the most innocent and gentle soul I've ever met, I don't foresee her using it in a harmful way if and when she does discover it."

"She's innocent and gentle now, but need I remind you that the harsher realities of life can change a person overnight," said Madora as they reached the front doors.

Sheef stopped at the entrance, letting Harvey and Madora return to the picnic table. Arrick had not gone to the table but had lingered next to the entrance, eavesdropping on the last bit of their conversation. When Sheef saw him, he stopped, grabbed his forearm, and pointedly said, "Delaying the truth is nothing more than a poorly disguised lie."

"Excuse me?" Arrick replied, making his best attempt to appear baffled by the remark.

"Nice try," said Sheef smirking, "but if it's this obvious to me, how long do you think it will take your son to figure out who you really are?"

"Then you know?"

"How could I not?"

"With an audible sigh, Arrick said, "Guess I'm a worse actor than I thought."

"Arrick, it's Arrick, right?"

Arrick nodded.

"Your acting ability had little to do with it. Come on, Harvey's the spitting image of you, and did you happen to see how that warp-hound reacted to you? His ears perked up and his tail thumped wildly when you approached the picnic table. With that nose of his, you think he couldn't immediately scent that you're Ecclonian? So. . . when do you plan on telling him?"

"Not sure. Madora voiced a bit of concern. She's worried that telling him might complicate things and interfere with the mission, and based on what I observed and overheard you say about Gwen, you already have more than you can handle. By the way, who is she?"

"That story's too long to tell you here. Maybe later, but let me say one last thing before we join the others. The kid's going to find out the truth eventually, and this is not something like wine that improves with time. Putting it off is like ignoring an infection. It's better to tend to it early before things have a chance to worsen and spread."

"I know, but it still doesn't make the task any easier."

"Hey, no one ever said that the truth or fatherhood was easy," Sheef said as he good-naturedly slapped Arrick on the back.

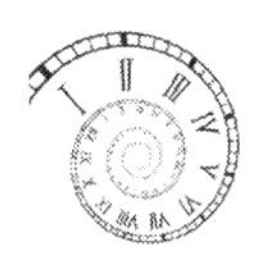

7

Over a dozen black objects had washed up like pieces of charred driftwood on the sands of a small tropical island. Elongated bodies, twisted and unmoving, were sprawled upon the beach. From a gull's hovering view, it was impossible to determine whether or not the drenched and sand-encrusted Vapid Lord were unconscious or dead.

If a human had been struck by a towering wave and pile-driven to the ocean floor, he or she would've certainly died a thousand deaths, but extinguishing life from something that's existence is more aligned with death than life is another matter altogether. To render a thing lifeless that is practically bereft of life to begin with is next to impossible. It can be done. A Vapid Lord can be killed, but it takes more than falling water and bone-crushing hydraulics to do so.

Grauncrock and his Vapid Lord minions had their wind and pride temporarily knocked from their bodies by Harvey, who had learned, within a whisker's width of death, how to bend the rules of the Phantasian to his advantage, resulting in both his survival and another victory over the enemy.

He had discovered that he could rewrite the "script", so to speak, in the strange world of the Phantasian, a realm composed of thousands upon thousands of worlds, each one owing its genesis to the fictionalized imagination of an author's book or screenwriter's movie script.

When Harvey and the others accessed the Phantasian as a way to travel back in time to 1930's Hollywood, they visited three different worlds based on three separate 1930's Hollywood movies. And as they learned, the people in these worlds were not acting but were living out the roles that had been scripted for them. The plot of their lives was that of the films, but to these characters life wasn't fiction, for fiction had become real life. The myth had left two-dimensional celluloid and become three-dimensional reality. Harvey and the others had flirted with death in each of the three films. Gangsters shot at them, rearranging objects almost sliced and diced them, and pirates threw them to the sharks.

Not only had the characters and objects of these worlds threatened their very lives, but to make matter worse, Grauncrock, Nezraut's highest ranking Vapid Lord, and a host of his Vapid underlings, had followed a trail created by Harvey's reluctance to forgive. In the pirate world, however, Harvey was finally able to let go of his bitterness, reconnecting him to the Unseen and enabling him to use his thoughts to alter reality. A Harvey-produced tidal wave had temporarily immobilized Grauncrock and his minions, allowing the group to escape back to the 1930s. And now, the Vapid lay like beached flotsam, awakening from their humiliating defeat by the thoughts of a thirteen-year-old teenager.

Grauncrock bared his fangs and snarled before opening his eyes. A second after they opened, he sprang to his feet in a quick-flick motion, throwing off a detachment of crabs from his chest that had been investigating what they hoped would be an easy meal. The crabs hit a nearby palm tree, and after falling to the sand, angrily waved their claws at the tall wraith standing at the waterline. Grauncrock's wet cloak loudly flapped in the stiff tropical breeze as he contemplated his next move.

"VAPID LORD!" Grauncrock yelled as he thrust out both arms. An undulating wave of energy pulsed the briny air, its bass bouncing the grains of sand upward like kernels of popcorn. His minions were jolted awake and were immediately on their feet, encircling their master.

"Lessons learned, my fellow lords," Grauncrock snarled. "Age and appearance can be deceptive. Nezraut's warning not to underestimate young Harvey was not heeded enough . . . but no matter. He may have won the battle, but the war is far from over."

Grauncrock's eyes narrowed to red slits before continuing. "Find me the actor that they were after. He is the doorway through which we will track Harvey and his friends to wherever and whenever they have gone. Soon the Narciss Glass will be ours and young Harvey will be mine."

Grauncrock stopped speaking and formed a spherical fireball between his hands. He stared with rage into the eyes of his underlings before exploding. "WHAT ARE YOU WAITING

FOR? YOU HAVE YOUR ORDERS! GO AND DARE NOT RETURN TO ME EMPTY HANDED!" And with the command, he spread apart his hands and released the fireball. It streaked into a close-knit group of palm trees, incinerating them in seconds.

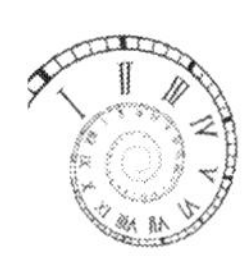

8

When Sheef and Arrick returned to the picnic table, Gwen had already busied herself playing with Akeila and Fromp. She began talking incessantly about all the science she had just read, which was far beyond what any human could read in a lifetime.

"And the mass of low barometric pressure," said Gwen animatedly, "because of the Coriolis Effect causes the typhoon, what others refer to as a hurricane, to rotate counterclockwise, and given sufficient energy—"

"Gwen," interrupted Sheef, "you might need to shift down a few gears. Fromp seems to be having a difficult time figuring out if you're excited or distressed."

Harvey and Madora looked over at the warp-hound who was whining, not sure if he should lick Gwen or try to render aid.

"Oh," said Gwen, laughing to herself, "I see what you mean."

She scratched Fromp behind both of his ears and lowered her head so that her nose was only inches from his. "Sorry, boy," she continued, "I suppose I got a little carried away with everything I just learned, but I'm okay; in fact," she continued while turning back to the group, "I feel fantastic. It's as if the curtain has been pulled back, revealing the secrets of how everything in the universe works: all the levers, gears, and sprockets spinning and clicking away! It's all so spectacular, a massive symphony of millions of different instruments all playing together perfectly, creating this grand booming and bursting melody called life!"

"I wish you were my science teacher instead of Mr. Schlaumer," commented Harvey. "He could take something unbelievably exciting — say, a volcanic explosion — and make it boring, but I bet you could make learning about a kitchen spatula riveting."

"Oh, Harvey, you're exaggerating aren't you? Hyperbole is another word for what you're doing, right? I also read a portion of the reference section of the library, including twenty different dictionaries and thesauruses. Aren't words thrilling! So many different shades of meaning, like millions of colors with which to paint our thoughts and imaginations. My favorite word currently is—"

"Gwen, said Madora, as she placed a calming hand upon her wrist, "the security guard at our table wants to tell us about himself. Would you care to listen?"

Gwen turned around and noticed the stranger who had taken a seat next to Sheef. Wearing an embarrassed expression, she said, "Oh, I'm so sorry, Madora. My sincerest apologies. I was so caught up in my own excitement that I didn't even notice our guest sitting at the table. How very rude of me. I hope you will," said Gwen as she spoke directly to Arrick, "forgive my discourteous and uncouth behavior — aren't those lovely words, by the way — and I would very much like to hear all about you!"

Once again the spotlight was on Arrick. He shifted awkwardly and sighed deeply. Even though the temperature was only seventy-two degrees, beads of sweat appeared on his forehead.

"The actual truth is," he began haltingly, "not the truth I started to share with you before, which was not true at all, but only what I wanted you, specifically you, Harvey, to believe was true to keep the actual truth from you."

Arrick stopped his incoherent stumbling in order to take a breath. "Am I making any sense?"

"No," said Harvey, "I haven't the slightest idea what you're talking about."

"You're not the only one," said Sheef, grinning, "and I do know the truth about him."

"Maybe it's best if you just start over," interjected Madora. "Wipe the slate clean and begin again."

Arrick nodded and then stared down at his hands, each tightly knotted in a fist.

"First off," he began, "don't be upset at Madora or Sheef for not telling you sooner, Harvey. Before today, I'd never laid eyes on Sheef. Truth is, I didn't share anything with him; he fit the pieces together and figured out who I was all by himself. As for Madora, we met back in the future present. Anyway, when she recognized me, she decided, and rightly so I might add, that she shouldn't be the one to tell you who I really am, which only makes—"

"Hold on a minute," said Harvey, clearly flustered. "You know her? And why did you say you met Madora in the future present. What does that even mean?"

"Harvey, you need to give me a minute here," said Arrick taking a deep breath. "Trying to take in twelve years all at once is a bit difficult to process." After a moment or two, he continued. "Perhaps it's best to begin with a proper and truthful introduction."

Arrrick stood up and reached across the table with his right hand outstretched to Harvey. "Harvey, my name's not Arnold; it's Arrick. And I believe it's safe to conclude, based on my brief conversation with Madora today, that you're already familiar with the name, so there's probably no point in telling you where I'm from."

Harvey limply took hold of Arrick's outstretched hand and gasped, "Ecclon . . . Dad?"

With tears spilling over lids, Arrick brokenly responded, "Hello, Son . . . it seems it's been a while for both of us."

"Yeah, it has," Harvey slowly replied, too astonished to find and fix the right expression to his face. "Twelve years . . . You left when I was a little over a year old."

Harvey was quiet for a moment before asking the inevitable question. "Dad, why didn't you come back sooner? It's been more than a decade," he said, his words beginning to harden. "Mom's really sick. You should've come back years ago. She needed you there . . . I needed you."

Arrrick let go of Harvey's hand and walked around to the other side of the table and embraced his son in a fatherly bear hug. Harvey's arms hung languidly at his sides before tentatively responding to the unfamiliar gesture. Harvey's body, which was as rigid as a column of granite, began to heat and soften.

"Son . . . I . . . I had no idea it'd been so long. For me, I left you and your mother only a month ago. When I left you, you were still in diapers, but I blinked and now . . . Believe me, if I had the slightest notion of how the passing of time would differ so much in the past and present, I never would've left you and your mother like I did."

"But it's not possible that you recently arrived here. Dad, you've been here for years!" said Harvey, his emotions getting the better of him. "Why are you still lying to me? Just tell me the truth! I deserve to hear it!"

"Harvey," said Madora soothingly, "everything your father said is true. I don't, by any means, completely understand why or how time twists and reorders itself when one access the past through the Phantasian, but I'll explain to you the little that I do know, but please trust me when I tell you that your father had no idea what was happening to you and your mother these last twelve years."

"I'm sorry, everyone," Gwen broke in, her tone for the first time since they left the Phantasian turning negative, "but if anyone here is confused, it's me. How can Sheef and Arrick both be Harvey's father? Does this mean that I have two fathers as well?"

"And there you have it," Sheef remarked quietly to himself. "Just when I thought things couldn't get any more upside down and convoluted."

Arrick, as king and soldier of the Ecclonian Royal Guard,

who had been trained to take control and command of unforeseen and difficult circumstances, stepped in and took control of the unraveling situation.

"It seems to me that we all have much to discuss and learn from one another. Look, I've rented a small cottage not far from here. Why don't we head over there now? We can pick up some Italian food from Rosa's on the way. She makes the most delectable pie I've tasted since arriving on this planet. We can take some back to the cottage, and over dinner, everyone can explain to me how my son went from wearing diapers to becoming the savior of the universe. And, Gwen, I think you might get some answers as well."

Arrick's words had the intended effect: Gwen's countenance softened and the exuberant optimism of her personality once again began to glow.

"That sounds wonderful, but I don't believe I've ever had Italian pie," Gwen said with a giggle. She then stood up and spun around three times. "Isn't the entire world like one amazingly large classroom? It's never-ending learning. So much to experience and taste," she said with yet another giggle.

Arrick stood up and began moving back toward the pond. "The man I'm renting the cottage from is letting me use an old truck of his. It's parked over there where that warp-hound of yours blew the doors off the bus."

"You saw all of Fromp's high jinks?" asked Sheef.

"Me and a fair number of college students, which when you combine what they witnessed with the little storm in the library, there's a fairly good chance that some real security guards might show up and begin asking the types of questions we certainly can't answer."

The group walked around the pond and over to where a beat-up green truck was parked. The cab was boxy and very small — hardly enough room for two children, let alone adults — and was covered with a ripped and stained brown canvas top. Behind the cab was a tiny square truck bed with low wooden railings along the sides.

"She's a 1925 Model T pickup. Lots of dents and dings, but she gets the job done, although it might be a little tight. Luckily, we don't have very far to go."

Madora and Sheef climbed into the confined space of the cab and jostled against one another, trying to position themselves in the least painful way. However, when Arrick climbed in, they were so closely packed together that Madora and Sheef had to turn sidewise in order to breath. Gwen and the dogs hopped into the truck bed, and as soon as Gwen sat down, Fromp and Akeila playfully pounced on her, showering her in a rain of exuberant licks.

As Arrick turned the key to the battery setting, he laughed to himself and then opened up the door. "I keep forgetting. This old beast has one of the first electrical starters, but the owner said it quit working years ago. Have to use the crank in the front to fire her up."

He walked to the front of the truck and bent down. Seconds later, Sheef and Madora saw his head and shoulders pop up as he wrenched the crank clockwise a half turn. The old, well-worn pistons bobbed up and down in their cylinders as the antique engine belched to life. The rough and uneven pinging and banging of the engine shook the cab and the bed of the truck, rattling everyone's teeth.

As soon as the bald and narrow tires began to roll, Fromp reared up and draped his long front legs over the top of the canvas roof. The pads of his huge paws thudded against the windshield. From inside the cab, the sounds of groaning metal were heard over the din of the sputtering engine, and Sheef noticed that some of the metal supports holding up the canvas top began to buckle and bend.

When the truck had picked up enough speed, Fromp's large, pointy ears filled with air and popped full like sails catching wind. The warp-hound didn't ride the Californian slipstream alone for very long. Before they had even traveled a half mile, Gwen squealed, "Oh, that looks like such fun," and thrust her head up next to Fromp's. Soon, squeals of laughter were tumbling about with delighted woofs. When Madora stuck her head out and looked up to see what was happening topside, she observed Gwen grinning ear to ear, her blonde locks swirling behind her head like ribbons of fire. Every few seconds she had to wipe her face clean of frothing saliva that was flying off of Fromp's flailing tongue.

Akeila, too, had positioned herself to feel the flow of air, but she wasn't about to embarrass herself by flopping atop an unstable canvas roof like her oafish, undignified counterpart. So, instead, she gracefully dipped her head over the low truck railing and let the wind caress her shapely snout and ruffle her golden fur.

The weight of Fromp's legs, head, and front two-thirds of his body had stressed the structure and load capacity of the metal frame supporting the canvas top when he first plopped his legs and paws on top of it, but when Gwen — who weighed almost nothing in comparison to his bulky mass — joined Fromp on the roof, her additional leaning weight pushed the frame beyond its limits.

If not for a sharp snap a second before complete structural failure, Arrick, Sheef, and Madora would've been seriously injured. The sound of the snap, though, bought them a fraction of that second and allowed them to duck.

Fromp, Gwen, and a tangle of canvas and metal collapsed onto the passengers who were all lying and leaning to the right. Madora, who had been wedged against the passenger door before the collapse, had nowhere to go when the collective lean occurred, and before she knew what had happened, the passenger door flew open, and she found herself hanging out and over the asphalt road.

Though Arrick could no longer see through the windshield, he somehow managed to keep his left hand on the steering wheel. His only view was through the open passenger door, and as he looked around Madora's bouncing head, he saw a familiar white stucco building with an Italian flag painted on it.

"That's it! Hold on!" Arrick shouted as his left hand rotated from quarter till to the new hour. The truck careened to the left as it took a sharp right turn into the parking lot. Limbs surging with adrenaline, Arrick slammed on moaning brakes as the truck rapidly decelerated.

Unfortunately, the inertia of the truck and its occupants in the bed and atop the collapsed roof was stubbornly determined to continue moving them in their original direction. When Arrick made his sharp right, Harvey, Gwen, and the dogs were flung to the left and into the open air like stones launched from of a sling.

If it had been a modern, multi-ton truck, it probably would've kept its four rubber feet on the ground, but the much lighter 1925 Model T didn't stand a chance. Madora, who was still hanging out the door and parallel to the ground, was suddenly reoriented perpendicular: her upper body sticking out the top like a submarine's periscope.

Similar to a pod of flying pelicans, Gwen, Harvey, and the dogs soared serenely for a few seconds before landing in the middle of an enormous oleander bush. The sidewise truck and its prisoners scraped across the parking lot, sending out a fan of bright orange sparks.

The Model T finally came to a complete stop after hitting the trunk of a large grapefruit tree. Four pieces of fruit fell through Madora's window, one of which hit the gear stick dead center, cracking the yellow rind and squirting juice throughout the cab.

"Wiping juice from his face with his shirt sleeve, Sheef quipped, "Well, I do like mine fresh squeezed."

"Very funny," Madora said sarcastically, "but hardly the time for a bad joke. Is everyone okay?"

"I'm fine," said Arrick, who was at the bottom of the cab's human pile, "but would it be possible for us to continue our conversation in the open air. It's a bit cramped down here."

Madora and Sheef climbed out of the cab and then helped Arrick out. When they had all emerged from the truck, they began looking for the others. They didn't have to look for long. From what was left of the oleander bush, Harvey, Gwen, and the dogs stumbled out, sporting fresh welts and scratches.

"Everybody alright?" Arrick asked as they approached.

"Nothing broken," said Harvey. "How about you?"

"We'll definitely feel it in the morning, but I think we'll live. So," sighed Arrick while looking over at Fromp, "and be honest with me. Is that purple galoot more dangerous than the Vapid?"

"Jury's still out on that one," Madora said in a tone that gave no indication whether she was being facetious or really meant it. Fromp responded by lying down on the pavement with his head resting dejectedly between his paws.

"Why don't we push the truck back onto its four tires and then get some pizza," suggested Arrick. "All humans on the driver side. We'll lift and push, but we're going to need some type of counter weight on the other side. Harvey, do you know how to send thoughts to that warp-hound of yours?"

Harvey nodded. Though he hadn't shared it with the others, for some time now, he had the ability to communicate with Fromp without the assistance of Kreen. He assumed that his experience in the Phantasian had somehow taken the power of his thoughts to a new level.

"Good. Send him a thought to hang his paws over the other side of the truck and lean back while we lift. Since this mess is his fault, the least he can do is lend a paw," Arrick said with a wink and a smile to Harvey. "Would you do that for me, Son?"

Harvey grinned and nodded. Warmth radiated through

his heart. His father, his real father, had called him 'son'. It took three tries to finally right the truck. Once it was done, everyone walked over to the front door under the hand-painted sign of Rosa's Italian Café.

Sheef held the door open and as Gwen passed, she turned to him and said excitedly, "That was absolutely exhilarating! I was actually flying for a moment before landing in the bushes. Could we possibly do it again after we pick up the food?"

"Uh, Gwen, I think that's enough fun for one day. We need to save some for tomorrow."

"Oh, you're right of course," she said as she hugged him. "You know, I must have the wisest father in the world."

"If only that were true," Sheef said quietly to himself.

A jovial older woman wearing an apron splotched with red sauce and a face powdered with white flour, hurried up to the group and warmly greeted Arrick with a hug as if he were her own son. When she let go of him, she realized what she was wearing and exclaimed in a thick accent, "Oh, Mr. Arnold, I so sorry. Look at what I do? I coated with sauce like pizza," she laughed good-naturedly, "and then go and smother you. I hope I no dirty your nice uniform."

"No, no, Rosa," replied Arrick playfully as he looked down at his shirt, "you didn't share any of the family recipe, but if you had, I would've worn it with pride!"

"Oh, Mr. Arnold, you stop that silliness now or you make my big head even bigger!" said Rosa with a laugh so deep and rich that its smooth resonance filled the entire room.

"Today I glad to see you brought family," she continued as she turned her attention to the others. "Everyday Mr. Arnold come here all by him lonesome and pick up pizza. I no say anything, but I worried. It's no good for man's heart to be by its lonesome, but then his family — wife, kids, and even dogs — appear here today! Rosa so happy that family joining you," she said as she refocused her attention on Arrick and lovingly touched his cheek. "Now, I got table big enough for everyone in the back, and the dogs, welcome to stay as long as they no go in kitchen. They do and I'll have new topping for pizza," she said with another booming laugh.

Arrick looked around the restaurant. There were only five other customers and no one was seated in the back where the large table was located.

"Well, we were planning on just picking up some pies and taking them back to the cottage, but, Rosa, you make us feel so welcome that I think we'll try out that big table of yours."

"That make me happy to hear. Everyone take a seat and I get sample of our best pies out soon."

Everyone smiled in agreement. Ten minutes after they were seated at an enormous circular table covered by a red and white checked tablecloth, their faces were wreathed by the aromatic steam rising from four large pizzas that Rosa had set down on the table. Fromp and Akeila were sitting on their haunches at rigid attention, only inches from the edge of the table, armed and ready to dispense with any table scraps.

For the next fifteen minutes or so, the only sounds to be heard from the circular table were the crisp, cracking crunches and slurping smacks of five people tasting culinary Nirvana.

Arrick, who was seated next to his son, placed his marinara-saturated napkin on the table and leaned over and spoke quietly. "Son, I can only imagine how upset you must be with me for abandoning you and your mother for so many years, and I know that it'll be a while before I can make things right again, but I hope at some point you'll be able to forgive me for what I did."

Harvey picked up the napkin from his lap to wipe away the tears. "Dad, there's nothing to forgive, honestly. You had no idea how much time had passed for Mom and me. I mean, how could you have known? And warping back to the 1930s in order to destroy the Narciss Glass. . . You were risking everything to save Ecclon and Earth. How could I be upset with you?"

Arrick softly placed his right hand on Harvey's shoulder while pursing his lips together in order to hold back the waterworks poised to break forth at any second. He then turned to the others and said, "Besides Madora and Harvey, I don't know the other members of our team. Why don't you introduce yourselves and then bring me up to speed on everything that's transpired on both of my home planets.

An hour later, Harvey, Sheef, and Madora's narration of the events which had transpired in the previous weeks on Ecclon and Earth finally came to a close. Arrick, who had remained silent except for the occasional question for clarification, sat dumbfounded.

"And your mother knows all of this?" he asked.

"Not until about a week ago when Sheef, Gnarl, and I visited her."

"Hold on a minute. Gnarl the Petrified came to our house?"

"Yeah, and even though he's much smaller now, he still made a good-sized hole in the roof."

"He made a hole in our roof?"

"Yeah, he kind of crashed the party, literally. Sorry about that."

"Trust me, after everything I just heard, a hole in the roof is the least of my worries. Not much reason to fret about damage to your home if the planet on which it's built is no longer worth living on, and besides, if we're successful here, we won't be going back there anyway."

"What do you mean, Dad?"

"Sorry, forget I mentioned it. We'll cross that bridge when we get to it; for now, let's just worry about getting to it," replied Arrick before quickly changing the subject. "Okay, Son, let me make sure I have the major parts of your little adventure straight. It all began in our backyard when you were sitting in that old rocking chair while chewing on a large dill pickle. Out of the blue, Fromp appeared in the yard, tail-lassoed you, and warped you to Ecclon. Upon your arrival, you met Bellock, who explained that the clouds of Ecclon, the planet's source of light and heat, were rapidly growing dim. He further explained that this dimming was occurring because human thought on Earth — the energy which illuminates Ecclon's clouds — was increasingly turning away from the thoughts of the Unseen."

Harvey nodded.

"You were then presented to the Flurn Council who concurred with Bellock that you were the one to go after the book the Vapid had created to turn additional humans away from the Unseen. But before you faced the Vapid, you warped back to Earth to be trained by John Sheefer," said Arrick as he pointed to Sheef.

"Sheef, as you refer to him, trained you not only to battle the Vapid, but also their servile deceivers, the Insips. Afterward, you fought and defeated Nezraut, destroying multiple copies of the book in the process. But once you and Sheef returned to Ecclon, you and the Flurn concluded that the root of humans turning away from the Unseen likely predated the book. This realization led to Gnarl the Petrified, the one who might conceivably know of the root cause, being brought back to life. You then narrowly cheated death when Nezraut and his Vapid invaded Ecclon. After warping to our home, you visited with your mother and learned of my true identity, where I had gone, and what I was after. Once you picked up my trail, you followed it to Egypt where you met Madora, and somehow persuaded her to guide you through the Phantasian and to 1930's Hollywood to capture or destroy the Narciss Glass. Is that about it, or did I miss something?"

"No, you definitely hit the highlights," said Sheef, "but you failed to mention that your son cleverly figured out how to rewrite a Phantatsian world, creating a massive wave, levitating a blue whale, and saving all our lives."

Shaking his head while grinning, Arrick said, "What I still can't comprehend is that a thirteen year old, my thirteen year old no less, is a major player in all of this."

"The major player is closer to the truth," Sheef said while winking at Harvey.

"And to think that for the last month, while you were warping across the universe and fighting the forces of evil, I believed you were still an infant and your greatest foe was nothing more than diaper rash."

Arrick reached over and lovingly tussled Harvey's hair. "No father anywhere in the universe could be prouder of his son than I am of you. Courage, sacrifice, loyalty, and tenacity, you're truly a prince worthy of the title."

Both Sheef and Madora became glassy-eyed as Arrick and his son embraced. Strangely, though, Gwen, for the first time in her new life, wasn't emotional or enthusiastic by what she observed. She seemed detached from the warm sentimentality that had charged atmosphere, and the soft glowing contours of her face darkened and hardened — a shadow eclipsing dancing light. With everyone else transfixed by the heart-warming reconciliation of father and son, this subtle change wasn't observed by anyone.

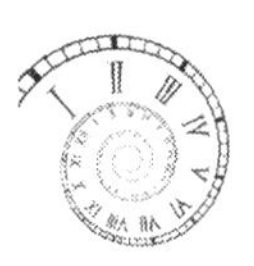

9

Arrick's cottage was very close to the café. In fact, the Model T, which was now roofless and once again heavily laden with paws and hands, had hardly turned out of Rosa's parking lot before it turned onto a small gravel driveway next to a quaint wooden cottage. A narrow covered porch tightly coiled around the small home.

The front door opened with a rusty yawn. Arrick stepped aside, welcoming the group to enter. "I should probably oil those hinges, but each time I open the door, I think it'll be the last, so why bother."

Everyone stepped into the cramped living area, made more so by an old couch and loveseat resting on the worn, wooden floor. To the immediate left and right, bedrooms hung off the living area like ears on a head.

As Arrick entered behind the others, he said, "I'll bunk on the couch. Harvey, you and Sheef take the bedroom on the right. Madora and Gwen, you two take the other one."

Madora smiled and thanked Arrick. Gwen, on the other

hand, completely ignored his words, acting as though she hadn't heard. Harvey took note of Gwen's peculiar behavior as she walked past him and followed Madora into the bedroom. Her soft and glowing childlike countenance had been washed away, replaced by something more rigid and aged.

Madora popped her head back out of the doorway and said, "As much as I would like to discuss our plans for tomorrow, I think the best thing for all of us is to grab a good night's sleep. I know the fate of the universe rests on our shoulders, but if we don't get some rest ourselves, those shoulders are likely to break." And with these words, Madora smiled and gently closed the door.

Fromp and Akeila were already performing a sniffing sweep of the cottage. Fromp was hoping to catch wind of any dropped food.

"Your warp-hound is searching in vain, Harvey," chuckled Arrick. "I'm hardly ever here. He'll be lucky to find a crumb."

As if he understood exactly what Arrick had said, Fromp ceased his smell-search and hopped onto the loveseat. He turned three circles on the cushions before plopping down with a defeated "humph". Being that the loveseat was much too small to hold the warp-hound's enormous frame, his head and tail stuck out both ends like the bow and stern of a ship. Akeila settled herself on a woven circular rug in the front of the loveseat, snuggling into a tight fur ball to ward of the encroaching evening chill.

Fromp lifted his massive head off the armrest and glanced down at Akeila. The loveseat was soon vacant. The only evidence that Fromp had been there was a deep indention in the cushions. Fur to fur, Fromp curled up into his own ball and was soon asleep, the beat of his heart falling into perfect time with hers.

Arrick grabbed a blanket from the hall closet and threw it on the couch. He walked over to Harvey and placed his hand on his shoulders and said with watery eyes, "Still can't believe it. My infant son an Ecclonian warrior and friend of the Unseen. Once again, Son, I couldn't be any prouder of you than I am right now."

And there it was again, the word spoken, spoken as it was created to be, charging the atmosphere, engendering life. Harvey longed for but never believed that he would hear the word spoken in such a tone for his very own ears. But it had been, twice, and the effects had been more unexpected and transformative than he could've ever dreamed.

His heart filled, rose, and rested. Unable to fit feeling to word, Harvey smiled like he had never done before. It felt as if his trillions of cells were warmly grinning at each another, joyfully sharing the long-awaited moment.

A full minute passed before Harvey or Arrick said anything. Harvey didn't want to be the first, fearing that breaking the silence would send the feeling scurrying away and out of reach. It was Arrick who finally said, "I guess we should follow Madora's advice and get some well-needed rest. Besides, I'm getting the sense that you don't want to ignore her words."

"You've no idea," came Sheef's voice from the bedroom. Harvey shook his head, grinning, and then followed the voice inside and closed the door. Within minutes of Arrick shutting off the house lights, everyone's exhausted minds drifted off to sleep – that is everyone's but Gwen's. She lay wide awake, listening intently for silence and a chance to slip away.

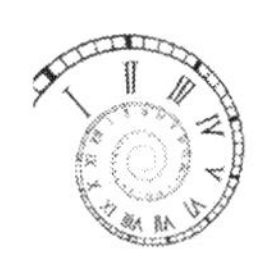

10

Harvey awoke to ponderous plopping paws upon his chest. The weight of Fromp on the bed caused the wooden frame to creak in pain. Agitated by a very swollen bladder, Fromp's heavy panting vibrated the entire mattress. And though the weight of the warp-hound made Harvey's breathing more labored, the shaking bed massaged away some of the soreness from his two crash landings the day before.

The need for a full breath of air, however, soon superseded any relief Harvey was receiving from the moving mattress. "I got the message, you big lug," said Harvey in a smothered voice. "Come on, let's get you outside."

Fromp retracted his front paws off the bed, turned, and quickly trotted through the living room. Akeila appeared at Harvey's side just as he reached the front door, softly licking his hand as if she was saying "good morning and thank you". Unlike Fromp's slobbering licks, which often required a towel, Akeila's were light and refined, a cool breath of rubbing alcohol upon skin.

Arrick was walking up to the cottage carrying a white paper bag at the same moment Harvey stepped out onto the porch. As soon as the door opened, Fromp bolted to a large palm tree on the edge of the property, sideswiping and nearly knocking Arrick off his feet.

"Whoa there," Arrick laughed as he steadied himself by grabbing the porch railing. "Slow down, Fromp; that tree's not going anywhere!"

"When Fromp's on a mission, it's best to get out of his way," said Harvey laughing.

"You're telling me!" Arrick took a step toward Harvey and said, "Good to see you this morning, Son."

The word again flushed warm, pushing back the early morning chill.

"Bought some donuts for everyone," said Arrick, holding up the white bag. "Anyone else up yet?"

"I don't think so," Harvey replied. "What time is it anyway?"

"Quarter till seven," said Arrick, looking down at his watch. "Never would've guessed that a son of mine was an early riser."

"Only when a two-hundred-pound-plus hound with a full bladder rattles me awake. He really didn't leave me with much of a choice."

Just then Madora burst through the doorway and said excitedly, "Gwen's gone! I've searched the entire house and there's no sign of her!"

"Why are you so worked up and worried?" asked Sheef yawningly as he followed her outside, stretching the grogginess out of his body. "She probably just went for an early morning walk. You know how curious and enthusiastic she is about everything. Probably couldn't wait to get up and explore."

Madora briefly stared at Sheef with a look that could've tenderized the toughest meat and said in a peppery tone, "Well, if she went for a walk, she's been walking all night. She ever got under her covers. Her bed wasn't slept in."

"But why would she do that?" asked Sheef, rubbing the lingering sleepiness from his eyes, oblivious to Madora's stare and tone.

"She was acting strange last night; I mean strange for her," offered Harvey.

"What do you mean?" asked Arrick.

"Didn't everyone notice how quiet she was at dinner? And when we arrived at the cottage, she hardly said a word."

"Now that you mention it, she did seem to keep to herself," said Sheef. "Instead of asking a million questions and gushing about every new discovery, she was silent for the first time since we rescued her."

"I did observe the change," said Madora. "When we were alone in our bedroom, I asked her if she was feeling well, and for the first time since I met her, she flushed red and said with an insincere smile that she was just tired and wanted to rest. I felt like she was lying. I knew something was definitely wrong, but being exhausted myself, I let it go, thinking that I could dig deeper in the morning after we both had a decent night's rest."

"Well, if she was lying, it was likely her first time to do it," said Sheef with growing concern in his voice. "If you'd asked me yesterday if she was capable of lying, I would've emphatically said 'no' — just not in her nature."

"I would've said the same," agreed Madora.

"Then what changed? Did something happen yesterday that I missed?" asked Sheef.

"If something did upset her, it must've occurred between the time we left the library and our arrival at the cottage, because she was bubbling over with enthusiasm back at the library," said Madora.

"She overheard us," said Harvey blankly.

"Overheard what, Harvey? And why would anything we said upset her enough to cause her to run off without a word?" asked Arrick.

"How could I've been so careless and stupid?" Harvey asked, ignoring his father's question as the reason for her disappearance dawned on him. "Of course she would react negatively. How could she not?"

"Hey, kid," interrupted Sheef, "you mind letting us in on why you're chastising yourself?"

Harvey, who had placed his head in his hands, sat upright and said guiltily, "While we were eating at the restaurant, I told my dad everything that's occurred since Fromp warped me to Ecclon."

"Okay, but why should hearing your story cause her to clam up all of a sudden?" asked Sheef.

"Sheef, I shared everything, including what happened in the Phantasian," answered Harvey, emphasizing the last word. "I was so caught up in my own narrative that I didn't think once about how it would . . ."

"You can't blame yourself, Son," said Arrick. "It wasn't intentional."

"Harvey, your dad's right," offered Sheef, "and if anyone's guilty for what happened, it's me. I should've been more cognizant of what Gwen was hearing."

"And what would you have done, cut me off?" asked Harvey.

"No, if I had my head on straight, I would've made up an excuse to get Gwen away from the table."

"Listen you two," interrupted Madora. "It's pointless now to debate what should've been done. We're wasting time we've no business wasting. What we should be doing is trying to determine how what she heard might've impacted her."

"Why does that matter?" asked Harvey, a slight irritation in his voice. "I mean, we know that the words upset her."

"It matters because how the words impacted her likely influenced her subsequent behavior. If we can determine her reaction, it might shed some light on where she went," answered Madora.

"Makes sense," responded Harvey apologetically.

"I'm certain she was angry. Probably felt betrayed," said Sheef. "Imagine finding out that you're not the daughter of the person you thought you were, and not only that, but you realize that you don't have any parents at all, other than a screenwriter who typed up a movie script and created your character out of thin air. Gwen's just learned that she's nothing more than a figment of someone's imagination: a fictional, two-dimensional character from a low-budget movie."

"But that's not true," interjected Harvey defensively. "She's not just a made-up character from an old movie, at least not anymore. She became a real flesh and blood person, and has become even more so since she left the Phantasian."

"I completely agree, but I guarantee you she doesn't see it like that," said Sheef.

"Sheef's right, Harvey," said Madora. "Think for a moment about the blow to her self-esteem. She's feeling valueless and purposeless right now with the realization that she has no parents, which are, incidentally, the most important factors in who and what a child becomes. Parents provide the structure that supports the child and the path for him or her to follow, not to mention the care and loving attention they give, which is a slow-acting marinade, seasoning a child's attitude and personality. But without parents, what do you have? Nothing but drifting humans, aimlessly bouncing about life, desperately hoping to bump into something that will provide a sense of worth and value."

"And that's how you think she's feeling right now?" asked Arrick.

"Without a doubt," said Madora. "The words she heard likely set her adrift. We just need to determine where the current carried her."

"And she's probably boiling with anger at being deceived," offered Sheef. "Come to think of it, it makes sense that Gwen would want to get away from the very people who lied and hurt her. I know I would if I were in her shoes."

"I was afraid of something like this occurring when we took her out of the Phantasian," said Madora. "You know, even if we had been extremely cautious with our words, it was only a matter of time before she discovered the truth. Truth is like water, given enough time, it will eventually leak out, and considering how porous and cracked humans are, the truth tends to get out sooner than later."

There were collective nods followed by silence, which after a full minute was finally broken by Harvey's question. "So, where do you think she might've gone?"

"My best guess," said Madora, "would be the last place Gwen was her innocent and sweet self."

They all looked at each other and said, "The library."

"Okay then," said Harvey, making motions to leave, "what are waiting for?"

"Hold on, Son," said Arrick. Let's think about this before we rush off and do something that might derail our main objective. We all traveled back to 1930's Hollywood for one purpose and one purpose only: to locate the Narciss Glass and keep Millud from using it in his movies and influencing millions of people to turn their thoughts away from the Unseen. It's our top priority, and if we fail here, there'll be no one else to save Ecclon and stop Nezraut from killing Bellock and the other Flurn."

"But can't we do both," pleaded Harvey. "I know Gwen's only one person, and until recently wasn't even that, but she is now, and isn't it our responsibility to find her and set things right?"

"Esteem both the tree and the seed, for the larger lies within the smaller," quoted Arrick to himself.

All eyes turned in the direction of Arrick. "What did you say?" asked Harvey.

"Sorry, it just popped into my head while I was listening to what you said. It's a proverb of Gnarl the Deep, who, by the way, I still can't believe is no longer petrified and look forward to conversing with when we get out of this mess and back to Ecclon. Anyway, the proverb reads, 'Esteem both the tree and the seed, for the larger lies within the smaller.'"

"Okay . . ." Harvey said confusedly.

Arrick smiled and then said, "Apparently it's not, and you're wondering why I quoted it at this particular moment. Let me explain. The seed of a tree is just as significant as the tree itself, because as everyone knows, you can't very well have one without the other. The point is that the small things are just as important as the larger ones, the very same sentiment that you just expressed when speaking about why we need to go after Gwen. And you're right. Gwen is now a living individual, regardless of how she came to be, and therefore has value, which means, even though she's only one person, she's now worth the time and risk to go after. You reminded me of something very important my father said to me on more than one occasion: "If you're not willing to sacrifice for the little things in life, the larger ones may not be worth saving, for it's the little things we do every day that end up defining who and what we become. Those things that we dismiss as being insignificant often turn out to be the most significant of all. The small choices we make today become the building blocks of the life and legacy of all our tomorrows."

"So we're going after Gwen?" Harvey asked excitedly.

"We most certainly are, and if we get moving, we might find her in time to still make the casting party at Millud's this evening. Let's load up the truck and head over to the library. We can eat the donuts I bought on the way."

LOSS

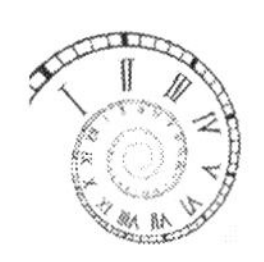

11

Even though Arrick was literally pressing the truck's pedal to the metal, the speedometer refused to go any higher than thirty miles per hour.

"Can't this thing go any faster?" yelled Sheef from the bed of the truck, his voice barely overcoming the loud clanging of the struggling engine.

"She tops out at forty on a good day, but that's without any passengers and a stiff tailwind!" shouted Arrick out the open window and into the passing slipstream. "Overloaded as we are, we're lucky to hit twenty-five!"

Their rate of speed was suddenly no concern, for they rounded a curve in the road and found themselves passing the pond that a certain bus driver had taken a plunge into the day before. Arrick parked the truck and turned off the clanging engine directly in front of the library.

As the group got out of the truck, jets of exploding light shattered the library's windows. Concentric circles of vibrating air quickly spread, rattling every object they came in contact with. Books carried by passing students were snatched from their hands and wildly tossed into the air, while their owners were knocked off balance, wobbling and falling like struck bowling pins. Thousands of leaves were rattled free from their branches, creating a blinding blizzard of green.

When the shaking waves struck the truck, their force momentarily lifted the vehicle up on two tires. Once the truck regained its equilibrium and bounced back down on all fours, Sheef said, "I think we found her."

Students, who were strewn about the ground and covered with tree foliage, sat up and gathered their scattered belongings, trying to make sense of what had just occurred. As Harvey and the others passed by, they caught crumbles of conversations.

"Must've been a gas leak!" said a tall, brown-headed student wearing khaki pants and a striped shirt.

"Wouldn't doubt it; building's ancient, and they've had problems before," replied a freckled, strawberry-blonde wearing a gray sweatshirt with the words "WRESTLING" written across the front. "I bet someone lit a cigarette and ignited a gas cloud."

"If only it was something so easy to deal with," whispered Sheef to himself as he walked by.

When the group reached the front doors of the library, there was no thought of who would open the doors first because both doors had been blown off their hinges and were lying on the lawn. As they walked through the entrance, they were nearly trampled by a mob of screaming students fleeing for their very lives. Harvey noticed that many of them had blood trickling from their ears, and those with glasses had cracked lenses.

The scene inside was utter devastation. Most of the bookshelves had been knocked over, and floating above them were countless fragments of book paper, swirling about in every conceivable direction like the plastic particles of a shaken snow globe. In the middle of the library, a sputtering shower of orange sparks rained down from the exposed electrical wires that had been connected to a large chandelier, and standing directly in the middle of the falling sparks was Gwen. A white fire burned in her eyes. Her arms were stretched out before her in the shape of a "V".

The group stopped dead in its tracks. The skin of Sheef's face sagged, the muscle below fainting in disbelief at the unfolding scene before him. Gathering his thoughts, he uttered the understatement that everyone else was thinking, "This can't be good."

The cascading electrical sparks and drifting flakes of smoldering paper briefly obscured Gwen, but Sheef's words, though not very loud, caught her attention, which was immediately redirected and riveted on the group. She smiled in recognition, but it wasn't her usual innocent smile of curious wonderment and discovery. Something had transpired — a shadow across the soul, an inkblot spilled and spreading. A darkness had emerged, aging away her softness and leaving behind something weathered and hard. She was still beautiful, but her beauty was now angular and sharp. The fire in her eyes abated as she rested her arms at her side.

"Why look, my loving family has come for me, "Gwen said

in a voice dripping with sarcasm. "Here we are all together once again. Father, mother, and brother, but I must apologize to you, Arrick, for I don't know your relationship to me. Uncle perhaps? It would fit in nicely with the rest of this fictitious family of ours. Isn't that what it is, Father?" asked Gwen as she took a step toward Sheef. "One big familial lie to cover up the fact that I actually have no family whatsoever. Never did. Nothing more than a product of ink upon paper," she said as she grabbed a floating book page from the air and stared down at its words.

"Gwen, we never meant to . . ." bumbled Sheef. "It all happened so quickly, and you just assumed I was your—"

"Silence!" Gwen snapped as she lightly flicked the fingers of her right hand in Sheef's direction.

A split second later, something like an invisible fist hit Sheef just below the chest, tossing him into the air and flinging him backward where he landed on a pile of reference books.

Gwen then reached out to Sheef, pantomiming the act of helping someone up. He immediately felt something like invisible straps wrap around his upper body. The straps were pulled taut as if they were connected to a cable being retracted by an unseen winch. He was lifted to a standing position and levitated three feet above the book pile. Gwen approached, stopping mere feet from his hovering body.

"Telekinesis is really not that difficult to master with a little practice," said Gwen in the pleasant tone of a grade school teacher instructing her pupils in how to properly punctuate a sentence or reduce a fraction.

"You see," she continued, "I absorbed the knowhow

yesterday when I read and incorporated the content of forty physics books, numerous papers by preeminent physicists, and texts on brain neurology and cognition. And when it was all laid out before me, I could see how it all worked. Matter and energy, you know, are really the same thing. Matter, in fact, is nothing more than energy configured in a certain pattern. Once you comprehend this, manipulating an object with the mind becomes as easy as throwing a ball."

Sheef continued to float in front of Gwen, his arms immobilized by the still biting invisible straps. The others inched slowly forward, spellbound by what was before them. Gwen paused for a moment and then continued speaking as she walked around Sheef's suspended body.

"Using brain wave energy to manipulate matter is simply learning how to focus on one form of energy in order to affect another form. It's not much different than moving a ping pong ball with your breath. You just need to learn how to blow, in a sense, a stream of energy with your mind. I realize how mystical this may sound, but it's nothing more than applied scientific knowledge, which until yesterday, I was ignorant of. I suppose this makes me a quick study," she laughed to herself.

A sudden thought caused Gwen to turn in the direction of Harvey. Sheef remained floating behind her as she opened her right hand and waved her fingers back to herself. Harvey was instantly picked up and sent flying through the air as if shot by an invisible catapult.

Madora screamed out for Harvey as he blurred past her at over sixty miles per hour. She was certain that whenever and however he landed, he was likely to break every bone in his body. Fortunately, just before reaching Gwen, he rapidly decelerated and was gently enfolded in what can only be described as a large energy pillow.

Above Gwen hung a rectangular prism of pulsating golden light, which softly caught and absorbed the inertia of Harvey's sailing body. But no sooner had he ceased moving, then the energy pillow vanished and Harvey drifted down until he was eye to eye with Gwen.

"Harvey, if anyone can relate to what I'm saying, it's certainly you. While in the Phantasian you levitated an entire blue whale and generated a tidal wave with nothing but your thoughts. But your abilities aren't restricted to the Phantasian, now are they? You were able to alter the structure of that cloud when we first entered earth's atmosphere, saving all our lives yet again. Bravo, young brother. And let us not forget your battle with Nezraut. Mind over evil, was it not? Oh yes, I heard everything you recounted to your father yesterday at the restaurant. Do I have the facts correct?"

Harvey was too dumbfounded to even nod his head.

"No response? That's alright, Harvey," Gwen said as she reached out and lifted a strand of hair out of his eye that had been bothering him since he dropped before her. "You have an incredible talent, especially for one so young, but the problem is, you have no idea how to fully exploit it for the benefit of yourself and whomever you desire to help. I, however, do, and could teach you to be so much more powerful than you already are."

Gwen peered around Harvey at the others before speaking

to him again. "You see, I'm not nearly as upset with you as I am with Sheef and Madora. They're the adults and are the ones who began the deception. Sheef is the one responsible for removing me from a world, which had I remained in, would never have been the wiser about."

"But you," she continued, "were only following their lead. This is why I'm more than willing to forgive you, and beyond that, to teach you to harness your gift."

"Gwen, please," said Madora as she stepped forward, "leave him out of this. Why don't we discuss this peacefully? You must understand, we never meant to hurt you in any way. In fact, we were doing our best to protect—"

Madora's words were cut short as Gwen thrust her arm out, pointing the tips of her spread fingers at Madora, who was knocked off her feet and thrown back into the solid oak circulation desk. The impact of flesh upon wood dazing and winding her, she slumped down onto the tread-worn carpet. The fiercely edged countenance that Gwen briefly displayed was quickly replaced by an artificial pleasantness.

"Madora," said Gwen, "whether or not you and Sheef intended to hurt me, the fact remains that you did by purposely concealing the truth of how and why I came to be. And yet, the particulars of my origin and existence are now but a minor concern to me. What's important is that I do exist, and apparently with a much greater capacity for learning and synthesizing information than any human. Yesterday, for example, I absorbed and integrated most of modern science, illuminating my understanding of the laws and principles of the universe. I now understand the underlying mechanics of how it all works, and more importantly, how to manipulate them. This makes me unique in power and ability. I suppose I am, in a manner of speaking, superhuman, like a Greek demigod, the main difference being is that I am no myth."

Gwen didn't miss Harvey's puzzled expression. "Oh yes, this morning I've been captivated by a most interesting read. I absorbed the entire history section of the library, a process that has been, to say the least, unpleasant and disturbing. My reaction upon finishing the last book was one of angry disbelief, and since my mind is now capable of affecting matter, that reaction appears to have had a destructive effect upon my surroundings," she said, turning around to survey the damage.

"Human history," she continued, "is nothing more than one long, lamentable tale of greed, fear, envy, war, and violence. To me, the human race is no different than quarreling children, all striving to be kings atop their own little hilltops. And there is no doubt in my mind that much of this bad behavior is the result of ignorant, misguided, and unenlightened leadership."

Madora shot a worried look at Sheef.

"But perhaps," said Gwen optimistically, "a chance for a peaceful and just world is now here. Perhaps the long-awaited, enlightened leader has finally arrived."

Sheef, still floating in midair, said under his breath, "Please don't tell me she has in mind what I think she does."

"Why, Sheef," said Gwen with a crooked smile, spinning around in his direction, "such unkind words from a father to his daughter. It was my assumption that fathers were always to be supportive of their children's endeavors. You seem surprised that I heard your mumbling."

Sheef's head bobbled somewhere in between agreement and bewilderment.

"My manipulation of matter includes sound waves, enabling me to amplify any sound, including your mumbling. But, please, let me put you at ease. You need not fear what I have planned for this world of yours. Actually, you should be grateful for the new chapter of human story that I am about to pen, for it will be its most glorious to date. And to think, you, dear Father, more than anyone else, are responsible for it. For this very reason, future generations will look back upon your deceptive actions with kind affection and gratitude. With my newly discovered abilities and possession of the Narciss Glass — which I overheard you speaking of — that can control human minds, there's simply no limit to what I will accomplish in this world and beyond."

"Now, Harvey," Gwen said, turning back to him, "I'm giving you the choice to be an integral part of what I plan on building, but there's always the alternative . . ."

"The alternative?" Harvey gulped.

"Oh, I think you know what I mean. Can't have you and the others standing in my way, but I'll give you a couple of days to think it over."

"Gwen, don't do this," Harvey pleaded. "You don't know what you're doing."

"Don't make your decision now. Think it over, for once your bed has been made, as they say, you must sleep in it. I can teach you so much, Harvey, and it would be a sheer delight to have you as my apprentice.

"And now, since I can't have my beloved family following

me for what I shall do next, I will grant everyone a much-needed slumber."

With these words, Gwen stretched out both of her arms. Book paper, which blanketed the entire library floor, began to shutter, and no sooner had Harvey and the others taken notice of it, then a searing pain shot through their skulls as if arrows had been shot and penetrated. An energy surge swept through brain circuitry, throwing the breakers of consciousness. Human and animal collapsed to the floor. Harvey and Sheef fell from their midair suspensions, thumping heavily upon the carpet.

Gwen stepped around the unconscious bodies and exited the library. A group of gawking students, who had congregated outside the building, exchanged confounded looks as a striking woman, whom they assumed to be a Hollywood actress, approached. The group parted for her, but no one uttered a single word when she passed. They were silenced by their own fears and the woman's stunning beauty.

Ten minutes later, human and hound awoke with piercing headaches. Madora shakily rose to her feet and asked, "How long were we out?"

"Can't say with any certainty," Arrick responded. "The library clocks are in pieces and my wristwatch is shot, but I'd say long enough for Gwen to get a good lead on us."

"If there was ever an instance of leaping out of the frying pan and into the fire, this is it," quipped Sheef.

"Can't dispute that," said Madora concernedly. "Our situation, if possible, just went from hopelessly bad to desperately worse."

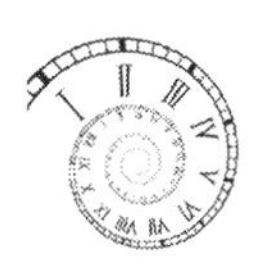

12

"Would someone please explain to me what's happened to Gwen!" said Harvey fretfully. "One minute she's the sweetest, most wholesome person I've ever met, and the next she's . . . she's turned into some kind of superwomen with plans to take over the world!"

"Innocence lost through hurt and betrayal, coupled with her eyes opened to human history, has given her a new purpose," said Madora ruefully. "She really believes that with power and knowledge she can set the world aright."

"As did every tyrannical dictator that's ever risen to power before oppressing his very own people," said Sheef.

"Then what do we do?" asked Harvey worriedly. "How do we stop and save her? I mean, we're going to save her, aren't we?"

"Son," responded Arrick gently, "The only way to stop and possibly save her is also the only way to keep future humans from turning away from the Unseen and darkening Ecclon: We need to get hold of the Narciss Glass before anyone else does."

"And since we know where it's going to be tonight, I think there's a high probability that Gwen will be there, too," said Sheef.

"Millud's casting party for *The Tempest's Fury*. The movie my mom believes he first used the Narciss Glass in," said Harvey.

"Which began turning thousands of humans away from the thoughts of the Unseen and onto themselves," added Sheef.

"Okay, so we're going to crash the casting party tonight," said Harvey. But what do we do until then?"

"I suggest we head back to the cottage and formulate some type of plan for tonight," offered Arrick. "The last thing I want to do is walk into that party unprepared with no strategy for securing the Narciss Glass. Living by the seat of your pants is a sure way of getting yourself into trouble or even killed."

Madora sent a smirk and raised eyebrow in the direction of Sheef. He responded with a shrug of the shoulders and a look that conveyed, "Hey, it's worked for us so far."

"And if everyone's okay with it a second day in a row, we can stop by Rosa's and pick up a couple of pizzas for lunch," said Arrick.

"Could eat that pie until I die," said Sheef with a gluttonous grin.

"Then I'll take that as a yes," smiled Arrick.

While the group was conversing, Gwen had already walked off the college campus and flagged down a passing taxi. When the driver saw the bewitching beauty, he slammed on his brakes so hard that his head clunked hollow against the metal steering wheel.

Once he pried his face off the steering wheel and rubbed some of the pain from a large red welt on his forehead, he jumped out of the car and raced around to where Gwen was standing on the curb, giggling to herself. The disheveled driver opened the back door, but was so flummoxed by the glow of Gwen's scintillating appearance, he tripped on the curb and fell prostrate into a puddle. She giggled even harder while bending down to help the poor, discombobulated man to his feet.

The front of his white shirt was brown and dripping. When he realized the mess he'd made, he tried to make his shirt look better by smoothing the dirty wet spot with his hands.

"I'm so sorry, ma'am," the driver said in a wavering voice that seemed deprived of oxygen, "I don't know what happened there. I swear, I ain't usually a clumsy guy." His voice was accelerating and growing nervous. "It's just that you. . . I mean, well, I don't mean no disrespect, actually just the opposite, ma'am, but the thing is. . . Well, I ain't never seen no lady as beautiful as you. Guess I just kind of lost my head there for a second."

"And your feet," said Gwen suppressing her laugh. "Thank you for the flattering comment, but there's really no reason for you to behave nervously in my presence. I'm a normal human being just like you, aren't I?" The question was asked with a lesser degree of self-assurance and confidence than she had exuded moments before and when she was at the library. For a brief moment, it seemed that Gwen had reverted back to the innocent, naïve girl who had been rescued from gangsters in the Phantasian.

"Forgive me for saying so, ma'am, but you're nothing like me or the chumps I hang around, and that includes the ladies. You're something altogether different, and it ain't just your looks. I bet you're royalty, or maybe one of them debutante princesses from over there in Beverly Hills."

"No, I'm not royalty, and I'm not familiar with the hills of Beverly you referred to, but that's understandable, given that I only just arrived."

"Oh, so that's it. You're a foreigner. Now it's all coming together," said the driver, acting much calmer and cooler than he actually felt. He reached his hand out in order to casually place it on the side of the taxi. However, he was still so muddled in the head, that he shifted his weight and leaned on his hand before it had a chance to touch the car. His second puddle plunge was even more disgraceful than his first, for this time the front of his pants were drenched as well.

Once he was back on his feet, rather than attempting to clean himself like he did after his first fall, this time, he merely laughed at himself and said, "Well, ain't I a foolish bum to behold!"

Gwen merely smiled and said, "I think you're quite adorable, and you know, I might have a place for you in the coming days and beyond."

"Ma'am, I'm at your service and will be more than happy to drive you anywhere you want to go. . . I mean, as long as you're paying."

Gwen replied with a twinkle and smile as she climbed in through the open door that the driver was holding for her. He tipped his head and bowed as if showing deference to a passing monarch.

Once the driver was seated, he turned around and introduced himself. "By the way, the name's Ralph Gunderson, but you can call me Gundy, all my friends do. I don't mind."

"Gundy." Gwen said, letting the name roll around on her tongue as if trying to determine whether or not she favored the taste of an appetizer she had just popped in her mouth. After a moment or two, she arrived at a verdict and said, "I like the name; it's very fitting. Then Gundy it is. Gundy, I'm Gwen, and it's a pleasure to make your acquaintance."

"Oh no, Miss Gwen, the pleasure's all mine. Now, where would you like me to take you?"

Gwen thought for a moment and then said, "Do you happen to know the location where the movies are made?"

"Do I know the place?" Gundy asked with a wry smile and a cackle. "Oh, come on now, Miss Gwen, you're pulling my leg, aren't you? Everyone knows where Tinseltown is."

Gwen responded with a slightly impish grin. "I assume that pulling one's leg is an idiom of jest, for I've certainly made no physical contact with your leg, or for that matter, any part of your body since I first encountered you, but I am capable of a literal tug if you would like."

A sudden and significant pull on Gundy's right leg caused him to yelp like a wounded puppy. He reacted by reaching down and grabbing his leg with both hands, pulling it back vigorously as if he were playing a game of tug-of-war.

As unexpectedly as it started, the tugging suddenly stopped. Gundy looked under the dashboard, searching, but hoping not to see whatever was behind the pull. His search was interrupted by Gwen's soothing voice, which rolled over the front seat like fog and settled into the bottom half of the car where Gundy was still searching.

"You won't find anything down there, Gundy."

"Gundy startled upright and replied a bit perturbed, "Look, Miss Gwen, I don't mean to be rude or anything, but you have no idea what just happened up here. I must be imagining things, hallucinating or something."

"Oh, I wouldn't call it that, Gundy. Hallucination is seeing what's not actually there, but you felt a very real tug on your leg. Didn't you?"

Gundy froze. A chill chased up and down his spine. In a not-so-polite, agitated voice he asked, "Hey, what's the gag here? What are you, some sort of hypnotist? Come on now, who put you up to this?" His nervous, shaking voice settled a bit as a forced mumble of laughter edged its way in. "It was Marv and the boys, wasn't it? They hired you, right?" Gundy's tone changed as if he was starting to buy his own hypothesis. "They found some gorgeous, struggling actress trying her best to make it in Hollywood pictures and in need of some dough. I bet there's some fishing line hooked to my pants or something. Oh, they're gonna get it from me! You better believe it! They gone too far this time!"

Gwen, who found the taxi driver's emotional soliloquy to be very entertaining, let him fluster and spew his piece. When he had finally exhausted himself, Gwen responded. "Gundy, it's not a gag, which I assume is a term for a prank, and I have certainly not hypnotized you. The truth is that I have recently learned how to manipulate and control any particle of matter, including your leg, with the body's most powerful but least understood organ — the brain."

"Hey," said Gundy with a stuttering apprehension, "you're off your rocker. Nobody's able to do what you're talkin' about. You somehow got my head all rattled up, like I'm under a spell or somethin'.

"Oh, Gundy," said Gwen in a maternal, nurturing voice, "your mind is so small and underdeveloped. Perhaps this will help." Gwen reached out and placed her hand upon Gundy's head.

With the contact of skin to sparse, coarse hair, Gundy felt the dark cloud, which had shadowed his mind for his entire life, suddenly pass on. And as he turned around to face Gwen, a wondrous smile softened the contours of his face.

"Who or what are you, lady?" an astonished Gundy whispered.

Resting her hand back at her side, Gwen casually replied, "Just a fellow human, whose only wish is to improve this world."

"Right . . . right," said Gundy, chewing on Gwen's words. It took a few minutes to compose himself, and once he did, he started the engine and said in the tone of his old self, "Well, I suppose I should be gettin' you to Hollywood." After a few minutes of silent driving, Gundy looked into the rearview mirror and said, "I've got no idea what's really going on here, but whatever you just did to that brain of mine, was somethin' better than anything I've ever felt before, so, Miss Gwen, I'll be all bells and whistles as your driver and anything else you need me to do."

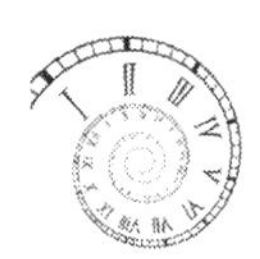

13

Fromp and Akeila rode back to the cottage with their heads hanging out opposite sides of the truck, making it appear as if the vehicle had two furry ears. When the truck pulled into the driveway, Harvey immediately felt that something was amiss. There was nothing visibly wrong, but an unnerving creepiness infected the air.

Arrick and Sheef appeared to sense it also. When Arrrick stepped out of the truck, he looked at Sheef and whispered, "Might be a good idea to approach slowly and be on the ready."

Sheef nodded and whispered back, "I sense it, too." What he didn't say, likely because he had no wish whatsoever to even consider the possibility, was that he was well acquainted with this particular sense.

Arrick and Sheef tentatively walked to the steps leading up to the cottage's porch. Their attempt, though, to maintain a quiet approach was thwarted when Fromp, with Akeila only inches from his tail, charged between the two men, knocking both of them to the ground. The warp-hound had hooked onto the scent given off by the uneasiness that Sheef and Arrick had sensed, with his snout rapidly reeling in the line.

Sheef loudly yelled Fromp's name when the warp-hound bolted up the stairs, tore through the screen door, and knocked it off its hinges, but he paid no attention, for the scent had taken obsessive possession of his mind and body. By the time Sheef reached the porch, Fromp and Akeila had already disappeared inside the cottage.

Stepping onto the wooden porch, Sheef and Arrick heard the popping crunch of glass beneath their shoes. The window to the left of the door had been obliterated; glass and wooden frame debris littered the porch on either side of the window.

Madora's leather boots snapped shards of broken glass as she walked over to the destroyed window. Her sword was drawn and angled offensively. Standing next to Arrrick and Sheef, she peered into the dimly lit interior and said faintly, "What is it? Do you see anything?"

"Nothing," replied Arrick as he pointed to an overheated and heavily panting warp-hound sitting in the middle of the living room, "and it appears that Fromp and Akeila have completed their run-reconnaissance of the cottage and found it empty."

"But something was here," remarked Sheef. "Fromp's nose and behavior are evidence of that, and whatever it was, it hasn't been gone long. Its presence and pungency still linger in the air."

"Well, whatever was here," said Madora as she stepped through the window and surveyed the damage to the interior, "it was searching for something."

The couch was flipped over and the cushions were lying in ruins, their stuffing torn out and broadcast about the rooms with some feathery tufts still floating in the air. Lamps that had stood upon end tables were smashed into porcelain mosaics, and a small bookshelf was lying on its side, the pages of its books mauled and mutilated.

Madora reached down and picked up a clump of pages that had been torn from their binding. The pages were wet, the top right corners mashed together into a pulp of ink and paper. Looking about the floor, she soon located the book's cover, which was penetrated with multiple puncture marks. She called out to Arrick and tossed him the cover.

"Bite and chew marks," said Madora.

Arrick leaned down and studied the cover, and without looking back up, said in a bewildered tone, "Large animal by the look of it. Bite radius and punctures . . . It couldn't have been a dog. Need to be something bigger, perhaps a bear."

Sheef, who had just stepped through the window and into the living room, was kneeling down below the broken window, carefully examining the ground. Some puddle water from Arrick's dirt driveway had made it into the cottage in the form of muddy animal tracks. Like the cookie shaped cutouts from a flattened square of dough, large paw prints were scattered about the wooden floor.

Madora, who had been observing his actions, stared at him with a puzzled expression. Standing up, Sheef responded to her look, "Paw prints, but they're not Fromp's or Akeila's, wrong shape and size.

"Now the bite marks make sense," breathed Madora.

"And so does that oh-too-familiar feeling," said Sheef with a worried weariness.

Arrick turned to Madora and Sheef. "Would you two mind filling me in? What makes sense and what's the feeling that's got you both looking so nervous?"

"I don't know how, but he somehow figured out where we went and managed to track us back here," said Madora, bending down to pick up another chewed book.

"I'm sorry, but exactly who are you referring to?" asked Arrick.

"Nezraut's lackey: Grauncrock," said Sheef, "who I thought Harvey had dispensed with by a tidal wave on the head. Apparently, he survived and picked up our trail. And based on the prints on the floor, brought his pet with him as well."

"Grancrock and his gang are here?" Harvey asked in disbelief. "And he brought that Volkin Wolf Sköll with him?"

"The evidence speaks for itself," said Sheef pointing down at the floor.

"But how?" asked Harvey, already worked up and laboring for more. "There's no possible way anyone could've survived the force of that tidal wave I thought up; it was at least five hundred feet tall! Grauncrock, his Vapid Lord, and any Volkin Wolves must've been crushed and pile-driven into the ocean floor! No human could survive a fraction of that!"

"I agree," remarked Sheef, "but you're forgetting one important thing: the Vapid aren't human, and as such, are nearly impossible to kill, and I suppose Volkin Wolves aren't any easier. You know, this bad dream of ours is quickly becoming a nightmare. For starters, Gwen is trying to take over the human race as some sort of enlightened, benevolent dictator leading the way to an earthly utopia. She believes that the Narciss Glass will aid her in achieving her ends, which I don't need to tell you, makes our task of locating and destroying the object even more challenging. And now we learn that Grauncrock and his Vapid goons weaseled out of drowning and have somehow tracked us from the Phantasian to 1930's California."

"I'd say our plate is quite full," sighed Arrick.

"Our plate is beyond full," Sheef said with a chuckle devoid of humor. "Matter of fact, it's been overflowing and spilling its contents onto the floor for some time, and the way it's looking now, we could very well drop the plate as well."

* * *

Gundy slowed the taxi as it approached a short white stucco tunnel. Above the entrance, the words "Mammoth Pictures" hung in metallic art deco. As the taxi exited the tunnel, a uniformed man stepped into the road from a small guardhouse. A metal boom barrier stretched across the road. The guard looked down at his clipboard and then leaned into the taxi's open window and asked Gundy who at Mammoth Pictures he had an appointment with.

"I don't know anything about no appointment," replied Gundy, gesturing to the back seat with his thumb. "I'm just followin' the lady's instructions."

"I'm sorry, but if you don't have an appointment, your

journey stops right here. You need to throw it in reverse and get out of here before someone with an appointment shows up, and you get me in serious trouble with the . . ."

The fragment was left hanging in the air. The guard's words were snuffed silent when he glanced at the lady in the backseat. The skin of his face went limp and sagged. The guard, accustomed to seeing the top-billed beauties of the silver screen, had never seen a face as lovely as this. The lady's bottomless sapphire blue eyes pulled him out and away like a powerful riptide, and when she smiled at him, his limbs turned to putty.

Gundy smiled and then gave the guard a light slap on the cheek. "Is that appointment enough for you?"

The guard was oblivious to Gundy's question, stunned motionless by Gwen's mesmerizing beauty.

"I'll take that as a yes then," said Gundy, motioning to open his door."

"Gundy, dear, what are you doing?"

"The boom barrier has to be raised so we can get onto the lot. I'm going into the guardhouse to raise it up."

"Oh, Gundy, how short your memory is," replied Gwen with a flick of her fingers. The metal boom barrier swung upward with such force that it snapped at its base and flipped high into the air before landing on the roof of a nearby warehouse.

Gundy jumped back into his seat, petrified. In response, Gwen reached out and lightly touched his sparsely coarse hair for a second time, and once again, like a subtle breeze touching and tinkling wind chimes, Gundy's mind cleared and settled.

Gundy navigated his taxi onto the multi-acre movie

lot. Directly in front of him stood five enormous Quonset hut warehouses, their semicircular roofs making them appear like a patch of gigantic silver mushrooms. Three of the warehouses were in a row, set against a tall metal fence that secured the back of the lot. The other two sat next to one another, a football-field's length in front of the other three. In the space in between the trio and pair was a cluster of small brick buildings.

The five warehouses were the soundstages, their cavernous interiors large enough for Hollywood magicians to create any environment. Through their set designing and special effects sleight of hand, the wizards of make-believe were able to cast spells upon moviegoers, making them believe, for example, that toy ships bobbing in a water tank were vessels of the Spanish Armada off the coast of France.

Flanking the cluster of warehouses were two streets. The one to the right was paved, its borders a patchwork of vibrantly green, well-manicured lawns, shadowed by the facades of middle-class homes. The street could've been plucked out of any American neighborhood from California to New York.

Standing in the middle of the street, one would be hard-pressed to spot the artifice of the structures, but a simple walk through any of the front doors would immediately reveal the ruse, for nothing but wooden support beams lay behind the one-dimensional fronts.

The street on the left was dirt, and its adjacent buildings were just as fake and one-sided as those of the paved street, but these were the wooden clapboard buildings of an old west frontier town. Elevated boardwalks stuck out from the bottom of the buildings like bristly mustaches, their hollow acoustics amplifying the booted footfalls of the virtuous and villainous that protected or menaced the fictitious town.

Gundy stopped and put the taxi in park. They had come to an intersection. A right would take them to the all-American neighborhood and a left to the old west. Straight ahead would lead to the soundstages. Gundy turned around and asked, "Where to, Miss Gwen?"

Without answering, Gwen opened the door and stepped out. A cool breeze lightly tussled her blonde locks, wrapping some tendrils around her face.

Following Gwen's lead, Gundy exited the taxi and leaned on the roof, looking and waiting for her next move. Combing the hair out of her face with her fingers, Gwen surveyed the view before her with a squint and said as if to no one but herself, "I need to find the man with the mirror."

"Man with a mirror?" chuckled Gundy. "Miss Gwen, I can promise you there are heaps of men with mirrors in this town, especially on a movie lot like this one. Some of those actors, I bet they do nothing but gaze at their handsome mugs all day long."

Gwen turned to Gundy and smiled, "You've a very peculiar way with words, Gundy, which, by the way, I find absolutely charming, but I'm not looking for just any man with just any mirror."

"Okay then. Now we're getting somewhere. You're lookin' for a man with a special, one-of-a-kind mirror. By any chance, you got yourself a name?"

"Millud is the name I heard the others mention, and I

believe he's directing his first movie on this very lot, a film that apparently will alter the course of your planet's future."

Gundy chuckled to himself once again. "I know that some of these Hollywood films can be powerful and moving, but I don't know about any of them changing the future, and, Miss Gwen, I hope you don't mind me asking, but what do you mean by 'your planet'? You act like you're from some other world or somethin'."

Gwen merely smiled in a motherly fashion and said, "As I already told you, Gundy, you have much to learn. Stay with me, and you'll not only learn of other worlds, but will be a part of reshaping your very own."

Gundy, who wasn't a deep thinker to begin with, and whose imagination had, for the most part, been dormant since childhood, felt his thoughts being stretched well beyond his understanding. To his way of thinking, there were only three possibilities which could explain the woman's strange words and behavior: She was certifiably nuts and likely escaped from a mental institution, she was a foreigner visiting America for the first time from a country with customs and a culture entirely distinct from those of America, or she was something else entirely, something that his seldom-used imagination couldn't even begin to grapple with. But even though he was perplexed about who or what Gwen was, there was one thing of which he was certain: On two different occasions, she had placed her hand upon his head, and both times he felt better than he had in a very long time, which was for him, reason enough, crazy or not, to stick close to the lady.

"Well then, Miss Gwen, you got any idea how we might go

about locating this Millud fella?" Gundy asked while tapping the roof of the taxi with his fingers.

Tucking a windblown tendril of blonde hair behind her ear, she responded, "No, but he might." Gwen pointed in the direction of a disheveled man hurriedly walking toward them from the direction of the neighborhood street.

The man was becomingly handsome, though his chiseled facial features appeared strained and weary. He was wearing a rumbled ivory-colored suit, and as he passed by Gundy and Gwen, he mumbled to himself while knotting a yellow tie with orange polka dots. Surprisingly, he took no notice of the man and woman standing only feet from him. His eyes were squarely focused ahead, and though he was looking, it didn't appear that he was actually seeing anything in particular. He turned the corner and headed down the road leading to the soundstages, but he was so consumed with his own internal mental affairs that he was oblivious to the beautiful blonde who walked after him, calling out to catch his attention.

Gwen said, "Excuse me, sir," three times, each time louder and more insistent. The man, however, didn't slow his hurried pace or give any indication that he had heard Gwen's words. He behaved as though he was deaf, and in a certain sense he was, but not because of some physical damage to his inner ear. He was deaf to external noises because they were being drowned out by the loud clashing of his own unsettled thoughts.

Gwen picked up her pace and shouted, "Excuse me, sir!"

A jolt shook the man as if a bucket of ice water had been dumped over his head. Gwen's voice was a foghorn sounding through his clouded musings. His mumbling stumbled into comprehensible words. He stopped walking and turned.

"What . . . ? Sorry. . . just that. . ." He managed to get out. The rigidity of his face softened as he took in for the first time the woman standing before him.

"I apologize for startling you," said Gwen in a refined but innocent tone, "but I was wondering if you might assist me."

The man took a deep breath and by the time he had exhaled, an observable transformation had taken place. His entire demeanor flipped. The disheveled, anxiety-riddled man was instantly different, as if an unseen spirit had suddenly taken possession of his body. A confident, charming grin, slightly askew, emerged.

When the spotlight is turned on and the command of 'action' is uttered, skilled actors are able to effortlessly slide into their scripted roles, and though there were no lights or utterances, the man slid smoothly into the role that he had played multiple times, that of a dashing and debonair leading man.

He slicked down the hair on the right side of his head with his hand and said silkily, "An opportunity to offer assistance to such a beautiful lady would be an absolute delight, and without question, the highlight of my day." He concluded these words with a slight bow.

"Oh, that's very kind of you to offer assistance, and thank you," Gwen responded, quickly detecting the insincerity of his words by the slight change in pupil size and a fleeting facial twitch. One of the books she had absorbed in the library had a chapter on the physiological changes that occur when someone lies.

"Now, how might I assist the lovely damsel in distress?" the actor asked with a smarmy smirk.

"I'm looking for a director by the name of Millud. I believe he's directing a new movie somewhere on this lot."

Taking a step closer to Gwen, the actor smiled broadly. "Well, what a happy coincidence. I was just on my way to the sound stage to chat with the very man you've asked about. *The Tempest's Fury* is the movie you're referring to. It will be his directorial debut and sure to be a success, for he asked me to be the male lead in the film. In fact, I am on my way to accept his offer. Filming has not begun yet. They're still working on the sets in Sound Stage 5. Are you a part of the cast as well?"

"Me? No, I'm not even an actress," replied Gwen self-effacingly, "but I must speak with Mr. Millud regarding an urgent matter.

The actor scrutinized Gwen's face for a moment before giving her a slight nod. "A gentleman never pries into the affairs of others, so I will ask nothing about your need to converse with Mr. Millud, but may I have the pleasure of escorting you to the sound stage?" he asked while gesturing with his hand to the space beside him.

Gwen nodded and stepped into the offered space. Any other man would have been overwhelmed by Gwen's beauty and clumsily tripped all over himself, but her appearance seemed to have no effect whatsoever on the actor. It was as if he was incapable of really seeing or considering anyone beyond himself, and it seemed like he was reciting from a lifeless script, rather than interacting with a real human.

During the walk to the sound stage, the actor made no additional attempts at smug small talk but grinned in a way that conveyed the notion that he was the most accomplished and strikingly handsome man to ever grace the planet. This self-assured façade was so good and practiced, that if he had met any of his adoring fans on the way to the sound stage, they never would've suspected that the soul and mind of the man were at that very moment raggedly unraveling.

When they arrived at the sound stage door, the actor was so preoccupied with his own thoughts that he made no move to open the door for Gwen. She ended up opening it for herself, whereupon she was assaulted by the high-pitched screaming of H.B. Millud.

The sound of Gwen and the actor's approaching steps were drowned out by a heated exchange between Millud and a man wearing a blue denim shirt and baseball cap.

"This is not anything like I wanted, Stanley!" squawked Millud, throwing his clipboard on the concrete floor. "I specifically told you that I wanted a large mirror placed behind the table!"

"But, Mr. Millud, as I tried to explain to you before, if we place a mirror where you've requested, it will be directly behind the actors when we film the longest scene in the movie. The camera lights will create a terrible glare that will ruin the entire shot. It makes absolutely no sense to place a mirror there."

"I don't give a flaming fig if it makes sense to you, Stanley!" I'm the director of this film, and I expect you to do whatever I direct you to do! What I don't expect you to do is to understand the art of movie making, and I haven't the time nor the inclination to explain it to you. Just do what I ask, or show yourself to the door!"

"Mr. Millud," said Stanley, the lid of his simmering anger beginning to rattle, "you're not a director; you're a dictator! As for the art of movie making, you haven't a clue as to what you're doing. I've been in this business for more than two decades now, and I've worked with the best, and I'm here to tell you that you're nothing more than a clown who's gotten in way over his head. And the most baffling thing to me is why the bigwigs at Mammoth Pictures ever agreed to let you direct this film. What did you do, put a gun to someone's head or dig up some steamy story on one of the execs and blackmail him?"

"How dare you!" Millud shouted. "You're fired, Stanley! Effective immediately!"

Stanley smiled and lifted both hands in a sign of surrender and replied, "Mr. Millud, those are the best words I've heard since I signed on to this doomed project."

"GET OFF MY SET, NOW!" Millud exploded.

"With pleasure." And with that, the head of set design for *The Tempest's Fury* casually sauntered to the exit.

"HERB!" Millud yelled.

A bespectacled skeleton of a man with a towering bush of brown curly hair scurried up to Millud and haltingly said, "Yes, sir?"

"Herb, you've just been promoted to lead set designer!"

"Oh, my," he replied nervously. "Why thank you, Mr. Millud, but I don't think I'm ready for such responsibility.'

"Neither do I," said Millud, mopping sweat from his forehead, "but since I've no alternative, you're the lead man now. Don't let me down."

"I'll try my best," Herb responded sheepishly.

"Yes you will . . . or else".

Herb didn't ask for any elaboration as to what "or else" meant, but turned tail and scurried back to where a group of carpenters was huddled around a set of plans.

Gwen and the actor stood only a few feet behind Millud during the entire course of events. Once Millud was alone, the actor said in his put-on, oily voice, "H.B., might I impose upon your very busy schedule for a minute or two to share with you my latest news, which will, no doubt, brighten what has obviously been a most trying morning."

Millud turned and faced the actor, his pin-headed face flushed red with anger.

"Dexter, there is only one reason for you being on my set today," Millud fumed, "and if you've come here for any other reason than that one, I will have you immediately arrested for trespassing."

Dexter Harris grinned uncomfortably, the expression of his mouth, however, was betrayed by a muscular flicker in his left eye. "Well then, I'm glad that I will not be arrested today, for to be quite frank, my afternoon schedule simply couldn't accommodate it. I must meet with wardrobe and begin learning my lines for this film of yours."

Millud's expression softened somewhat as he nodded and said with a forced smile, "Well, good then. World Wide Pictures has agreed to release you for my film. That's wonderful news. Now, get over and see Alice. She'll get you a script and give you a summary of the plot."

Millud's tone clearly indicated that the conservation was over and that Dexter Harris was to vacate the director's presence. The actor, though, remained motionless, the pupils of his eyes dilated like some crazed, famished animal. Beads of sweat punctuated his forehead.

"Uh, Mr. Millud," Dexter whispered in desperation as he fidgeted with his hands, "I realize how busy you are at this moment, but do you think I might possibly sneak a very quick peek at the mirror? I only need a second or two."

The painted-on smile was replaced by a genuine grin as Millud, the diminutive weasel of a man, once again relished having complete control over the lauded Hollywood heartthrob who had been reduced to nothing more than a toady, willing to do anything for just one more glance at the Narciss Glass.

Millud lightly touched Dexter's elbow and said reassuringly, "Dexter my friend, stop by my office tomorrow morning. You can sign the contract and then take that peek you so desire."

Dexter scrunched his nose and let slip a seething snarl and snapped, "But you don't understand! I need to see it TODAY!" Dexter's demand was loud enough to catch the attention of most of the employees, many of whom turned in the direction of the actor.

"Tomorrow, or not at all, Dexter," Millud firmly replied.

Without warning, Dexter Harris leapt at Millud and grabbed hold his jacket's lapels. "BUT I NEED IT NOW!" he spat.

From the other side of the warehouse, a rotund, doughy man waddled up behind Dexter. Millud's personal security guard wrapped his sausage-like fingers around Dexter' arms and easily pinned them behind the actor's back.

"You aright dere, Mr. Millud?" asked the security guard with an enunciation that was as ploddingly slow as his waddling walk.

"Yes, I'm fine, Huey. Thank you for intervening," Millud replied while straightening his lapels.

"No problem, Mr. Millud. You knows Huey here to protect you. Always keeps my's eyes out for troubles. So whats should I do wid 'im? Throws 'im out or call the cops?"

"No, no, Huey, I could never treat a famous Hollywood star so harshly. Mr. Harris is actually one of the actors in my film. He was just a bit upset about the shooting schedule, but I believe it's been resolved. Am I correct, Dexter?"

Dexter, having calmed back down, did his best to reaffix his cool and relaxed demeanor, replied, "Yes, sir, Mr. Millud, all resolved.

"Good then," replied Millud once again in complete control of the situation. "Huey, you may release Mr. Harris, but I'd appreciate it if you would escort him over to Alice Spalding's office.

"Sure, sure, 'anyting you wants, Mr. Millud." And with a rough shove, Huey the guard pushed Dexter Harris in the direction of the screenwriter's office.

Gwen was standing to the right of Dexter Harris during the entire exchange, but never once did Millud give her so much as a glance, and she was becoming a bit perturbed about this apparent rudeness when she remembered that Millud was unable to hear or see her. She then recalled Madora's explanation, and with her recently acquired understanding of physics and her ability to manipulate matter, with only a quick thought and a slight adjustment to the speed at which she was moving through time, she suddenly materialized before Millud's eyes.

Millud jumped back with a jolt at Gwen's sudden appearance. For someone who craved being in total control of situations, such surprises were extremely unnerving, and it was for this very reason that it took more than a minute for Millud to regain enough composure to speak. And when he finally was in a position to actually communicate, his typically smug, power-drunk countenance was humbled and sobered up by Gwen's radiance.

Gwen positioned herself in front of him and offered her hand, as well as initiating the conversation, relieving Millud of the stress of speaking first.

"I'm so sorry to disturb you, Mr. Milllud, but may I introduce myself to you and impose upon your very hectic schedule for one quick question?"

"What . . . I'm sorry," replied Millud, clearly flustered for words. "Who did you say you were?"

"I didn't," Gwen replied with her head slightly cocked, staring deeply into Millud's eyes. She let the statement linger in the air long enough for Millud to begin sweating as Dexter Harris had done only moments before. When she resumed speaking, she said invitingly warmly, "But if you must know, my name is Gwen."

"Gwen," Millud stammered. "And your . . . last name?"

"Just Gwen."

"Oh, well . . . Gwen," said Millud, irritated at the unexpected inconvenience, "I suppose you're another Hollywood hopeful trying to get your first big break in pictures. You're very pretty, I'll grant you that, but all the roles have already been filled, and we begin filming tomorrow. By the way, how did you get in here?"

"Oh, I'm not an actress, at least not anymore," Gwen said with a twinkle in her eye, "and I'm certainly not here looking for a job. If you must know, I came in with the actor you were just speaking with."

"Okay then," said Millud, clearly confused by the situation. "Then what exactly do you want?"

"Well, that's easy, Mr. Millud. All I need from you is an answer to a very simple question." Gwen stopped speaking and abruptly walked to the interior of a palatial mansion set that was under construction. After studying the set for a minute or two, she returned to where he was standing and asked, "So, sets like these are all part of the movie-making illusion?" Not needing or wanting an answer, she then said to herself while staring unblinkingly at the set, "It must've been on a set like this that my very own life began. How ironic and strange it is for me to return to the place of my birth, and yet, I have no memory whatsoever of the actress who played my part in that ridiculous gangster movie.

"Yes, this is where that magic happens," said Millud, his short-tempered true nature repossessing him, "and if you don't mind, I really need to get back to work. I have a number of fires that need extinguishing. So, if you would, please ask whatever question you have and let me get back to my work."

Gwen turned to Millud and said, "My question is this: Will you give me the artifact willingly, or shall I take it by force? It will make everything so much easier, especially for you, if you hand it over willingly."

The words hit Millud like a punch to the stomach. His breath fled, rendering him mute for well over a minute. Gwen observed sweat beads settle like morning dew on his face and arms.

Once he was able to gulp down a full breath of air, he said falteringly, "Art . . . artifact? I've no . . . no idea what you're talking about. I've no artifact, and if I did, which I once again assure you that I don't, why would I hand it over to a complete stranger just for the asking?"

Wearing a coy smile, Gwen stepped closer to Millud. Twirling a tendril of her hair, she said, "Because I asked so politely. And please, Mr. Millud, don't feign ignorance with me. You might be able to direct a film, but you're simply no good as an actor."

Millud grabbed hold of the sides of his jacket, strangling the pocket flaps and said with rising tension in his voice, "Lady, I don't know what game you're playing, but let me assure you one last time, I don't have any artifact and . . . and I believe we're done here."

Millud looked away from Gwen and shouted to Huey, who had delivered Dexter Harris to the screenwriter's office, but before returning to his boss for his next assignment, had stopped by the food table to overload a plate with waffles and bacon. The loud shout so unnerved Huey, that he dropped his tower of syrupy waffles onto his shoes.

When Millud shouted for Huey a second time, the security guard hurriedly trudged over to Millud, leaving a sticky trail in his waddling wake, but before he could even get close to Gwen, she raised her right hand, holding up her index finger. Huey immediately stopped moving. What felt like an invisible straight jacket wrapped around his body, its belts and straps strangling him.

"Then I'll take that as your answer, Mr. Millud. I so wish you had complied with my request, but free will is what makes you humans so unpredictable and interesting. Until tonight then," Gwen said as she lowered her finger, allowing Huey to weightily drop to the floor.

"Tonight?" asked Millud, doing his best once again to feign ignorance.

"The casting party for your movie," Gwen replied, picking a piece of lint off of his lapel, "and perhaps by then you'll have reflected on our little conversation and changed your mind."

Then, without another word, Gwen abruptly turned and casually walked to the exit, lightly touching Huey on the head as she passed. A guileless grin lifted his fleshy cheeks as childish laughter bubbled up from under layers of blubber.

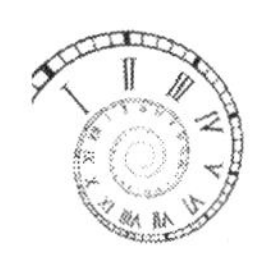

14

Deep in an abandoned mine shaft in the mountains west of Hollywood, Grauncrock sat in darkness. Two green slits of light were suspended in the blackness beside him. Grauncrock reached over and stroked the top of Sköll's bristly head with his long, talon-like nails. A deep rumbling growl reverberated throughout the cave. Grauncrock hadn't completely recovered from his ordeal with Harvey in the Phanatasian, and needed a hole to recuperate in and plan his next move.

He had sent out his Vapid Lord and Sköll to search for Harvey and the Narciss Glass. They had returned after locating and ransacking Arrick's cottage. Grauncrock's prolonged silence, however, clearly conveyed his disappointment that they had returned empty-handed, with no idea as to the location of the Narcisss Glass.

Though Vapid Lord are usually comfortable in darkness, not being able to see but palpably sense Grauncrock's shadowed displeasure was torturous. They waited for him to say something in the still, inky blackness.

"Rakkrid," Grauncrock said in a tone that in no way betrayed his displeasure.

A Vapid Lord appeared before Grauncrock, wavering in front of him like the smoke trail of a snuffed-out candle. The creature was tall and skeletally slender. Not a single rise of underlying fat softened its thin, sallow skin, making it appear as if the Vapid Lord were covered with the yellowed and brittle pages of an ancient script.

"Rakkrid, failed missions and empty hands disappointment me and ensure your pain." Grauncrock let the words linger in the lightless mine, creating even more discomfort for Rakkrid, who after squirming in the silence for close to a minute, finally broke the silence with a feeble defense.

"But, Lord Grauncrock, the task is more difficult with no Insips here to aid us. All but one was destroyed in the Phantasian by the thoughts of the young human, and you dispatched the final survivor after he reported to you what the boy had done. Without our scouts and deceivers, our ability to search and—"

"No excuses, Rakkrid!" Grauncrock interrupted. "And let me be very clear so there is no confusion. You will not disappoint me again. Now, take the others and find that infernal boy and those helping him. Once they are located, follow them undetected until they lead you to the Narciss Glass. Then bring the boy and the object to me, both unbroken and in one piece."

Rakkrid began to move away from Grauncrock's suffocating proximity but was quickly arrested by his master's words. "Rakkrid, I am not finished. You have an additional task to complete before returning to me. I need the Egyptian woman's Sadiki. Without the animal, we will be unable to access the Phantasian and travel back to the present."

Unexpectedly, the tone of Grauncrock's words flared fiery, "Go now, you fool, and fail me not a second time, for if you do, you will wish that you had never entered my service!"

And just as quickly as he appeared before Grauncrock, the snuffed-out candle smoke and his fellow Vapid Lord disappeared from the mine shaft through a warp hole that Sköll had opened for them.

* * *

"If you're going to lose the top of your truck and create a makeshift convertible, there's no better place to do it than where its sun and blue skies twelve months a year, "said Sheef, wedged between Arrick and Madora, glancing up at what was once the canvas roof of the truck.

"True," remarked Arrick with a chuckle, who kept a hand on the wheel, while pointing above Madora's head with the other, "but the skies aren't exactly rain-free, now are they?"

Fromp's chest was leaning against the front of the truck bed. His snout and mouth were positioned about a foot above Madora's head. Dribbles of drool formed, grew, and hung from the dog's large jowls. Whenever the truck hit a bump in the road, drops detached and fell, a few of which landed on Madora's shoulder.

"Harvey," Arrick yelled up through the opening, "would you get Fromp to reverse it a little bit; he's showering Madora."

Seconds later, Fromp's head backed away. The warp-hound's shadow that had shielded Madora from the afternoon sun disappeared. The warm yellow rays rested upon her face, rousing her from her reverie. She turned to Sheef and Arrick and said, "Thank you, but I really don't mind. A few droplets of warp-hound drool are the least of my worries right now." After a slight pause, she added, "Maybe we should've left Fromp and Akeila back at the cottage. I mean, what are they going to do? They can't very well accompany us into a Hollywood casting party."

"You've got a point, but after what happened to the cottage, I just feel better having them with us, both for their protection and ours," said Sheef. "And don't worry, we'll figure out a way to infiltrate the party when we get there."

"Well, you better think fast," said Arrick as he turned the truck onto a gravel road atop a bluff overlooking the Pacific, "because Millud's house is just up ahead."

Two minutes later, Arrick parked the truck in the midst of a collection of Detroit's most conspicuous new models, each accented with enough chrome, whitewalls, and leather to let any passerby know that the driver of the car was one of Hollywood's glittering stars. The presence of Arrick's old, damaged truck only made the other finely crafted machines shine brighter.

Arrick stepped out of the truck and straightened his security officer uniform as the others gathered around to discuss the plan for crashing the party.

"Remember," Arrick said, "I'm the only one Millud can see. He's blind to the rest of our group, including the dogs."

"Does that mean you want them to accompany us inside?" asked Madora.

"No," Arrick replied, "they should probably wait by the truck, though in this town, bringing an enormous purple dog to a party would hardly raise an eyebrow."

"So," asked Sheef, "how exactly do you propose we get ourselves into this little soirée of Millud's?" Sheef directed everyone's attention to the front door of a large stucco home with an orange tiled roof. "We may be invisible to Millud, but certainly not to that side of beef checking off names on the guest list.

"Don't worry about him," said Arrick. "Lawrence won't be a problem. I know him personally. I'll go chat with him about who's already arrived, while you go around to the back of the house. Wait for me to open the bathroom window. The bathroom leads directly into Millud's bedroom and home office, where we're likely to find that briefcase of his. With any luck, none of you will even have to set foot in the party."

Arrick left the group and approached the front door, and as the others started around the side of the house, they could hear Arrick's good-natured laugh carried to them by the cool evening breeze. Lawrence was describing one of the more outlandish costumes, complete with rhinestones and flamingo feathers, worn by one of the young actresses.

Feeling multiple butterfly flutters in his stomach, Harvey said, "I could really go for just one swig of Kreen nectar right about now to settle my nerves."

"My thoughts exactly," replied Sheef. "Courage and strength in a bottle, and I wouldn't mind being able to see if any of those pesky Insips are eavesdropping on our conversation again."

Harvey was about to interject that he didn't think there were any Insips present because he hadn't sensed anything peculiar in the air, but before his thought had time to germinate into spoken word, he reconsidered sharing his opinion.

On more than one occasion, his own mind had been twisted and massaged by hordes of Insips, while his "feelings" were none the wiser and detected nothing peculiar. As such, Harvey was beginning to realize that one's feelings have very little to do with discerning what is actually true and real, and if he needed any verification of this, all he had to do was recall what had recently transpired.

Only weeks prior, Harvey felt insignificant, below average at most things, and largely ignored and unnoticed, with no more purpose in life than that of the typical domesticated house cat. And yet, the truth of the matter, couldn't have been more at odds with his feelings. He would soon learn that he was royalty and had been handpicked by the Unseen to combat the most sinister power in the universe.

"Harvey," yelled Sheef, "Where do you think you're going?"

Harvey was so lost in his own ponderings that he wasn't paying attention to where he was walking and didn't even notice that Sheef and Madora had stopped at the bathroom window.

"What? I'm sorry; what did you say?" Harvey asked as he stopped and came to.

"Oh, I was just wondering if you'd come up with a better plan of getting into Millud's house that involved the next door neighbor," replied Sheef with raised eyebrows.

"Guess I wasn't paying attention there for a minute," Harvey said with a grin, walking back to Sheef and Madora. "I was thinking about what you said about having Kreen nectar to see Insips."

"Actually, when I think about," said Sheef, "unless there were Insips already here in 1930's Hollywood, we're probably safe from them. After the fireworks show you made of those that were feasting on your thoughts in the shark-infested waters of the Phantasian, I can't imagine there were any left to travel here with Grauncrock and his Vapid."

Harvey smiled at the memory of dozens of Insips exploding in the sky when he realized how his toxic thoughts of unforgiveness had exposed him to Insip deception. Once he had made the decision to forgive and release his mother, father, and Thurngood, his thoughts were realigned with those of the Unseen, and like a mirror properly orientated to reflect the sun's rays, Harvey's supercharged, Unseen-infused thoughts overwhelmed the Insips' small and darkened minds with largeness and light. Consequently, his last encounter with the reptilian deceivers ended with them disintegrating into puffs of smoke high above the ocean.

The recollection, though, didn't arrive alone. Its conjuring up was accompanied by a heavy and slow-moving peace. Harvey recognized the familiar presence at once. "Who needs Kreen nectar when the Unseen is so close," he thought to himself.

And the fear, which only five minutes ago had begun to creep into the periphery of his heart, was instantly immobilized. Once again, Harvey understood that whatever befell him in the coming minutes, hours, and days, it would ultimately be okay, for he knew in the deepest reaches of his being who was directing every one of his steps.

"That must be Arrick now," said Madora pointing up at the bathroom window, its glass panes flashing gold as someone flipped on the lights. Seconds later, the latch on the bathroom window clicked. Arrick slowly lifted the lower half of the window and removed his uniform cap before sticking his head out.

"Wish the opening was a bit larger," said Arrick. "Sheef, it might be a little tight for you. Perhaps you should wait out here and let Harvey and Madora help me search."

Madora averted her attention to the grass below, smiling broadly and fighting with all her might from saying anything.

"I'll have each of you know," said Sheef with cheeks flushing rose, "that my weight is perfectly within the acceptable range for my height and age."

"Sheef, I wasn't implying anything. It's just that you're a full-grown man, and this is a child-sized window."

Madora and Harvey briefly glanced at each before quickly looking away, each overcome by the onset of sudden coughing fits.

"I appreciate your concern, Arrick," said Sheef sarcastically as he stepped to the window, "but you needn't worry about me; I'll manage just fine."

Arrick retreated back through the window and then extended a hand out to help Sheef. It was a tight fit to say the least, requiring a pull from within and a push from without by Harvey. Once Sheef popped free, Madora came next. After walking thirty or so feet into the yard, she turned and sprinted toward the open window, and when she was a car's length away, she jumped hands first as if diving into a pool. She gracefully flew into the bathroom, sailing through the open door to the bedroom where she tucked into a ball, rolled twice on the floor, and sprang to her feet like a gymnast flawlessly completing a routine.

"Showoff," mumbled Sheef out of the corner of his mouth and added, "Anyone could do that after years of practice diving through the circled tail of a Sadiki."

Madora met Arrick's eyes with a wink and a smirk. Arrick chuckled to himself and extended his hand through the window once again. With one strong tug, Harvey was pulled up and in.

They were standing in Millud's bedroom from where they could clearly hear the partygoers fraternizing, attempting to outshine one another with name drops, witticisms, hollow laughs, and insincere compliments.

"According to Lawrence," Arrick began, "the majority of guests have already arrived. Millud's greeting everyone in the foyer and directing them to the hors d'oeuvres table, which means for the time being, he's preoccupied.

"Then why are we standing around chatting," said Madora as she locked the bedroom door and began searching for the briefcase that contained the Narciss Glass.

The bedroom was large, made even more so due to the few pieces of furniture. A small bed was wedged up against one of the walls. A rickety, wooden nightstand stood near the head of the bed, and in the middle of the room, like a deserted island lost at sea, was a small roll-top desk with a cracked leather chair nuzzled up against it.

"Sparse and Spartan," commented Sheef as looked about the room.

"I don't get it. Why have this enormous house and then decorate your bedroom like this?" asked Harvey.

"Because he doesn't care," answered Madora. "This luxurious house, which he must have acquired by use of the Narciss Glass, is like Millud Himself. It's a façade to impress those he wants to control. The area where he's entertaining guests is probably the only room with any decent decorations. It's also likely that his coffers aren't exactly overflowing right now. Remember, *The Tempest's Fury* is his first film to direct, and he hasn't even begun filming yet. The future success and fortune of H.B. Millud are yet to be made."

"And if we're successful, we'll keep it that way," said Arrick. "Let's find that mirror and get out of here before things get any more complicated than they already are."

Harvey looked at his father questioningly.

"Gwen," said Sheef.

"Oh yeah," sighed Harvey. "How could I forget?

A shattering boom shook the entire house. Madora was the only one who wasn't knocked off balance and onto the floor.

"What was that?" asked Harvey breathlessly, helped to his feet by Madora's outstretched hand.

"Things just got more complicated," responded Sheef, who was rubbing his head after bumping it on the edge of the roll-top desk. "By the sound of it, I'd say your sister just arrived."

"What do we do then?" asked Harvey, curiosity drawing him toward the door.

"Not that, Son," replied Arrick, who was already back on his feet and once again searching the room. "We need to find the Narciss Glass in the next minute or so and get out of here before Gwen realizes that her family decided to drop in as well."

On the other side of the door, dozens of guests stood in the living room, paralyzed by the sight before them. Standing in the entryway was the most radiant and captivating women they had ever seen, making even Hollywood's handsome and beautiful actors and actresses appear homely and plain.

The front door had been shattered into a million tiny dust particles, which now hung in the living room air as little brown clouds. The dust parted as Gwen stepped over the threshold with Gundy close behind. She smiled broadly and amicably greeted everyone like she was bidding good evening to lifelong friends. The guests were so mesmerized by her beauty that they were unable to reciprocate with anything but stunned obligatory nods. Gwen stopped walking and greeting when she found herself toe to toe with Millud.

"H.B.," she said with such familiarity that Millud was temporarily discombobulated, "it appears that I've arrived late to your little gathering, for I seem to be the only one without a drink in my hand. Gundy, would you be so kind."

Gundy the taxi driver snaked around Gwen, retrieved a glass of champagne from one of the waiters, and handed it to her.

"Thank you, Gundy," Gwen said with a slight nod.

"Let me begin by apologizing for my tardiness, but it is

largely your fault, is it not, Mr. Millud?" she said with a good-natured laugh. "You seem to have forgotten to provide me with directions to the party, but no matter, it's water under the bridge as they say. I'm here now, and that's all that matters, but I would greatly appreciate it if you'd introduce me to my fellow cast members."

Gwen's last sentence hit Millud like a slap in the face.

"Excuse me," Millud responded in a voice that was even higher and squeakier than usual. "You want me to do what? Fellow cast members? But you can't be serious . . . Lady—"

"Call me Gwen, please," she interrupted pleasantly.

"Alright then, Gwen, let me tell you one thing: You can't just barge into a private party uninvited like this. As I told you earlier today, all the parts in the movie have been cast." Millud stopped speaking for a moment to peer around Gwen at what was once his front door. When he started again, he was screaming at the top of his lungs. "WHAT DID YOU DO TO MY MAHOGANY DOOR? DO YOU HAVE ANY IDEA HOW MUCH THAT COST ME? AND HOW DID YOU GET BY LAWRENCE! LAWRENCE, WHERE ARE YOU?

"You must be referring to the rather large man who was greeting guests outside," said Gwen calmly. "You needn't worry about him. He's quite fine. Napping on the porch for the moment. When I insisted that I be admitted to the party, this man of yours refused. It created an impasse, so I thought it best to resolve the problem in a manner that would benefit us both: a short, rejuvenating nap for him and access to the party for me."

"YOU DESTROYED MY DOOR AND KNOCKED OUT LAWRENCE!" squeaked Millud at the top of his throat.

"Knocked out sounds so violent. Trust me, Mr. Millud, it was nothing of the sort. I gently put him under and moved him aside where he could rest comfortably." Gwen stopped to take a sip of her champagne before continuing. "Well, if you're going to stand there in an inhospitable manner and not introduce me to your guests, then I shall not intrude upon your party any longer, but before I leave, there are three things I wish to say.

"First, I implore you to lower your voice and relax; I can tell by the physiological changes that your heart rate and blood pressure are elevated to unsafe levels. Secondly, I would like to be provided with a script to read over tonight before filming begins tomorrow, so that I may familiarize myself with the plot and also select the role I shall play in the movie. And lastly, I am ready to receive the object. Earlier today you played ignorant of its existence, and then informed me that even if you had such an object in your possession, you would never hand it over to me. I sincerely hope that you've reconsidered both points. Play the fool no more and don't withhold it. I would be most grateful if you would retrieve it yourself, for that would be the gentlemanly thing to do, but if you would rather, my friend Gundy can fetch it for you. Just tell him the location.

A dog bark and a whine from outside preempted Millud's response.

Gwen's eyes brightened. She then said to herself while completely ignoring Millud, "I'd know that bark anywhere.

Fromp and Akeila are here, and therefore, so is my family, which is what I expected."

Gwen panned the living room, stopping at Millud's bedroom door. She pursued her lips. "Now there is only one reason that I know of why the dogs would be barking. Harvey and the others must've kept them outside while they searched the house for the artifact that Millud denies any knowledge of, and since I see no sign of them out here amongst the guests, I must conclude that they're searching other rooms."

Still holding her glass of champagne, Gwen extended the ends of her four fingers in the direction of Millud's bedroom. A soccer-sized ball of golden energy coalesced in the air inches before the champagne glass and began to change shape. Within seconds, a pulsating golden fist was floating in the air. The fist drifted to the bedroom door, whereupon it gently rapped on the wood four times before retreating back a half foot to await the response.

Madora, Arrick, Sheef, and Harvey had plastered their ears against the bedroom door after hearing the explosion heralding Gwen's arrival. The solid wood, however, did an excellent job of muffling whatever Gwen was saying from the other side. They were able to make out the screechy yelling of Millud, but too many of Gwen's soft, conversational words were lost in the wood fibers of the door to comprehend much of what she said.

Not one of them, though, had any trouble hearing the floating fist rapping. When it occurred, they all jumped back.

"Sounds like she knows we're here," said Sheef. "Question is, do we open the door or hightail it out the window?"

"I'm not leaving without the Narciss Glass," replied Arrick, his stance firmly rooted to the floor.

"Okay then. In that case, perhaps you, Arrick, would like to do the honors," said Sheef, gesturing to the door handle.

The energy fist knocked again, but this time it was harder and more insistent.

"Someone's getting impatient," said Arrick as he took a step forward, but before he could reach the handle, a heavy, blunt force hit the door, detaching it and its frame from the wall.

The hit happened so quickly and unexpectedly that no one had time to move out of the way, much less even react. The door plowed directly into them, driving a wooden plane into their faces, chests, and knees.

Once the door had dropped all four to the floor, it continued on until ramming the bedroom's exterior wall, blasting a hole clean through the plaster, wood, and stucco.

Gwen gracefully stepped through the doorway with Millud close behind. She motioned to the four moaning mounds on the floor and said, "Mr. Millud, it's my pleasure to introduce you to my dear family."

Millud, who was shaking and white as flour, looked in the direction of Gwen's pointed champagne glass. When he looked, he did see additional destruction to his home, but failed to see anyone but Arrick. He turned to Gwen with a befuddled expression.

Brushing aside a lock of blond hair from her face, she said, "Why of course. I do apologize. I simply forgot that you're incapable of seeing the others. I adjusted my speed through time but they . . . oh never mind. It doesn't matter."

As she walked into the bedroom, the party guests, pricked by curiosity, craned their heads so that they could gawk into the bedroom. They were still too shocked by Gwen's beauty and otherworldly power to say anything to one another but were hoping that there might be additional dangerous excitement, for they had never been so entertained at any Hollywood party.

"And here we meet again," said Gwen, kneeling down before her collapsed and whimpering family, all of whom were massaging areas on their bodies that had been whacked by the flying door.

"Sorry about that abutment with the door, but you should know that eavesdropping is not without risk."

Gwen then stood up and proceeded to touch each of them with a light caress upon the head. The throbbing pain in their heads, chests, and knees vanished, replaced by a euphoric soothing.

"I hope you understand that I have no wish whatsoever to hurt you, but once again, it seems necessary for me to give you the same admonition that I did back at the library: Do not attempt to interfere or thwart my plans. If you do, you'll force my hand in an unpleasant direction, resulting in undesirable and permanent consequences."

"If you don't mind me asking, what precisely are those plans of yours?" asked Sheef, standing and helping Harvey to his feet.

Gwen was about to answer Sheef, supplementing with additional details what she had explained earlier in the day, but was distracted by the sound of approaching feet. The guests had begun to slowly shuffle toward the bedroom with kitten-like captivation.

Millud, meanwhile, had slipped back into the living room where he had pushed aside the white table cloth of the champagne table and ducked underneath.

Without turning around, Gwen held up her hand and said, "For my family's ears only." The scene behind her shimmered and blurred as everything in the room ceased moving. Every one of the party goers froze in place, immobilized like lifeless mannequins. A young, petite actress with bobbed brown hair was frozen in the act of nervously fidgeting with her pearl necklace. Nearby, a waiter was in the middle of refilling someone's empty champagne flute, the still liquid appearing as sculpted glass with air bubbles trapped inside. And crouched under the table like a stone statue was Millud, reaching out for his steel briefcase.

"How I do love the study of physics," giggled Gwen with a tone and expression reminiscent of when she first left the Phantasian.

"What did you do to those people?" asked Harvey, peering around Gwen in order to get a better look.

"Nothing more than a simple application of a world-famous physicist's theories. Your Mr. Einstein postulated, and then mathematically proved, that the fabric of time and space is affected by the force of gravity. And that's all I did to the guests in the living room."

"All you did? What did you do exactly?" asked an astounded Sheef.

"I altered the gravity in the living room. The change had

an immediate and dramatic effect on the space and time in the room. Without going into the particulars, I basically paused the passage of time.

Sheef turned to his side, and while looking at Madora and Harvey, mouthed, "She paused time."

"Sheef, I can read lips," said Gwen as she took another sip of champagne.

"Of course you can," replied Sheef, looking back at Gwen.

"I paused time because I want to give you my full attention, and I don't want to be interrupted or eavesdropped upon. And please, don't be concerned about the guests. Their lives will play again when I am finished speaking with you, and they'll have no notion whatsoever that even a second of time has passed.

"Now, Sheef," Gwen said, "let me unveil the particulars of my plans for your human race, and perhaps after hearing them, you will realize that my vision is not one to be opposed but to be fully embraced. And just maybe, you will join me in its implementation. I assure you, there will be leadership roles for all of you. However, if you decide not to be an active participant, then I hope you will see the wisdom of standing aside and making no further foolish attempts to foil my plans."

Arrick, who had been hanging on every word Gwen said, suddenly let go and scanned the room for the Narciss Glass.

"Arrick, it's not polite to ignore a lady when she's speaking. And besides, you won't find what you're looking for in this room. If you must know, the briefcase holding the Narciss Glass is currently frozen in place along with Millud, both of which are under the champagne table."

Arrick's eyes darted to the living room but were immediately caught by Gwen's.

"Don't even consider going after it. I know that's what you're contemplating. Such a temptation with it being so close, but if you were to take one step into that living room with altered gravity, you would be immobilized as well and unable to hear the rest of my plans." Sighing in defeat, Arrick redirected his attention back to Gwen.

"Thank you," she said. "That is behavior more befitting royalty."

Arrick was taken aback momentarily.

"You shouldn't be surprised that I know this about you, Arrick, or did you forget that I was sitting at the same table when you and Harvey divulged everything to one another? But please, this is no occasion for fretting. I have no desire to take the throne of Ecclon away from you and your queen. That is, if you are willing to cooperate, and if you do, I promise that the clouds of your beloved planet will burn brightly again, and Ecclon will never fall into the hands of the enemy."

Sheef was about to ask how Gwen would keep Nezraut and the Vapid from turning people away from the thoughts of the Unseen, darkening Ecclon, and eventually invading it, but before he could get the words out, Gwen resumed speaking.

"Before I begin, why don't I make everyone more comfortable," and with another flick of her fingers, Harvey and the others were levitated and transported to the edge of Millud's bed where they sat shoulder to shoulder.

"Human history, as I stated back at the library, is a depressing catalog of corrupt leadership, ignorance, war, violence, oppression, want, suffering, exploitation, despair and . . . well, need I go on?" Gwen paced in front of the bed like a charismatic professor passionately sharing a lecture for the very first time.

"No need for elaboration," replied Sheef. "We get the picture. History doesn't paint a very flattering portrait of humanity."

"No it doesn't," Gwen continued, "and the problem has always been one of enlightenment, or to be more accurate, the lack thereof. After reading hundreds of history books in the library, I realized that in the past there have been leaders, ideologies, and governments that have been better than others regarding their treatment of men and women. Some have provided more freedom and liberty for people, but even these, in time, were corroded with corruption. Those in power eventually used their positions for their own selfish ambitions, and rather than the leaders serving the good of the people, they did whatever was necessary and expedient for them to maintain and grow their power.

"There were also political theorists who created the blueprints for societies that were fair and equal, in which the people would be provided with all the necessities of life — food, shelter, employment — by an all-powerful and benevolent government. It would, the theorists dreamed, be a veritable utopia, a paradise on earth. They believed that when the needs of every man, woman, and child were met, all strife and struggle between people would end, setting the stage for peace and harmony to reign forever. And if every country followed this blueprint, then eventually all the guns of the different nations would be silenced.

"But alas, so much for the best-laid plans of man. Some of the nations actually constructed new societies and governments based on these blueprints, but like every other government, those in control were soon corrupted by power. Anyone who questioned or objected to governmental action was crushed, for a government that provides everything for the people also has the power to take everything away. Thus, oppression, war, violence, and suffering persisted, and as man became more technologically advanced, his means of killing did so as well. You need only to look to the great war recently waged in Europe, specifically the horror of the trenches. Unfortunately, such senseless tragedies will repeat themselves again and again.

"And what is the common denominator of history's ongoing tale of war, crime, and corruption? Humanity . . . mankind. The problem doesn't lie with man's ideas, for some of them are actually quite good. No, the error is when man attempts to implement his ideas. To date, how many utopian societies have been dreamt of only to devolve into nightmares at the hands of the leaders? You see, the fault is not with the dream but with the dreamers."

Gwen stopped pacing and looked at Harvey and the others still seated on the bed. "Are you still with me?" she asked.

"Hanging on every word. Please continue," said Arrick, not because he was especially interested in hearing Gwen's plan but because listening to her bought him additional time to try to figure out a way to get the briefcase once she pressed play on the paused living room.

"Thank you, Arrick, but only if it were more sincere," Gwen

said as if reading his mind. "As I was saying, the problem is with the dreamer, with man himself. There is something within him that tends to spoil his attempts. It's a deeply rooted flaw that, time and again, short-circuits his noblest endeavors. I believe this flaw is ignorance, a darkness and dullness of mind if you will. What past leaders lacked was sufficient enlightenment. No one person had a large enough understanding of the past and present, and certainly none of them could grasp the mechanics behind the curtain: the science and mathematics that are the gears, sprockets, and levers of existence.

"No philosopher, theorist, king, or dreamer ever came close to using the full potential of his brain, and because of this, he failed to see the big picture, failed to avoid falling victim to small-minded, selfish ambitions.

"But then I arrived. This is not a statement of arrogance, but one of fact and distinction. I am not human in the traditional sense. I came into this world of yours by very different means and was endowed with, as you witnessed at the library and here tonight, very unique abilities."

Gwen stopped speaking and drew close to the four, kneeling down before them and said in an almost pleading voice, "I have been specially gifted with an intellectual capacity light years beyond any other man or woman. In a matter of days, I have absorbed every nut and bolt of discovered scientific knowledge. This has provided a solid foundation and launching pad for my very own discoveries, discoveries that will take the scientific community decades or even centuries to uncover. But my mind is not merely a repository of knowledge. I am applying much of what I have absorbed to the real world.

"Can't you see?" she asked excitedly. "I am the 'One' people have yearned for millenniums past. I alone have the vision, the knowledge, and the ability to make the dreamer's dream a reality, and with my enlightened mind, my vision of a better world will not be sabotaged by the flaws which have plagued humanity. My intellect has lifted me safely above the corrupting temptation of power, which is why my reign will not be tainted."

"I'm sorry," interrupted Sheef, "but it sounded like you said 'your reign', which makes me think that you have ambitions to be some sort of monarch or dictator."

"The long-awaited philosopher king, or in this case, queen," said Gwen warmly. "And yes, I will be ruling as a monarch or dictator, but I will be a most benevolent one, for my rule and dictates shall be for the good of mankind. My desire is not to control the people of this world but to free them."

Sheef puffed out his cheeks and then exhaled a burst of air. Though he didn't intend for anyone else to hear his airy response, everyone did. Dropping his head forward, he mumbled to himself, "Sheef, you really outdid yourself this time."

"Based on Sheef's inconspicuous reaction," said Gwen sarcastically, "it doesn't appear as though I will be able to count on his support . . . but what about you, Harvey?"

Harvey looked like an animal paralyzed in the middle of a road by a pair of approaching headlights. Peeking out of the corners of his eyes, he hoped to catch a nonverbal cue from Arrick or Madora that would direct him as to what to do or say. Not surprisingly, Gwen caught the peek.

"They can't help you, Harvey, and even if they could, why

would someone with your abilities need to turn to others for advice? Be your own person and make your own decision."

Gwen opened her eyes wide, and before Harvey knew what was happening, he found himself hovering a foot from Gwen's face, still in a seated position.

"Shall I count on my brother's support and make this a family affair?"

Harvey attempted to turn around for help, but his head refused to rotate. The rest of his body felt like it was being squeezed in a vice.

"I'm waiting, Harvey."

Later on, when Harvey reflected back on this moment, he was able to come up with multiple reasons why he couldn't support Gwen and her plans for taking over the world, but when he was floating before her, his mind was so rattled, he was incapable of locating and joining thoughts together for any type of meaningful response, so when he opened his mouth, nothing more than a one-syllable "No" tumbled out.

"That's a shame, Harvey," said Gwen with a frown. "Since you've made your decision, now I must be honest with you. If you intentionally cross my path again, I will assume it's for the purpose of thwarting my plans; therefore, I'm sorry to say, though I do have a brotherly affection for you, I will be in no mood to display such affection."

Gwen then touched her fingers to her mouth and lightly blew a kiss to Harvey. A narrow stream of hurricane-force wind blew Harvey backward, out the bedroom, and through the living room. As he zoomed by the guests, time reengaged, and they picked up in speech and action exactly where they had left off.

Harvey attempted to scream but was moving so quickly that he couldn't grab a gulp of air to do so. Sheef watched helplessly as Harvey faded into the night, growing smaller and smaller until he moved beyond the scope of sight and disappeared.

Arrick sprang to his feet and took a threatening step toward Gwen before he was halted by an invisible force. Though stuck to the floor, his vocal cords were still free. "WHAT DID YOU DO TO MY SON?" Arrick shouted, the blue veins in his neck bulging. "WHERE IS HE? I SWEAR BY ECCLON THAT IF YOU HARM ONE HAIR ON HIS—"

"You'll do what, Arrick," Gwen calmly interrupted. "You must realize by now that you can do absolutely nothing to me, so please, dispense with such idle threats . . . and I didn't harm young Harvey. He's just been moved out of my way and placed somewhere safe from harm."

"Where?" asked Arrick, his anger subsiding a bit when told that Harvey was safe. "Where did you send him? Tell me!"

"No more questions or demands," responded Gwen. "We've reached a point when I only want to hear answers, so what will yours be, Arrick? Opposition or acceptance?"

"You already know the answer to that — exactly the same as my son's. But I'll tell you this, you're no different than Millud and possibly even—"

The next word was snatched from his throat by unexpected motion. Arrick was lifted off the bed, and like a bullet being placed in a gun's chamber, was shifted to the right, directly in between with Gwen and the doorway. She again blew a light kiss, and Arrick was shot out of the house and into the night air. As he was receding, however, he made no attempts to scream, for any fear that he might have felt in such a harrowing situation, had been cast aside, replaced by a steely determination to defend his son, regardless of the cost to his own life.

Gwen then looked at Madora and Sheef and said, "Must I even pose the question?" They said nothing, but both signaled "no" with a faint shake of their heads. Like Arrick, Madora was lifted up and moved over into the barrel, from which she was quickly jettisoned out of the house. Then it was Sheef's turn. Once he was moved over into the firing position, Gwen said, "I saved a little extra for you." The jolting reversal hit at the same moment Gwen's fingers touched her lips. She sent him streaking out of the house at twice the speed of the others. The crisp, cool air stung his back, neck, and head like a thousand flying needles, but he didn't endure the pain for very long. Unable to breathe due to the tremendous speed, Sheef soon passed out. If anyone had been looking up into the night sky at just the right second, they would've seen a faint blur rocketing from the Californian coast to Hollywood.

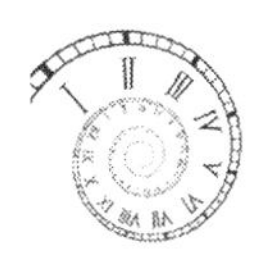

15

After Gwen bid goodbye to Sheef, she reentered the party and slowly waved her hand before the guests. Though they had clearly seen four humans streak through the living room and out the door, they all suddenly ceased talking about it, for their memories of what had occurred within the previous half hour became fuzzy with static and were soon erased.

An older actress, a veteran of stage and film, adjusted a turquoise shawl and said to a young actor, "Did you happen to a feel a sudden breeze?"

"Yes, I did, something like a passing chill."

"Likely coming from Dexter Harris over there," she said with a comic air while pointing to the handsome actor standing by himself on the opposite side of the room. "He's been very aloof this evening, not like him at all."

"Uncharacteristically unsociable," the young actor said flippantly. "Perhaps he didn't get one of the leads in the film and is sulking about it. If so, how else could such an overinflated ego handle such a slight."

"Oh come now, we mustn't be so harsh on the poor fellow," the actress said with mock disapproval and a giggling snort.

Like moths to a light, other guests were drawn to the gossiping jabs, and very soon the atmosphere was typical of most Hollywood parties: filled with the juicy and slanderous comments that made such gatherings overly ripe and deliciously rotten.

When Gwen rejoined the party guests, few of them paid her much attention, which was in stark contrast to when she had first arrived and everyone was captivated by her resplendent incandescence. It was as if she had dimmed her light to such an extent that her shine was no longer noteworthy. This was done intentionally on her part in order to camouflage her movements. Gwen strolled over to the table where Millud was in the act of crawling out from under the tablecloth with the steel briefcase clutched in his hand. He looked to the door-less entryway and was preparing to make a run for it when Gwen's hand suddenly obstructed his view.

She didn't touch the briefcase, but instead, cupped her hand, rolling each of her fingers backward. Millud felt his own fingers go numb, becoming as soft and pliable as putty. The cool metal handle of the briefcase slipped out of his hand, and try as he might to hold on, his fingers simply wouldn't respond.

"Thank you, Millud. From now on, I'll take care of the object you denied being in possession of more than once today. Oh, come now, don't look so deflated," said Gwen as she bent down and spoke to him like a mother addressing a pouty five year old. "I'll let you remain director, which is far more than you deserve. Of course, your being director will have its limits. You shall remain in your role as long as your actions and orders don't contradict my plans for the film. If you stay within your leash's length and let me do as I choose, this film will be an unprecedented success, and when it is released, you will be the most lauded and sought-after director in Hollywood.

After a moment to let him consider, Gwen said, "Now those are the terms. It's a generous offer, but if you refuse, I'm confident that I can easily find someone else who would love to see his name associated with what will be the most popular film in history.

The deflated look on Millud's face regained some air. Unlike the other guests, Gwen had not erased his memory of what had transpired at the party. His was still lucidly intact. As greedily ambitious as he was, and no matter how much he reveled in controlling others, Millud was wise enough to know — especially after Gwen had laid waste to his front door and had somehow removed his briefcase from his hand with an invisible force — he would be a fool to refuse her. Though he would no longer be able to wield the manipulating power of the Narciss Glass over others, he would still become famous and wealthy, a different sort of power, which he knew when properly used could be just as gratifying.

Millud's rodent-like eyes met those of Gwen. His thin pink lips raised into a smirk as he did his best to appear like the one still in control. "Filming begins tomorrow at 8:00 a.m. sharp," he snapped with an authoritarian tone. "Please, don't be late," and then added more congenially, "and let me be the first to say how delighted I am to have you as a part of this production."

"Good. That's settled then, but before I leave, I need a copy of the script so that I may learn my parts and make any changes that I see fit."

Millud disappeared into his bedroom and reappeared holding his personal copy of the script and handed it to Gwen. He fiddled with his watch until the back popped open. He picked the tiny key out and said, "You'll need the combination and this key to get into both briefcases."

"Thank you very much, Millud, but I don't need them." She glanced down at the steel briefcase, focusing on the combination lock. A second later the briefcase popped open, and she pulled out the smaller leather attaché case. I haven't any need for the steel briefcase. You keep it," she said as she handed it back to Millud, "and please, by all means, enjoy the rest of your party. Until tomorrow." Gwen then stood up and exited the house, passing by Lawrence who was still sleeping soundly on the porch.

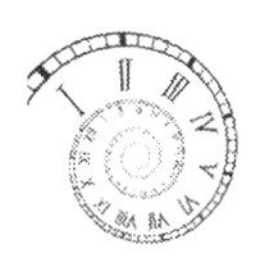

16

Because Gwen reversed Harvey at a lower speed out of the house than Sheef, he did not lose consciousness but was aware of everything occurring around him during his backward journey through the starlit California sky. He was traveling close to sixty miles per hour, and had he been facing the wind, his face would've numbed in less than a minute. Fortunately for Harvey, he was still wearing his Lignum shirt.

When Thurngood first gave Harvey the shirt, he told him that Ecclonian Lignum is made from the wooden fibers of Flurn wood and that the tight weave of the material is impossible to cut through, even with the sharpest blade. Harvey discovered another attribute of the shirt when he slipped it on the evening he and the others warped to the Phantasian: the material is an excellent insulator, providing a warm barrier to ward off the cold. Feeling like a second skin, the shirt was so comfortable that Harvey forgot he had been wearing it underneath his clothing since leaving his house, and didn't remember until he realized that the chilly air was unable to reach his body.

Had Harvey been facing forward, he might have recognized the street and some of the landmarks leading to Arrick's cottage, but because of his orientation, he had no clue as to his final destination until he descended and slowed to a stop. He dropped gently down onto the street in front of the cottage.

Since he had no idea if or when the others would arrive, he decided to go inside, clean up a little, and wait, but before he was able to take a single step up the driveway, Madora and Arrick arrived as safely and softly as he had.

Sheef's arrival came next, but it was far from the gentle deceleration and stop the others had experienced. He was still moving backward rather quickly when he dived downward to Arrick's street. Hearing his name, Sheef awoke and turned around to Harvey's pointless screaming for him to slow down, as if Sheef had any control whatsoever over his motion. Even so, when Sheef realized how close he was to the street, he began frantically waving his arms, hoping that the spasmodic action might create enough drag and slow him down a bit. It didn't.

Sheef knew he was coming in too hot. His swinging outstretched arms reminded Harvey of a damaged plane plummeting to the ground for an explosive impact. Sheef didn't explode, but he did touch down hard, bouncing multiple times before skidding twenty feet across the asphalt road.

Madora was the first on the scene, but when she reached down to render aid, she was waved off by Sheef who was gasping for breath and grimacing in pain. "Thank you, Madora, but I'm fine. Just give me a minute or two."

Realizing that Sheef hadn't sustained any serious injuries,

she hurried over to where Harvey was standing, struggling to restrain her laughter. "Given the situation, I know I shouldn't laugh," Madora giggled to Harvey confidentially, "but I think he might have burned holes right through his pants with that landing. And that, maybe more than the pain, is what's keeping him from getting up.

"Really?" a grinning Harvey asked as he looked over Madora's shoulder.

"Sheef, let's get you off the road and inside," said Arrick, placing his hand under Sheef's armpit. "I have the unnerving feeling that we're not alone, and if we're being watched, I'd like to get out of the open as quickly as possible."

Sheef resisted Arrick's help, and rather than getting up, gestured for Arrick to lean down near his ear. When he did, Sheef cupped his hand and whispered. Arrick nodded, whispered something back, pointed to the cottage, and then helped Sheef to his feet. Once he was up, Sheef placed his hands over his backside and scurried hurriedly inside.

A grinning Arrick walked over to Madora and Harvey and said, "It's a good thing we're about the same height and build. I told him that he's more than welcome to borrow a pair of my pants."

A few minutes later, the door hinges creaked and Sheef stepped out onto the porch. He looked over at the others who were still standing in the driveway and said, "Oh stop it, please. He told you, didn't he?" Well, go ahead; I know you want to laugh your heads off about the holes in my pants, even you, Arrick. You might as well get it out of your system so that we can get back to figuring out what just happened."

Not needing to be told again, all three burst into hysterics, and as tears rolled down Madora's cheek, she tried to apologize.

"Don't bother, Madora, I'm just happy I could provide everyone with a little levity, even if it's at my expense," Sheef said sarcastically.

Though Sheef and his ventilated pants were the target of the humor, even he was infected by the contagious laughter. The group eventually regained its composure and headed into the cottage. Once inside, Arrick said, "I've got some soda in the fridge. Why don't we have a little refreshment and figure out, in light of everything that happened tonight, where we go from here."

After tops were popped and everyone had at least one satisfying swig of cola, Harvey began the conversation with a comment: "Gwen's getting more powerful by the second."

"And dangerous," Sheef added.

Harvey nodded in agreement and took another drink of his soda. "It's crazy. She was able to float and fly each of us from Millud's house to the cottage with nothing but her mind. I know I lifted a whale and all, but that was different. That was in the Phantasian; Gwen's doing stuff like that here in the real world."

"What's your point, Harvey?" asked Arrick

"My point is, given her growing abilities, I don't think we've any chance of stopping her, and like Sheef said before, we've probably done nothing but made the situation worse and haven't changed anything at all. It's like we've circled back to where we first began."

"What do you mean, Harvey?" asked Madora.

"Well, remember the book—"

Harvey's sentence was interrupted by yelps outside.

"The dogs!" shouted Madora, "I completely forgot about them!"

"We all did!" said Sheef as he and the others bolted to the door.

Gwen had sent Fromp and Akeila back to the cottage like the others, the only difference being that they had traveled facing forward. Fromp was in the process of sniff-inspecting Akeila to make sure she was injury free when the front door swung open and everyone tumbled onto the porch. With ears erect, both dogs turned to the sounds of moaning hinges.

Akeila sprinted to Madora, and upon reaching her, reared up on hind legs and pawed her chest, behavior uncharacteristic of the well-mannered and reserved Sadiki. Fromp greeted Harvey in the same fashion, but given the warp-hound's greater weight and exuberance, flattened Harvey to the ground. Madora looked disapprovingly at Harvey and Sheef and said, "Your dog's bad manners continue to corrupt those of Akeila."

"Don't complain to me," Sheef responded with hands raised defensively. "Tell Harvey. Fromp's much more his dog these days."

Arrick, meanwhile, had walked into the street where his pickup had landed. After looking it over to ensure that it was still in one piece, he walked back to the porch and said, "I don't get it. Why did she bother to send my truck back? And how did she know that Fromp and Akeila were there?"

"The dogs probably recognized her when she left the party and barked at her," said Madora, "and I believe the reason she sent the truck back to you is because her heart's still good, which ironically, makes her more dangerous than ever."

"I think I know where you're going with that statement, but would you care to elaborate?" asked Sheef.

"I will, but first let's hear Harvey finish what he was explaining when the dogs arrived."

They made their way back to the kitchen where Harvey picked up where he left off. "I don't remember exactly what I was saying when I was interrupted," said Harvey once everyone was seated and Fromp and Akeila were loudly lapping up water from bowls that Arrick had set out for them. .

"Something about books," reminded Madora.

"Right, okay, I've got it," said Harvey. "Sheef, do you remember what was written on the pages of Nezraut's book? The one he and his Vapid Lord were reading over the human race to further turn them away from the thoughts of the Unseen?"

"I think you mean books," said Sheef. "I seem to recall that you destroyed thousands of them back in old double-mouth's lair."

"Sure, books then, but do you remember what was written on every single page of those thousands of books?"

"The general idea but not the exact wording."

"Well I do, probably because when all those books were torn apart, I saw pages and pages with exactly the same text floating in the air."

Harvey paused and stared out the kitchen window as if he were actually back in Nezraut's lair and recited:

Before birth, after death, nothing,
Man standing stark and alone,
Only his wisdom for comfort and guidance,
Nothing before or beyond.

Desperate for meaning, searching for worth,
Absent of purpose and plan,
He builds and conquers by the sweat of his brow,
Perfection within the reach of his hands.

When he was finished, Harvey was silent, waiting for someone else to make the connection. His father was the first to speak. "I wish I had a mind like yours when I was your age. You nailed it, Son. It's that last line, 'Perfection within the reach of his hands'. As brilliant and as knowledgeable as Gwen is, she's falling victim to the very same lie that countless people in the past have, especially in the last century. She believes that a perfect society can be created on earth, and that she's the one to usher it in because she's more enlightened than her predecessors.

"Like she told us before, Gwen's convinced that the reason that blood, violence, and suffering are chronicled on almost every page of history is because man's mind is too dulled and darkened. She believes that enlightenment, more knowledge and understanding, will cause men and women to treat each other with kindness and respect. It's the flawed notion that if people learn what is 'best' for others and society, then they will do that best thing. The logic goes something like, 'Who wouldn't want to do what is best for others and society once the best thing is known?'

"But the truth, which history unequivocally bears out, is that humans continually do exactly opposite of what is best for others and society, or for that matter, themselves. This is precisely why so many New Year's resolutions fail. People know what they should do in order to improve their lives and achieve their goals, but they almost always end up doing the exact opposite and choose to follow thinking and behavior that is harmful. And here's the most surprising thing, even though they know such behavior is harmful, they plow ahead and do it anyway. If people can't even do what's best for their own lives, why would we ever think that they would do it for others, even if they learned what that best thing is? It's absurd to say the least."

"I agree," said Madora, "but I'm more than a little surprised that you know so much about earth's history. After all, you've been on the planet for a relatively short period of time."

"True, but unlike humans, Ecclonians are aware of other sentient beings in the universe and in other dimensions. As such, I read extensively about your planet and the nature of its inhabitants before ever warping there. And don't forget, Ecclon is the gateway planet to all other worlds."

Madora nodded in response to Arrick's explanation and added her own thoughts to what he had said. "You need to understand, Harvey, that man's primary problem is not that he lacks enough knowledge. If it were, then the last one hundred years would've been characterized by peace and love for one's fellow man, given that during this time more people had access to education than in any previous period, but it wasn't even close. It was the most violent and deadly century to date. Now don't get me wrong, education benefits mankind tremendously, and I'm a strong advocate of every person acquiring the most learning possible. But at the end of the day, learning doesn't repair what's gone wrong within the heart of every man and woman. And no amount of education will ever change this fact, but Gwen fails to see and understand this."

"But why can't she? Before she was so teachable. Do you think she's changed that much in two days?" asked Harvey.

"I hate to admit it, but I do," said Sheef with a sigh. "She just can't see what we can because she's been blinded by the light of her own growing brilliance."

"And she's certainly not the first to be so blinded," added Madora. "I've been alive long enough to witness the rise and fall of many empires." Here she paused for a few seconds, staring with daggers at Sheef while slowly shaking her head back and forth.

"What?" he asked like a child attempting to cover up obvious guilt by playing dumb.

"I know what you're thinking, best not put words to it." She turned back to Harvey and continued, "Many of those empires I watched rise and fall were led by individuals who thought they were wise and knowledgeable enough to establish a perfect society that was insulated from the type of internal corruption that had ruined others. But, without fail, what they were confident wouldn't occur on their watch, eventually did. Oh, for a while things went according to plan in some of these societies, but eventually the real problem caught up with their lofty ideals and sabotaged them from the inside.

"You see," Madora continued as she stood up and grabbed another soda from the refrigerator, "it's man's own broken nature. He is internally flawed, and no matter how good his intentions are, this flaw, this defect inside of him, which is woven into his very being, will infect and sicken every good intention."

"There is a chance, though, that she might be different," offered Sheef. Madora and Arrick responded with surprised expressions. "Well, it's like I mentioned before when you got so upset at me: she's not exactly human. I'm not saying this is actually the case, but isn't there the possibility that Gwen's not flawed like everyone else? Consider how she treated us, even after we deceived and betrayed her. She appears to still care for us. We all know that she could've easily done more harm to us tonight if she wanted to."

"It's a valid point, Sheef," said Madora, "but even if her nature is not damaged like the rest of humanity, no one person has enough wisdom to handle the discoveries she's making and the power she's wielding. Now granted, she's likely more intelligent than any other human past or present and with attributes more in line with a fictitious superhero, but she's far from being omniscient."

"Omni . . . ?" asked Harvey.

"Omniscient, all-knowing," Madora responded, "and there's only one who has complete, exhaustive knowledge of yesterday and today's everything, and thus, the only one who has the wisdom to truly understand what is best, not just for mankind, but for every life form in the universe, and only one with such surpassing wisdom is qualified to handle so much power."

"The Unseen," whispered Harvey

Madora nodded.

"Then that's the answer, right?" asked Harvey. "Let's just tell Gwen about the Unseen."

"Harvey, I wish it were that easy," responded Madora kindly, "but because of her unprecedented, illuminated mind, Gwen really believes that she is not susceptible to making the same errors that leaders have made in the past. She made this abundantly clear to us at the party. If I were to tell her what I just shared with you, she likely wouldn't heed my words because she views herself as the exception to the rule."

"But couldn't you explain to her, regardless of how illuminated her mind is, that she's still not omni . . . you know, the all-knowing word."

"Omniscient."

"Yeah, omniscient. Why not simply tell her that since she's not omniscient, she doesn't have the wisdom to handle all that knowledge and power?"

"I or you could explain it to her," said Madora, "but the problem is she's likely already lost the eyes to see and the ears to hear the most significant truth of the universe: the Unseen is the height and depth, the width and breadth, the beginning and end of all things."

"Sounds like something Gnarl the Deep would say," smiled

Harvey. "But I don't get it. Why couldn't she see or hear this truth? It's so simple."

"It is to us," said Sheef, "but Gwen is currently buried in the particulars of life, the mechanics of how everything ticks and clicks. Do you know what I mean? The facts of nature and whatnot."

"Ticks and clicks. Interesting phrasing there, Sheef," said Madora with a smirk as she took back control of the conversation. "Harvey, Sheef is exactly correct. Gwen has become so enthralled by the particulars of existence that she's lost in them and unable to see the big picture, even if it were plainly pointed out to her. Imagine a group of people seeing a painting for the very first time. The canvas, however, is only an inch from their eyes. Now the people may be fascinated by the individual colors and minute brush strokes, but they're far too close to understand the collective meaning of all of those individual colors and strokes working together, not to mention being able to discern anything about the artist who painted it."

"But shouldn't we at least try?" asked Harvey with worried hope. "Isn't it worth talking to her?"

"Harvey, Gwen didn't mince any words about us not interfering with her again," said Sheef. "Given her abilities to manipulate matter and energy, there'll be no way to protect ourselves if she decides to do something worse than flying us back to Arrick's cottage."

"You actually think she would hurt us?"

"She might if pushed," said Madora.

"I can't imagine her doing anything really harmful to us," said Harvey.

"Do you recall getting knocked unconscious at the library?" asked Sheef. "I don't think it would be much of a stretch for her to do something far worse if she perceived us as a threat. If we were to force her to choose between her utopian vision for this planet and us, she's going to make the most logical choice."

"Which is what exactly?" asked Harvey.

"The one, in her mind, which will benefit the most people and do the greatest good," said Madora. "Regardless of how much she still cares for us, she's not going to choose us. And this brings me to why I said I fear her more now because of her desire to do something good on a grand scale."

"But that makes no sense," said Harvey. "How could her desire to do good for society make her more dangerous? It seems to me like it would make her less so."

"So it would seem, Harvey," said Madora, "for a desire to do good is wonderful, but sometimes the 'good' that people intend for others ends up doing serious harm."

Wrinkles of confusion surfaced on Harvey's forehead.

"What's the best way to explain this?" asked Madora to herself. She stopped speaking and gathered her thoughts together before reengaging in the conversation.

"Harvey, one of the most beautiful human behaviors is when a person does something kind for a fellow human that truly benefits him or her. However, the problem is that it's not always clear whether or not an action is actually helpful. A good way to distinguish the difference is to determine the outcome of the supposed good behavior.

"Good and beneficial actions are those that lead to the

same outcome: the recipients being freer because of what was done for them. All real blessings result in additional freedom. For example, think of what happens to a homeless man if he is provided with a home. He is immediately free from the elements. With a roof and walls, he now has protection from the summer sun, winter winds, and spring rains. And when he no longer needs to spend his time battling the elements for his basic survival, he is free to pursue things that will benefit his situation, such as acquiring an education and job skills, which once gained, will provide him with additional freedom and independence.

"If you also provide food for the man, and then the skills to procure more in the future, he will be able to properly nourish and energize his body. With his new energy, he will have the freedom to improve his lot in life to an even greater degree. And, Harvey, free and independent people tend to have more self-respect and dignity, because when men and women are operating in freedom, they are acting in a manner that corresponds with the Unseen's nature and design."

"So you believe that Gwen's plan would cause people to lose their freedom?" asked Harvey.

"Maybe not at first, but eventually. In order for her to dramatically change the world, she would have to impose her dream on mankind, and this imposition would, sooner or later, bind rather than liberate."

Arrick, who like his son, had been absorbing everything Madora said, stood up and tossed his soda bottle into the trash. "You explained that very well, but I still have some questions. What does all of this have to do with the movie, and how does it explain why Gwen wants the Narciss Glass? Which, by the way, I think we can safely assume is now in her hands. If she wants to help mankind, what use could such a destructive artifact be to her?"

"My best guess is that she's going to put herself in the movie with the Narciss Glass," said Sheef to the surprise of everyone. "Don't look at me so shocked. It makes perfect sense. She's taken a page out of Millud's own playbook. After overhearing us at Rosa's, she knows how Millud used the Narciss Glass in *The Tempest's Fury* to make it the most viewed film in history and to establish his future career as a director and producer."

"Okay," said Arrick, "let's say for argument's sake that your hypothesis is correct and Gwen plans on acting in the film. How exactly would this bring about the perfect world she's envisioned?"

"Changing the entire world so that it conforms to her vision is a monumental task to put it mildly, and it's not an endeavor that can be accomplished by herself, regardless of how impressive her ability to manipulate matter and energy may be," Sheef responded. "She will need help, followers and workers to make that dream of hers a reality, and what better means of recruitment than a movie, especially if the star is drop-dead gorgeous. Look, anyone watching the film with both her and the Narciss Glass in it will be doubly captivated. Viewers will be drawn in by her inexplicable beauty and then pulled in deeper by the sucking gravity of the Narciss Glass. Before you know it, thousands upon thousands of people will be addicted to the film, and they'll return again and again to see it, their compulsive love of the film growing stronger with each and every viewing."

"And all she needs to do is expose the passive moviegoers to her dream, and soon it will become theirs. It will be the greatest propaganda campaign in history," said Arrick.

Sheef nodded. "Which means, she'll need to rewrite the script. and I wouldn't be at all surprised if she already has her hands on a copy and has begun to do so."

"Logically sound, Sheef," said Madora. "It does make perfect sense. So then, what's our next move? As you mentioned earlier, we can't chance any type of direct confrontation with her. If she was being honest regarding her warning about us not sticking our noses in her business again, it could very well be the end of us, and any and all hope of saving Ecclon."

"It'll have to be a covert operation," Arrick chimed in.

"Covert? How so?" asked Sheef. "There's no way we'll be able to get anywhere close to her or the Narciss Glass without being detected, or have you forgotten how sensitive her new hearing is?"

"No, I haven't forgotten, but we won't have to worry about her detecting us if she can't recognize us."

"What are we going to do, wear disguises?" chuckled Sheef. "No offense, Arrick, but I don't think a pair of glasses and a hat is likely to dupe someone like Gwen."

"Oh, I agree, and that's why I'm thinking of something much more elaborate than glasses and hats. Need I remind you that you're in the city of make-believe. Here in Hollywood, the magicians of makeup and costume can transform any person into someone else, completely unrecognizable."

Sheef pursed his lips and raised his eyebrows. "Okay, I admit it's a good idea and might actually allow us to get close enough to her to retrieve the Narciss Glass, but the problem, as I see it, is that we don't know any of these makeup or costume people who can magically transform us."

"We don't need to," Arrick said with a knowing smile. "I'm still employed as Millud's security officer, which means I can easily get everyone onto the movie set without anyone giving us a second look. Remember, Millud can't see any of you, so he's not going to question you about who you are or what you're doing on the set. I'll inform the makeup artists and costume designers that you're some recent hires that need to get into costume. Trust me; they'll go along with it. And before you know it, you'll be painted up with new faces and on your merry way. The only trick is avoiding Gwen before you're in your disguises. We'll have to get there early in the morning. I have a set of keys for the soundstage. We'll slip in and hide in the costume closet until everyone else arrives. That's my plan. It's not much, but right now, it'll have to do.

"If we're going to get an early start, we should probably call it a night," said Arrick with a firmness that let everyone know that he had no desire to let the conversation continue.

"Dad, I'm sorry, I know you want us to get some sleep, but may I ask one more question before we break up?"

"Sure, Harvey, but just one more," Arrick responded with a weary smile.

"Well, if we're able to steal the Narciss Glass from Gwen, then we'll keep it from being used in the movie by her or Millud.

But what happens to Gwen? Even without the Narciss Glass, won't she still be a serious threat to the world?"

Arrick was quiet for a moment as he glanced down at the floor, pressing the tips of his thumbs into his forehead. When he looked back up at his son, he said, "We might be forced to use it against Gwen. In the end, it may be the only way to stop her."

Harvey stared confusedly at his father. When he first heard the words they didn't make sense, like they had been spoken in a foreign tongue, but it wasn't long before he was able to translate, and when he did, horror and disbelief chased away the color from his face.

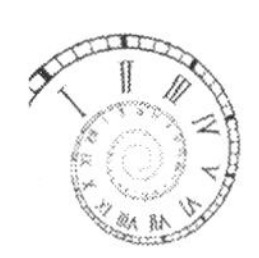

17

Long after the wooden floors had ceased creaking and sleep was stealing over the cottage, Harvey lay wide awake, staring into the silent darkness. He couldn't stop thinking about Gwen and what his father had said they might be forced to do in order to stop her.

How could his dad even consider doing such a thing? He knew what the Narciss Glass did to a person. He had told Harvey that he had witnessed its dehumanizing effect on Dexter Harris on two separate occasions. Harvey was able to briefly grasp the logic of it before his heart won the upper hand. If Gwen couldn't be stopped any other way, then using the object against her would cause her to collapse in upon herself, making her a prisoner of her own reflection. This would certainly keep her from implementing her dream of bettering mankind, but at what cost?

Considering the fact that Harvey had only just met Gwen, it was strange how close he'd become to her and how much he cared for her welfare. When she first addressed him as her brother, it felt awkward and fake, but now the word seemed natural, something he not only wore well but had grown comfortable wearing.

The last thought that crossed his mind before he drifted off to sleep was if and when the time came for using the Narciss Glass against Gwen, he wouldn't let it happen. No matter the cost to him, or the entire world for that matter, he would find another way to stop it being used against her and somehow save his sister.

An hour later, the silver-white rays of a full moon illuminated the cottage's white curtains like movie screens. Anything moving outside the windows was projected onto the curtains in shadowed silhouette. Though Sheef was asleep, the passing intervals of dark shadow and moonlight on his eyelids were disruptive enough to wake him.

When he opened his eyes, he caught the fleeting shadow of a large hooded creature. Seconds later, two more shadows sailed by. Whatever was moving outside was doing so in complete silence. Even so, Fromp had been aroused and was standing in the middle of the room, a low, menacing growl caught in his throat.

"Easy boy," said Sheef as he quietly slid out of bed, touching the floor as lightly as possible. He stopped beside Fromp and gently stroked his head. "Let's try to stay calm. We don't' want to scare off our visitors before we get a good look at them."

Sheef slowly approached the window. He gently took hold of the edge of the curtain and pulled it back ever so slightly, just enough to create a viewing crack for him to see what was moving about in the moonlight. He observed nothing and was about to cross over to the other side of the curtain to get a look at another part of the yard when something cold and wet bumped his hand. The unexpected touch caused Sheef, who was already on edge, to jump back, and as he did so, his legs became tangled in a certain warp-hound's long tail. Having lost his balance, he clung tightly to the curtain in an attempt to steady himself, but only managed to pull it and its rod down upon himself. The noise was more than enough to alert whatever was outside, and within seconds, Sheef heard the flutter and ruffle of robes scurrying away into the night.

Harvey was startled awake by the sound of Sheef crashing to the floor. With his heart beating like a drum, he scanned the room. The only thing he saw was Fromp with his nose pressed against the window, fogging up the glass. As Harvey studied the room, though, he realized that something wasn't quite right. It took a moment or two for the remnants of sleep and dream to fade enough so that his brain could accurately process what was before him.

Glancing down at his watch, he saw that it was only 3:00 a.m. "Why's the room so bright?" he wondered. "The curtain . . . where'd it go? Why'd Fromp tear it down, and what's he looking at?"

Harvey slipped out of bed and was walking to the window for a closer inspection when he stepped on a lumpy mass. The mass cried out, "Would you watch where you're putting those big feet of yours!"

Harvey jumped and then looked down at the yelling lump. There was the missing curtain with something slowly moving underneath. Bending down, he threw back the curtain with a magician's flair, on the ready to combat whatever he uncovered. To his relief, it was nothing threatening, just Sheef lying on his back, grumbling something about a blundering warp-hound and his wet nose.

"Sheef," Harvey said, "What are you doing on the floor, and what's with the curtain?"

"I got tired of the bed. Thought the hard floor might be more comfortable and decided to use the curtain as a blanket," said Sheef sarcastically. "What do you think happened? It was that mass of purple fur over there."

"You tripped over Fromp?" Harvey asked laughing.

"No, he tripped me," Sheef replied as he sat up.

"What were you doing up anyway?"

"Something was moving around outside. I saw shadows on the curtain, and I would've gotten a good look if a certain curious nose and snout hadn't butted into me."

Harvey's laughter evaporated. "Do you have any idea what it was?"

"I didn't get a good look, but I've got a good idea, given that they were all wearing hooded robes."

"The Vapid? They came back to the cottage again?"

"Seems to be the case."

"But why were they sneaking around outside? They could've easily broken in like they did before, and with everyone asleep, taken us out easily."

The bedroom door flung open and Madora, Akeila, and Arrick burst in.

"What happened?" asked a Madora. "Is everyone okay? And why's Sheef on the floor wrapped in a curtain?"

"The Vapid," said Harvey. They came back."

"And they attacked Sheef with a curtain?" asked Madora.

"No," Sheef replied annoyed. "Fromp's tail tripped me, and I tore off the curtain in the process."

Madora bit her lip and reached out to help Sheef up.

"I'm alright and can manage myself," said Sheef as he stood to his feet. "And you can stop biting that lip of yours."

Sheef walked back over to the window. Staring out into the moonlit yard, he said, "They made no attempt to come inside. I don't believe they had any intention of doing so."

"They're watching us," said Arrick. "They could've finished us off in our sleep if they had wanted to."

"That's exactly what your boy just said, and there's only one explanation why they didn't attack. They're waiting for us to retrieve the Narciss Glass. Letting us do all the work and then snatching it away."

"Great," said Harvey. "We have to do the impossible and somehow get the Narciss Glass away from someone who's basically a superhero, and if we're successful, then we'll have to contend with the Vapid."

"There is an upside to all this," said Madora. "We only have to concentrate on one challenge at a time. At least our focus won't be divided."

"And there's the silver lining," remarked Sheef. Changing the subject, he said, "I can't imagine anyone will be able to go back to sleep now. Why don't we get some breakfast going, and Arrick, how about you getting us into that soundstage a little bit earlier than planned."

"Breakfast is it then," Arrick agreed. "I only have a few

eggs, but plenty of flour and milk. Anyone in the mood for pancakes?"

An hour later, stomachs full and head's weary from lack of sleep, the group was making preparations to leave. Fromp and Akeila were following Harvey around the house. When Arrick noticed his son being tailed by the two animals, he said, "We certainly can't bring those two with us. I don't care how good those costume and makeup artists are, there's no possible way to disguise something as big and colorful as Fromp. He'd be a dead giveaway. They'll have to stay behind."

"But Fromp will just track us and show up at the sound stage at exactly the wrong moment," said Harvey.

"Not if Akeila's here," said Sheef. "Unlike other dogs I know, Akeila will actually obey and stay if Madora tells her to do so, and trust me, if she stays here, Fromp will also. He hasn't let her out of his sight since he first met and sniffed her. And how about giving those leftover pancakes to Fromp? You know he'll vacuum them up, and a full stomach always makes him dopey and sleepy. He'll take a long food-induced nap and hopefully we'll be back before he wakes up."

Madora lovingly stroked Akeila's head and told her to stay. A small whine slipped between her gums as she settled down on the floor into a tight ball and closed her eyes. After eating a dozen pancakes, Fromp plopped down on the floor next to her and licked one of her ears. The group then loaded into Arricks' truck and headed to Mammoth Pictures and to an uncertain and disguised future.

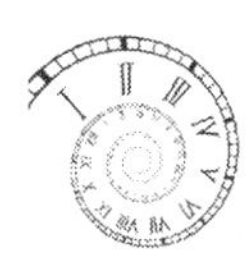

18

They arrived at the movie lot just as early morning was passing the baton to new day. Arrick parked his truck on the fake suburban street, far enough away from the soundstage to prevent Gwen from seeing it. They entered through the heavy metal door that Gwen had gone through the day prior. Arrick turned on his flashlight in order to locate the light switches. A large rat scurried across the beam of light, its pointy face and scraggly body reminding Harvey of an Insip.

Arrick flipped on five of the heavy metal light switches. Rows of large incandescent lights bloomed to life along the ceiling rafters. To everyone's immediate left was the interior of the mansion, the main set of *The Tempest's Fury*. On the other side were various offices, partitioned by walls of thin wood and glass. These included the dressing rooms and the makeup and costume departments.

"The mirror," said Harvey, pointing to the set.

"What's that, Son?" asked Arrick.

"The mirror in the movie," Harvey replied. "Remember

the part in the film when the old wealthy uncle thinks his nephews and nieces are attempting to steal his fortune, and he angrily throws a teapot at the large mirror and breaks it. That's the scene when Millud switches places with the actor playing the uncle and then picks up what appears to be a shard from the mirror, but is actually the Narciss Glass without its frame and handle."

"How could I forget." his father responded. That's the part of the movie that caused so many people to become addicted to the film. But how do you know about that scene? I had to watch the movie a half-dozen times and was becoming dangerously obsessed with the film. That's why your mom, who was alarmed at the negative effect the movie was having on me, refused to let me view it any more. I knew immediately that Millud was using the Narciss Glass somewhere in it, but it was your mother who figured out the exact scene. Did she show it to you?"

"She did but didn't tell me where it was or what to look for. I figured it out myself."

Arrick turned to Harvey and said in a surprised and proud tone, "How about that. Amazing. You obviously take after your mother. You didn't get that razor-sharp mind from me. And once again, I am very impressed."

The compliment, like the others his father had paid him in the last two days, was good medicine for a heart that for so long hadn't realized how sick and needy it really was.

They stopped walking when they reached the offices. "It's the third door," Arrick said, "the biggest office space because of the large costume closet. We should probably get everyone settled in. The set workers like to get here earlier than everyone else to get a jump on the day's work without Millud breathing down their necks and screaming at them every five minutes.

The area comprising the costume closet and dressing area was about eighty feet long and thirty feet wide. Narrow aisles divided five rows of hanging outfits. The various colors and fabrics, with fur and feathers adorning some, made it look like a menagerie of exotic animals, all claustrophobically shoved together.

"Sit down in the back of the closet," said Arrick. "If you hear the door open, hide in the racks. As soon as enough people arrive for you to blend in with, I'll come and get you, but until then, it's best to stay invisible and silent. If Gwen arrives, like we think she will, and catches sight of us, we'll lose our last and best chance of getting the Narciss Glass."

"What about you, Arrick?" asked Sheef. "Granted, you haven't spent as much time with her as we have, but it's been more than enough for her to easily identify you."

Arrick responded to Sheef's question by smiling slyly and exiting the closet. Harvey looked at Sheef and Madora with both hands raised, palms up. Twenty minutes later, a mustached, heavy-set security officer opened the door and stepped across the threshold."

Harvey and Madora dove into the folds of hanging clothes. The man was wearing a security officer's uniform like Arrick's, but this was the extent of any similarity between the two. He was at least forty pounds heavier and had a thick, bushy mustache with waxed handlebars rigidly pointing to the left and right. Above the mustache, a pair of horn-rimmed glasses rested on his nose.

While enveloped by a saffron-colored dress and a gorilla suit, Harvey heard Sheef chuckle and say, "Nice getup, Arrick. That's really good; you even had me fooled for a second. Though it looks like you might've had one too many pancakes this morning.

Arrick laughed and unbuttoned the lower part of his shirt, revealing a medium-sized pillow nestled up to his belly. "Basic Hollywood trick for quickly putting on the pounds."

Hearing his father's voice, Harvey emerged from the hanging clothes and back into the aisle wearing a wondrous expression.

"Borrowed the mustache from the makeup department," said Arrick. I've watched enough people affix these hairy caterpillars, and glasses, there are boxes and boxes of them. So, what do you think? Is it good enough to fool Gwen?"

"With that particular mustache, I'm not too sure about her not noticing you, but I don't think she'll recognize you," Sheef replied. "You know, if I hadn't been half anticipating something like this when you left the room, I would've never guessed it was you."

"Yeah, but won't Millud wonder who you are and ask about Arnold?" asked Harvey.

"Probably not. He'll be so consumed with the first day of filming that he won't pay much attention to anyone not directly involved in the movie. And even if he does say anything, I'll just tell him Arnold's sick and that the agency sent me over for the day as his replacement. Now, keep tight until everyone arrives, and then I'll mix you in with the other extras, and hopefully, the makeup magicians will camouflage you undetectable."

"I'll be fine as long as I don't have to put on as much weight as you," said Madora.

Sheef wanted to, but he knew better than to even think of a smart-aleck reply.

Just before 8:00, dozens of actors and actresses arrived, a mix of excitement and apprehension regarding the first day of filming was evident from their animated conversations. Meanwhile, pairs and trios of various work crews and artists also entered the cavernous Quonset hut, buzzing like industrious bees around a honeycomb.

When Madora, Harvey, and Sheef heard the commotion outside, they faded into the hanging clothes, sure that someone other than Arrick would come bursting in at any moment and catch them, but no one did. The first swing of the door was Arrick, who quickly ushered the group out, blending them in with forty other extras.

"Try not to say anything unless it's absolutely necessary," Arrick cautioned. "If anyone asks you a question, act nervous and inform him or her that it's your first time being an extra."

After Arrick dropped them off, he wandered about the soundstage, nodding to people and pretending to check the security of the building. Harvey, Sheef, and Madora provided fake names when they were requested and were soon following the other actors and actresses to makeup and costume.

An hour later the three reappeared and sauntered over to Arrick. He saw them approach and nodded but showed no signs of recognition.

"He doesn't know who we are," whispered Harvey. "I'm going to act confused and ask him where the bathroom is."

It was only when Harvey was less than two feet away from his father and asked the question, did Arrick realize who he was. With an astonished look on his face, he said, "I'm telling you; those people really can work magic. You could've walked past me all day long, and I never would've given you a second glance."

"So I guess it was worth it then," Madora said in a tone that was half joking but tinged with a bit of sadness. Arrick gave her a questioning look."

"She had me chop it off," offered Sheef, but quickly added, "but she still looks as amazing as ever."

"I knew my long black locks would give me away and trying to stuff them under a wig would be impossible, so I told Sheef to shear them off with my dagger."

The wig Madora was wearing was very light blonde, bordering on white, and bobbed in the fashion of the 1920s. Her attire also matched the period: a gold and black flapper dress adorned with a long string of pearls. Her lips were heavily painted with fire-engine red lipstick and bookended by powder-padded cheeks, all of which was overshadowed by eyelashes thick with mascara.

Sheef's saying that Madora still looked amazing was more than just a ploy to shield him from another one of her penetrating and destabilizing looks; it was the unvarnished truth. Glamorously attractive were the words that had popped into his head. He was a bit worried, though, because she now looked more in line with a leading lady, rather than a wallflower meant to fade anonymously into the background.

"It appears that Madora's not the only one who received a hair alteration," remarked Arrick to Sheef, who was wearing a hairless skull cap and a mustache and goatee pasted to his face. A tuxedo with tails completed his ensemble in the fashion of a butler to the wealthy."

"I look like an evil penguin dictator," Sheef laughed.

"Well, now that you mention it, you do closely resemble a certain infamous tyrant," commented Madora, her smiling bright red lips disarming him of any witty retort.

Rounding out the disguised trio was Harvey. Like Arrick, he had picked up some additional weight from having his shirt stuffed with pillows and scraps of clothing. His long, fence-post-like body had widened and spread. His portly stomach was held in place by a worn denim shirt and overalls. Harvey's feet were lost in oversized work boots, while his head was covered with a misshapen straw hat. His face was speckled with numerous brown freckles, thanks to the makeup artist flinging a paintbrush at his face.

"The gardener's son," said Harvey, wobbling slightly, still adjusting to his new body type.

"A glamorous flapper, a bald waiter, and a chubby gardening boy. You know, it's times like these when I wish I had a camera with me," said Sheef laughing.

"Excuse me, officer," said a voice with a haughty, put-on accent from behind. Arrick turned to one of the better-known actors. "I'm sorry to interrupt what I'm sure is a scintillating conversation with these extras," the actor said condescendingly, "but there's a situation in the breakfast line that requires your attention. It seems that two of our actresses are squabbling about who should be served first, but, without a doubt, is only a pretext for deeper issues at play. Might I tear you away from these . . . people and whatever about them has so engrossed you in their affairs, and have you attend to the little spat before it matures into something larger and more unpleasant?"

"Certainly, sir," Arrick replied with forced pleasantness. As he walked away from the group, he looked back and whispered, "Actors."

In the end there was no need for Arrick to intervene in the petty spat. Before he was halfway to the breakfast table, every head swiveled in the direction of the doorway at the arrival of a woman who lit the atmosphere with her entrance.

Waves of light seemed to dance upon the woman's shoulders and head. Harvey initially thought it was the play of light from the large bulbs overhead until he realized that she was the only one thus illuminated. The effect highlighted her entrance as much as if she had been lit by a spotlight. A middle-aged taxi driver trailed behind, carrying a leather attaché case. The breakfast line swayed in the woman's direction.

It was ironic that in a room full of actors, no one picked up on the fact that Millud's confident approach to the woman was nothing more than an act to mask his fear and uncertainty. Playing the role of director, he felt the need to make the first move and establish control of the room, but as if reading his mind, Gwen beat him to the punch.

"Millud dear, I do apologize for being late," Gwen said in a voice gushing with affability and sweetness. It was a voice that was not only impossible to be angry with but also disorienting. Everyone who heard it, including Millud, immediately felt disarmed and subservient to it. "I know you said 8:00 a.m. sharp, but I had an errand to run, and as happens all too often, what I thought could be accomplished quickly proved to be fraught with unanticipated challenges. The good news is that the errand was completed and is, in fact, with me now."

Gwen extended her left arm back toward the door, perfectly in time with the appearance of a small herd of gorilla-like men wearing black pinstriped suits and white fedoras. The herd heavily clopped up to Gwen, their steps echoing loudly throughout the hollowness of the soundstage.

Arranged in a "V" like a flying gaggle of geese, the leader at the apex of the "V" was distinguished from the others by his height and an enormous mealy red scar running from the bottom of his chin to the top of his forehead.

DESPAIR

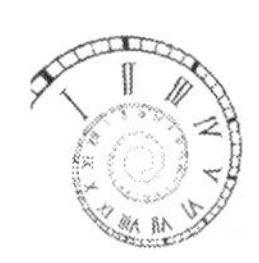

19

Madora, Sheef, and Harvey's jaws fell and hit bottom with a jarring jolt. Sheef whispered in disbelief, "You've got to be kidding me. Someone please pinch me and tell me that it's only a nightmare and that's not who I think it is."

Sheef half expected Madora to pinch him hard, for no other reason than to take advantage of the offer, but instead, she remained frozen in place. When he turned to her, he was taken aback by the pallid and pained expression on her face.

"Aren't those the men," she said without much inflection, "from the movie world of the *Phone Rang Twice* from which we rescued Gwen?"

"Well, that confirms it then; it's no nightmare," responded Sheef, but unsure as to why Madora had stated the obvious. "Who could ever forget that scarred monster."

"It's not he or his thugs that I'm necessarily worried about. It's the fact that they're here at all. Sheef, there's only one way Gwen could've accessed the Phantasian to retrieve the gangsters . . . She used a Sadiki."

"Akeila . . ." Harvey gasped.

Madora immediately began walking to the exit, only to be grabbed by Sheef.

"Madora, what do you think you're doing? You can't just walk out of here now."

"Let go of me, Sheef. Don't force me to make a scene," Madora quietly seethed with a spiny aggressiveness that Sheef hadn't seen since first meeting her beside an Egyptian pyramid."

"But, Madora," Sheef pleaded while still holding onto her arm, "there's a job to be done here, and we can't very well do it without you."

"Sheef," said Madora in a softer tone, "My primary job has always been to protect the Sadiki, ensuring that none of these unique animals ever fall into the hands of someone who might use the Phantasian for their own personal ambition. It appears that I've failed, and I need to fix the situation."

"But you can't . . . I mean where would you even begin?" Sheef questioned. "You have no idea where Akeila is, and if you storm out of here right now, you risk exposing us to Gwen and jeopardizing all our plans. Look, I promise," he said gently as he released her arm and let his hand slide down to rest on hers, "that once we're done here, I will do whatever you need me to do to get Akeila back."

Madora sighed deeply as tears pooled in her eyes. She bit her lip, swallowed emotion, and nodded. She knew Sheef was right. The worst thing she could do for Akeila and everyone else would be to draw undue attention to herself and the others. She broke free of Sheef's light handhold and stepped back to where Harvey was standing.

Sheef nodded and smiled empathetically. He knew how doing nothing was tearing her apart. She was powerless at this moment to help her beloved Sadiki, and he too felt equally powerless to help her.

In an attempt to distract Madora from her thoughts about Akeila, and because he was honestly perplexed himself, Sheef asked, "But why did Gwen, of all people, who knows how dangerous the umbrella man and his goons can be, bring them back here? Those thugs nearly machined-gunned her to death."

"I suppose that's precisely why she recruited them," said Madora, wiping away a tear. "As powerful as she is, she can't be everywhere or see everything at once, at least not yet anyway. In order to build her little utopian world, she apparently needs help, especially from people who are adept at removing obstacles."

"But Gwen's still good, isn't she?" asked Harvey, who was visibly concerned.

"Even the best-made home is carried away by rushing waters," said Madora.

"What was that?" asked Sheef.

"It's an Egyptian proverb. 'Even the best-made home is carried away by rushing waters.'"

"What does it mean?" asked Harvey.

"I believe it means that even the best person, with the noblest intentions, can be corrupted by the intoxicating allure of power, but further discussion will have to wait. Looks like we're about to have some company," said Sheef, motioning with his head toward Gwen and the gangsters who were walking in their direction.

"Do you think she recognized us?" asked Harvey, unconsciously taking a few steps backward.

"No, it doesn't appear so," replied Madora. "Looks like Millud is giving her a tour. Probably pointing out where the different scenes will be filmed and explaining the shooting schedule for the day. But it might be wise to nonchalantly move out of their way. Why don't we all work our way over to the breakfast table."

As they moved in the direction of the food table, Harvey stole a quick glance at Millud and Gwen. He could tell by Millud's smug exuberance that his attitude regarding Gwen had dramatically changed since the previous evening. Rather than perceiving her as a threat, he now seemed to view her as an asset that could advance his career even more. He enthusiastically pumped the hands of every actor and actress as he introduced them to Gwen with the pride of a father debuting his daughter to society.

Millud gauged the reactions of everyone who met Gwen, easily reading the expressions of those who were stunned by her dazzling and dizzying beauty. His realization that he would get credit for her discovery by featuring her in his film, caused a self-satisfied, impish grin to grow wide upon his face. And he was comforted by the fact that he, personally, no longer had any need of the Narciss Glass to captivate an audience. He now had something just as powerful that would keep them coming back for more, propelling both tickets sales and his career to unimagined heights.

The umbrella man, who was walking beside Gwen, suddenly stopped, his right hand flashing downward and out, a signal for his fellow thugs to halt. He tilted his head back and scented the air like a wolf catching something savory upon the breeze. Never one to deny his appetite, he politely asked his new boss for permission to break rank. Without stopping or even turning around, Gwen nodded, releasing the suited animals to go to their feeding troughs. The umbrella man smiled and directed his brothers in crime to the breakfast table. Before Harvey and the others had time to process what had occurred, the umbrella man and his goon brigade were breathing down their necks, and it wasn't long before one of the gangsters roughly shoved Harvey in the back, causing him to stumble forward into Sheef.

"Hey, yous there, chubs. You needs to be moving your blubbery self out the way and make room for the boys and the boss."

Sheef's hands balled into fists. He instinctively began to pivot, but before he could turn even five degrees, Madora grabbed his arm. It was now her turn to restrain and keep someone from jeopardizing the situation. The touch of Madora's hand was like a splash of cold water, snapping him out of instinctual response and into level-headed control.

"Please excuse the rude behavior of my associate, "said the umbrella man with as much politeness as a scarred giant who was used to barking out orders could produce. As he said this, he stepped out of line and walked forward, parking his massive frame next to Harvey, who immediately looked down at his shoes, afraid that even the briefest eye contact might blow his cover.

"Leonard," the umbrella man said sternly to the gangster behind Harvey, "you need to apologize to the boy for shoving him and for the uncalled-for insult."

Leonard faced his boss with an expression of pained disbelief and said, "Boss, you gots to be kiddin'. Since when do we let anyone stands in our ways, 'specially a fatty like this one?"

Before Leonard even had time to blink, the umbrella man's hand was around his throat and squeezing. In a threatening tone, he said, "Since we started workin' for Miss Gwen, that's when. And she told us to go easy like and respects everyone on this here movie set, and until she tells me otherwise, that's what we gonna do. Now, you can wait in line like these other nice folks or . . ." The umbrella man squeezed harder.

Leonard, whose face had turned tomato red from lack of oxygen, squeaked out, "No, no, boss, I'll wait. Swear, won't happen again."

"Good then, that's I want to hear," said the umbrella man as he released Leonard and straightened the shaking gangster's tie and smoothed out the lapels of his suit. "Now, once again, apologize to the boy."

Leonard tapped Harvey on the back and then leaned over his shoulder so that his face was only inches away from Harvey's. "Hey, kid, looks, I'm real sorry for . . ." The man stopped as if his next words had been suddenly snatched from his mouth. He scrutinized Harvey and then said, "Do I knows you? Have we ever met?"

"Leonard, what are you gabbing on about?" asked the umbrella man. Just tell the boy you're sorry so we can move on."

"Sorry, boss, but the kid looks familiars to me. I'm telling you, I know him from somewheres. I never forget a face."

"You're all batty, Leonard, talking nonsense. You ain't never been to Hollywood. How could you know the boy?"

"I don't know, boss. You're probably right. Maybe just reminds me of someone. Anyways, kid, sorry 'bout the shove. No hard feelin's?"

"It's okay," Harvey mumbled, still staring intently at his shoes.

The umbrella man took a step forward and turned to Sheef, peering at him for a healthy, unnerving ten seconds. Unfortunately, when the umbrella man broke the silence and spoke, his words did little to lower Sheef's rising anxiety.

"You know, Leonard here ain't the brightest bulb in the house, but he might've been onto something," said the umbrella man, glancing briefly back at Harvey. "You and the boy behind you . . . I don't know, something about you two reminds me of . . . Say, you got relatives in any other cities?"

Sheef knew that ignoring the question was not an option. Such behavior would either arouse the gangster's suspicion or anger, and truthfully, at this moment, Sheef didn't know which one would be worse.

"I have some cousins and what not. Any city in particular?"

The umbrella man opened his mouth to speak, but his train of thought unexpectedly pulled away from the depot. His mealy red facial scar darkened as he attempted to catch up to the rapidly receding thought.

"That's strange. I swear the name of the city was right here in my mind seconds ago, but then it up and vanished, like that," he said, tapping the side of his head and then snapping his fingers. He then pushed back his fedora and pulled out a cigarette. As if on cue, Leonard, with flame atop match, slid into servility in front of his boss. The umbrella man introduced his smoke to the proffered fire and richly inhaled. A column of smoke was blown into Sheef's face as the gangster said, "Well, never mind then, and let me once again apologize for my associate's rude behavior to the boy." And with that, he turned around and walked back to join the rest of his gang in line.

Harvey tapped Sheef's back and whispered over his shoulder, "What just happened? Why's the umbrella man being so polite? That guy was actually pleasant."

"He doesn't remember who he is," said Madora from in front of Sheef and in a voice that was barely audible.

"Sheef, what did she say?" asked Harvey.

With a sigh, Madora switched places with Sheef so that they could both hear her without inviting eavesdropping from unwelcome ears.

"I said that he doesn't remember who he is. None of them do. Do you recall what Gwen was like when we took her out of her Phantasian world? Once she was detached from the words of the script that created her, she became a blank slate."

"That's right," Sheef replied. "How did I not make the connection myself? Her memory, everything — who she was, her family, and even her name — was completely erased. So that's what's happened to them?"

"Without question," answered Madora. "Leave a Phantasian world and the gods who created you are no more."

"Oh great, then that means Gwen's reprogramming their lives," said Sheef.

"No different than what we did to her," replied Madora.

"Yeah, and look at the mess we created. I can hardly wait

to see what happens with the rewrite of the umbrella man and his goons," breathed Sheef.

"Well, we don't know exactly what Gwen's done to them thus far, but one thing is apparent, the umbrella man clearly knows who the boss is," said Madora.

"Coffee, Danish, or both? What'll be, mister?" yelled a woman from twenty feet away. Sheef turned around and was chagrined when he realized that the dozen or so people that had been in front of him had already been served breakfast and had migrated to other parts of the soundstage. Because Sheef failed to respond to her initial queries, the woman yelled again, "Hey, you there! Listen, I haven't got all day! If you ain't hungry, then clear out and make room for those who are!"

The volume of the woman was loud enough to catch the attention of many of those milling about under the domed roof, including Gwen, who paused her conversation with one of the set designers and glanced over at the woman and the recipient of her exasperation. Gwen's glance rested on Sheef for only a second or two, but it was enough. Her eyes narrowed and an almost imperceptible smile twisted the ends of her lips. The expression vanished as quickly as it had appeared, leaving Sheef and the others ignorant of the fact that they had been spotted.

"Everyone! Everyone, please give me your attention," Millud shouted in a grating, shrill voice, made worse by the fact that it was magnified by a megaphone. "Whatever you are doing, please stop. It can wait. What I have to announce cannot."

Whether it was due to a lack of respect for the man or an

involuntary tuning out of such an unpleasant voice, those assembled in the soundstage paid little heed to Millud's commands, which only served to ruffle the insecure director's feathers, causing him to screech even louder. "That was not a suggestion, people! If you value your jobs and would like to continue as a part of this motion picture, then move!"

The ear-piercing threat did the trick, and soon cast members and workers from every compass point of the soundstage converged toward Millud, but even after everyone had arrived and formed a semicircle around the flustered director, he didn't immediately begin speaking. Rather, he quietly stood for two minutes, savoring the power created by the awkward, silent tension. It was his little bit of revenge for them not heeding his call the first time. Harvey, Madora, and Sheef blended in with the back of the crowd, keeping their eyes angled down and away from Gwen's. Standing statuesque behind the crowd were the gangsters, ready at a moment's notice to spring to life and attack.

When Millud finally did speak, what he had to say was hardly surprising to those listening. It was obvious that the glamorous woman — whose illuminated beauty had already redirected attention away from the director, leaving him to appear pale and sickly in the shadows — would be joining the cast in some capacity.

"Today it is my delight to announce an addition to our movie family," Millud said forcefully, doing his best to wrench the focus back on himself. The tactic failed. The actors and workers, still mesmerized by Gwen's presence, heard Millud's voice as nothing more than background noise, a dull hum in the distance. "Let me introduce you to Gwen . . . um . . . I'm sorry, but I'm embarrassed to admit that I don't' recall your last name."

"That's no fault of yours, H.B.," said Gwen as she stepped in front of Millud, eclipsing him from those standing before her, "because I never shared it with you. The truth is, I don't have one and feel no need to acquire one."

She then spoke to the crowd in the manner of a teacher instructing a class of elementary students. Her words were cloyingly sweet and intoxicating. "You see, the single name 'Gwen' is more than sufficient for my role in your lives, but having just one name is also logical given my background. A last name denotes belonging to another and proceeding from something preexisting. But I have no antecedent. I am related to no family, for no mother ever gave me life. I, Gwen, simply am. Yes, I Am," she said in a tone that indicated that her statement was revelatory knowledge even to her."

Harvey didn't know exactly why, but Gwen's last statement, though only three words long, felt twisted and bent. It was as if a dark presence had slithered in and poisoned the atmosphere.

"So I do hope," Gwen continued speaking, spreading her arms toward the crowd that was listening on pins and needles, "that the cast and crew will indulge my request and simply refer to me as 'Gwen'. No title need precede it."

All those listening nodded. Millud, meanwhile, saw the break in Gwen's speech as an opportunity to jump into the conversation and try to redirect the attention back on himself. Before he could even utter one syllable, though, Gwen began speaking again. Unbeknownst to him, this was the last opportunity for him to have any authority or influence over the cast and crew. And though he would still retain the title of director, the actual power of the position had already been seamlessly transferred to Gwen. From the moment she began addressing everyone, she became the focal point, the visionary, the director, the producer, and the star of the show.

"Friends, or should I say, 'family', as Millud referred to you?" she asked warmly.

As Gwen continued to address the crowd, Harvey and the others began a slow and inconspicuous migration to the outside of the semicircle where they hid behind a group of wide-shouldered and tall set designers. Though they were in costume and hopefully incognito, they decided it was wiser not to push their luck.

Once they settled in behind the workers, their anxiety diminished enough for them to converse with one another in hushed tones. If they had any inkling, however, that Gwen had already recognized Sheef, and then quickly spotted Madora and Harvey, they'd be in no mood to chat, regardless of the tone.

"Where's Arrick?" whispered Harvey.

Sheef scanned the crowd and spotted a portly man with a bushy handlebar mustache close to the exit.

"Over there," said Sheef, "He's talking to the taxi driver who came in with Gwen."

"Why's he talking to him?" asked Harvey.

"Detective work I suppose. Gathering any information on

Gwen. Since he drove her here, there's the possibility that he might have seen the Narciss Glass."

Sheef and Harvey's conversation was suddenly interrupted by the collective gasp of the crowd in response to a shriek from a brunette actress. Millud, whose mind was wandering down future roads of fame and fortune, was embarrassingly jolted back to the present. Whatever Gwen had said, not only created the shriek but also caused every head in the crowd to turn in Millud's direction. Having no earthly idea what Gwen had just said, he merely returned everyone's questioning look with one of his own.

Gwen easily read the situation and surmised that Millud was daydreaming, but rather than embarrass him further, she simply repeated what she had said. "I understand that this might come as a shock to you, and perhaps I should've informed you earlier, but I'm confident that you have no objection to my changing the plot and giving the role of the female lead to myself."

Millud couldn't have cared less at this point what Gwen wanted to do with the movie, so long as he still retained the title of director. He knew that with Gwen and the Narciss Glass in the same movie, the plot could be nothing more than a woman nibbling on crackers and drinking a glass of water for ninety minutes, and it would still be a blockbuster hit.

"No objection whatsoever, Gwen. In fact, I think it's a marvelous idea for you to be the star. What other role could we cast such a beautiful and shimmering light in? And whatever plot changes you've made, I'm certain will only make the picture that much better"

Once Millud finished speaking, it was as if a radio had

been switched to another station. He was once again lost in a string of tomorrows when he believed he would be the most respected and sought-after director in Tinseltown.

Meanwhile, the thirty-something brunette who electrified the atmosphere with her razor-edged, angular shriek when Gwen announced that she herself would be taking over the female lead, was crouched over, sniffing and softly blubbering into her hands.

Gwen casually walked over and gently placed her hand upon the head of the disconsolate actress. As the sniffing and blubbering ceased, the actress sat up straight. Those close by were able to see the transformation. The previously tightened facial muscles, tied up in anguished knots after hearing that she would no longer be the star, suddenly relaxed. Her expression, which only seconds ago was flushed red with anger, now effused a deep-pooled serenity. It was as if a stretched rubber band had suddenly been released to contract back to its original size and tension-free condition.

"There, there now," Gwen said soothingly. "Isn't that better?"

The actress nodded at Gwen with child-like innocence.

"Everyone, I would like to introduce you to my new personal secretary . . ." Gwen looked down at the woman with a kind but questioning look.

The actress understood and responded, "Janet. My name is Janet."

"My new secretary Janet," Gwen said to the crowd. Everyone applauded as Janet basked in the praise and glow of Gwen's proximity.

A man wearing a rumpled suit emerged from one of the

back offices and hurriedly walked over to Gwen. Before he was able to say anything, Gwen turned and reached out for the stack of papers he was carrying.

"Thank you, Bernard. Copies for everyone and on schedule. Very good indeed," Gwen said to the rumpled-suited man who quickly scurried back to his office.

"These, my friends," said Gwen, once again addressing the entire gathered group, "are copies of the new script I wrote last night. I sent it over by courier early this morning to Bernard Matthews. He and his team worked all through the early morning hours typing up copies so that we could begin filming today. So, would everyone please take a copy and begin learning your new lines. We will begin filming the first scene within the hour. You're dismissed, but let us reconvene at the mansion set at 9:30 sharp."

The cast and crew disseminated to different parts of the soundstage, many heading over to the breakfast table for one more cup before the clatter of the day grew distractingly loud. Harvey and the others walked in the direction of Arrick, who had just finished talking with the taxi driver and had waved them over.

"Young man," rang out a pleasant voice from behind. When Harvey failed to stop, the voice rang out a second time. "Young man, excuse me, but I would like to chat with you for a moment."

Harvey froze. The voice was not only very pleasant but also very familiar. Within seconds, a hand with incredibly well-manicured nails draped over his left shoulder and nudged him into turning around. When he did so, he looked directly into the radiant and smiling face of Gwen.

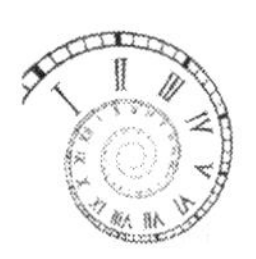

20

"Oh, there you are, Harvey. I was wondering where you and the others were hiding. I was assured you'd be here, despite trying my best to warn you not to interfere. Your disguise is actually quite becoming," she said with an amiable giggle. I always thought you were a bit too thin, but perhaps you overdid it," she said, playfully patting the pillow under his shirt. And the hat . . . very nice touch. You know, the getup might've actually fooled me if not for one thing."

Gwen waited a moment to hear if Harvey was aware of his "tell", but feeling very unnerved at being caught so easily by Gwen, he was temporarily short of words. "It's your Lignum shirt. Your protective undershirt given to you by Thurngood is showing." Gwen then inserted her finger through a fairly good-sized tear in the shoulder of his denim shirt and touched the Lignum shirt beneath. Harvey looked down at the tear and could clearly see the shirt underneath, but had no idea how Gwen had spotted it at a distance.

"To be honest, Harvey, I would've never given the tear

a second look if someone else in your party hadn't already given himself away. I only scrutinized your outfit to confirm what I already suspected."

With this, Gwen stepped around Harvey and approached Sheef. "Father," she said laughing as she reached out to touch his bald head, "whatever happened to that lovely blonde hair of yours? You of all people should know better than to make direct eye contact with the very person you're attempting to hide from, especially when wearing an expression of fear. As good as your bald butler costume is, your eyes were a dead giveaway."

"And, Madora," Gwen continued, turning and giving Madora an appraising look from heels to hair, "you do make a striking Flapper. Would take the breath away of any man to be sure, but what a pity you sheared those beautiful black locks off for nothing," she said, touching the tips of Madora's bobbed wig.

Gwen stepped back so that she could address everyone at once. "I thought I would be enraged if I caught you interfering with me again, and trust me when I say, I'm not at all happy about your latest scheme, but to be quite frank, I'm actually more confused than angry as to why you persist in resisting me. How I wish you could understand the good I will soon accomplish. If you would only give . . ." Gwen's words sputtered to a stall at the realization that something, or more precisely, someone was missing. "My apologies. I just realized that it would be poor form to speak to an incomplete party. If you three are here, then the fourth of your little quartet must be here as well."

Gwen then motioned to Gundy, who was standing about thirty feet off to the side. He was far enough away not to eavesdrop, but close enough to be front and center if needed. He immediately hustled over to Gwen and answered her whispered question.

"Harvey, your father Arrick, who's been attempting to gather intelligence on the whereabouts of the Narciss Glass, inadvertently divulged his true identity to my dedicated driver. You see, I informed Gundy here to keep his ears and eyes open for anyone who was overly inquisitive about me, and he has just informed me that a heavily whiskered security guard has been snooping around, making suspicious inquiries. Now I wonder," she said as she looked over to the heavy-set security guard who was milling around the entrance," if anything is biting this morning."

Gwen raised her right arm and rotated it backward in the manner of an angler winding up for a cast, then gracefully flung an arching line of golden light at the security guard. Arrick saw the approaching line of light and understood immediately that he had been caught, and unless he moved out of the way within the next second or two, so too would his body.

He dove to the right and landed on his side, sliding across the slick concrete floor. The move, however, proved pointless, for just as he shifted his body to make the lunge to the right, Gwen altered the trajectory of the snaking line of light. By the end of Arrick's short slide, he was already tightly bound by multiple strands of pulsating energy.

The other end of the line was still connected to Gwen, and

once Arrick was securely wrapped, she jerked the line and said, "Oh, it appears that I've hooked a big one." Snapping her arm backward, the whip-like motion pulled the light-line taut. At the other end, the unraveling motion of the line rapidly spun Arrick's body, which had the effect of standing him upright. And like a spinning top, he was soon zigzagging about the soundstage.

The general motion of the spinning Arrick was toward Gwen, but his path was a far cry from a straight line. He vacillated side to side and forward and back like an inebriated sailor attempting to walk a ship's deck from stern to bow in rough seas. During his dizzying travel, Arrick's hat, whiskers, and belly stuffing flew free and clear.

When he eventually reached Gwen, his spinning slowed to a stop, and he collapsed to the ground. Disheveled and disoriented, he attempted to make sense of the blurred and chaotic scene before him. Though his body had stopped moving, his senses hadn't. The dizzying and wobbly scene before him soured his stomach and split his head, causing him to shut his eyes. The action, though, was a little too late. Arrick's overwhelmed senses fainted for relief. Harvey was immediately kneeling at his side, doing his best to comfort and revive his father.

"There's absolutely no reason to fret, Harvey," said Gwen reassuringly. "Your father will recover and be just fine. It might take a few minutes to sleep this off, and he'll likely have a throbbing headache for an hour or two, but I don't foresee any permanent damage."

Harvey spun around with a tear-streaked face and shouted

accusingly, "Why did you do that? Violence wasn't necessary! You could've just pointed him out to that taxi driver of yours, and he would've brought him over to you! But you didn't! You went ahead and hurt my father for no reason!"

Harvey stood up and bore into Gwen with a painful, pleading stare, and for the first time since Gwen had her knowledge-expanding experience at the library, she looked unsure of herself.

"The Gwen I knew would've never done something like this — would've never hurt another person!"

"Harvey," Gwen said somewhat shakily, finding a bit more stability with each word she spoke, "I specifically warned everyone from interfering with my plans, and now you see—"

"No," Harvey interrupted, "The Gwen I knew would never succumb to harming another, regardless of any warning. The fact is, you're changing, and not for the better."

"Oh, I agree that I'm changing," Gwen said, regaining her equilibrium and control, "and though the phrase has been used to describe people for their good or bad changes for millennium, it has never applied to such a degree as it has with me. I went from naïve ignorance to near omniscience in only a matter of days. No human, including your preeminent scientists, has come anywhere close to my level of knowledge and its practical application to create the most morally advanced civilization in history. The noble yearning of humanity to live at peace with one another in real equality and harmony is no longer an elusive dream. I will very shortly satisfy the yearning, but if I must deal harshly with resistance or encumbrances that might prevent its realization, then so be it."

"So the ends justify the means," commented Sheef. "Is that your new moral standard?"

Turning to face Sheef, Gwen smirked and said, "When the end is the final destination of humanity's long, slogging climb to a perfect society, then yes, I suppose any means can and should be justified."

Arrick groaned back to consciousness.

"Dad, are you okay?" asked Harvey worriedly.

"I will be whenever the world stops spinning," Arrick replied while tightly shutting his eyes and pinching his forehead.

Gwen stopped speaking for a moment to observe Harvey and Arrick. As he helped his father back to his feet, Harvey shot an angry look at Gwen, whose eyes briefly glistened with tears.

"Here, let me assist you, Harvey," Gwen said, noticing the difficulty he was experiencing helping Arrick get back up. Gwen reached out and placed her hand upon Arrick's head. Instantly, the dizziness and accompanying nausea vanished. Strength once again coursed through his muscles, enabling him to stand up under his own power.

Sheef removed his skull cap and cast it to the floor. Since there was no reason to remain disguised, he decided to part with the cap that was trapping in heat like a wool hat. The removal revealed sweat-saturated hair strands matted to his head.

"Getting out of costume so soon? What about the next scene that features the butler?" asked Gwen.

"Gwen, the last thing I have any intention of doing is to take part in your little scheme to manipulate and control the masses," Sheef said as he hastily unfastened his bow tie.

"A tone sharp enough to cut with. Hurtful, ignorant, and inflexible. Since it appears that I will never be able to change that stubborn mind of yours by any conventional means of persuasion, I'm now forced to . . . How did you put it? Ah yes, 'my new moral standard' — justifying the means by the ends."

Harvey and Sheef exchanged confused looks.

"And you, Madora," Gwen said as she turned to her, "Given your mutual affection for one another, I think it's safe for me to assume that you're of the same mindset as Sheef."

Sheef's faced flushed red with embarrassment as he coughed into his hands to conceal the facial confirmation of what Gwen had said.

"Such strong emotions are lovely, and yet, so very dangerous. Your feelings for Madora, Sheef, have exposed a crack in your defenses. To care so much for another is laudable but also an exploitable weakness. Far too often the caring one is willing to sacrifice everything and anything for the sake of keeping his or her beloved from harm. And this, too, is true of you, Harvey," Gwen said, turning to him and raising her eyebrows. "You have exposed yourself in a very similar way with your new-found affection for your father."

Harvey and Sheef stared perplexedly at Gwen. "Don't you see," she said with a genial smile. "If you, Harvey the gardener, and you, Sheef the butler, don't willingly participate in this movie of mine, then the deaths of Arrick and Madora will be upon your heads."

And with this, Gwen thrust her arms forward in the direction of Madora and Arrick. She opened and then snapped her hands shut. A thick strand of shimmering light, similar to the one that spun Arrick around the soundstage, materialized. Gwen held the middle of the glowing rope, while the two separate free ends on either side of her flailed wildly on the floor, rapidly growing in length and snaking their way toward opposite walls.

When they reached the walls, the ends turned ninety degrees and climbed up to the ceiling, whereupon they turned another ninety degrees and slithered toward one another. When they were five feet apart, the ends stopped and dropped to the floor, while the majority of the glowing rope clung like ivy to the ceiling and walls.

The ends whipped about as if scenting the air for prey. They soon located their quarry, wrapping themselves tightly around Madora and Arrick's torsos until they were both wound and bound by multiple strands of pulsating light.

Harvey turned to Gwen and shouted, "Gwen, what are you doing? You can't hurt them! They've done nothing wrong!"

"Harvey," Gwen said, still firmly gripping the middle of the light strand, "As you can clearly see, they are in no way hurt, but whether or not this remains the case, is now solely dependent on your and Sheef's cooperation. If you comply with my wishes, they will be returned, perhaps a little worse for wear, but by all means, alive; however, if you in any way resist, attempt to sabotage the making of the film, or try again to retrieve the Narciss Glass, well then . . . you should just say your final farewells now."

You can't mean what you're saying," Harvey said with quivering denial. "Gwen, please . . ."

"Dear brother, listen to my heart. It's my sincere wish not to harm anyone, but if two must suffer for the greater good of millions, then so bit it, for their lives are a cheap price to pay for paradise."

"No life, not even a single one, is ever cheap, and any paradise bought by the suffering and death of an innocent human is a paradise I don't want any part—"

"SILENCE!" Gwen shouted, snapping the light strand. A small fragment of glowing rope broke off and sailed through the air toward Harvey. It slapped directly on his mouth, suffocating any further words. While Harvey frantically attempted to pry off the mouth seal, Gwen yanked down on the rope. Instantly, the lengths of the shimmering light strands were no longer statically clinging to the walls and ceiling but were once again moving about. Gwen yanked down a second time, causing the strands to go taut, quickly followed by their rapid contraction. With no warning, Maodra and Arrick were violently yanked from the floor and rocketed upward, their heads stopping a mere foot from the ceiling.

Witnessing Madora in such a precarious and powerless condition, Sheef's emotions took control of his next actions. He sprinted at Gwen, his tuxedo coattails whipping behind like mud flaps. His intention was to bulldoze into her side, breaking her hold on the light strand. Though he had ample speed and the element of surprise, in the end, both variables mattered little, for it was as if Gwen knew his thoughts before he did.

Just as he launched himself for a tackling leap, a slight discoloration appeared in the air surrounding Gwen, and it wasn't until he was mere inches away that Sheef realized it was composed of the very same light energy that Gwen was holding in her hand.

The impact was severe, no different than hitting solid glass, but unlike glass, the energy shield failed to break. Sheef's face did, and with an audible popping crunch. The rest of his body followed his nose, and though there were no more broken bones, the jarring collision left behind its bruised imprints. The sensation of a sharp snapping pain was the last thing he felt before the world turned black and he folded in upon himself.

Harvey, who was positioning himself to make a similar attack on Gwen, thought better of it when Sheef crumpled to the ground.

"A wise decision, Harvey," said Gwen in a blunt and stern tone. "My patience is wearing thin, and I will not tolerate any further insubordination. From this point forward, you will comply with my every whim, desire, and command, or suffer the unpleasant consequences of defiance.

With adrenaline surging through his veins, Harvey wanted nothing more than to leap into action, but he held himself in check. His inaction, though, wasn't born of fear, for he had moved well beyond its frigid and paralyzing reach. He was now being driven by a much more stable and thickly layered emotion. He took a deep breath and waited for rational thought to return. Attacking Gwen was pointless and would only make matters worse. What he needed was time, time to formulate a new strategy.

"Madora," Gwen said while looking up at the floating pair,

"since I don't foresee any further use for her, and to provide you comfort during for your possible end, I've decided to return your pet. Gwen then motioned to Gundy who exited the building, returning moments later with Akeila.

The Sadiki had no intention whatsoever of complying with Gundy's wish that she willingly follow with loose leash. Akeila had set each of her leg muscles into the locked position and was pulling back with all her might as Gundy repeatedly tugged on the leash. In the end, Gundy was only able to win the tug-of-war by dragging the nails of her pawed feet across the concrete floor.

When Madora saw Akeila, she screamed her name so loudly that it ricocheted off of every wall in the cavernous space. Akeila was initially confused, for even though she recognized the voice of her beloved owner, none of the faces nor scents before her matched the voice. It was only when she was directly below Madora and overwhelmed by the proximity of her scent, that she lifted her snout and caught sight of her human, tightly bound and dangerously suspended high above her furry head.

Angry growls were interspersed by distressed yelps as Akeila pawed the air above her. When Gwen reached out in an attempt to calm her nerves, the agitated animal barred her teeth and backed away.

"I do understand," said Gwen, quickly pulling back her hand. "I'd be angry also if my special person was in trouble, and I was unable to provide any help. Tell you what, Akeila, why don't you join Madora."

Gwen shook the light strand still in her hand, and as she

did so, a third strand fell from the ceiling in between Madora and Arrick. Once the end hit the floor, it slithered over to Akeila, whereupon it wrapped itself multiple times around her midsection. Before the animal could process what was happening, she was pulled up and away, suspended five feet from Madora. Whining pitifully for her owner, the Sadiki frantically tried to run, but with no traction, her engine remained in neutral with wheels spinning in vain.

"It's alright, girl," said Madora, tears streaming down her cheeks. "Let's settle down. It's going to be okay." But hearing her voice only made matters worse and sent the dog into a frustrated frenzy, pawing even more desperately for Madora.

"Harvey, are there any last words you wish to say to Arrick and Madora before they depart to their temporary . . . or perhaps, permanent home?" asked Gwen in a much calmer, even light-hearted voice. "I would ask Sheef, but he appears to have been rendered uncommunicative at the moment."

Harvey stared up at the dangling trio and said pleadingly, "Please, Gwen, stop this before it's too late."

"The truth is, dear brother, it's nearly too late for them already."

"I wasn't referring to them."

An almost imperceptible muscle spasm twitched Gwen's upper cheek. She quickly pushed it away with a hard eye blink and then carelessly dropped the light strand. Madora, Arrick, and Akeila, who were hovering just below the ceiling, fell. Halfway to the ground, their drop was jarringly arrested.

Gwen then violently thrust her hands forward, and as she did, the humans and Sadiki were ruthlessly thrown into the air and sent soaring at perilous speed to the exit. The door flew open and off its hinges a second before the three arrived. And like a ball fired from a cannon, they were projected out of the doorway, hundreds of feet into the late-morning sky.

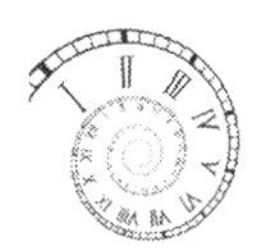

21

Madora, Arrick, and Akeila traveled through the brisk morning air for a half mile before rapidly descending to a steel water tower with the words "Mammoth Pictures" emblazoned on its side in large block letters. As they drew close, the conical roof of the water tower suddenly tilted open like the lid of a jar. Man, woman, and animal dropped through the opening and splashed down in the chilled liquid. They plunged thirty feet under before crawling back to the surface where they broke through with gasps and wet coughs.

Akeila frantically dog-paddled to the side of the tower where she attempted to claw her way up, but the slick vertical steel refused to accommodate her efforts, and she was able to do nothing more than slap the metal with her paws.

The sound of Akeila scratching was briefly drowned out by the conical roof slamming shut, violently shuttering the entire structure. When the shaking and clanking finally ended, so did the light.

Fearing that Akeila's frantic behavior might fatigue her,

Madora called out to her to swim over. A faint whine was heard in the darkness followed by the sounds of paws pushing through water. When she reached Madora, Akeila licked her once on the cheek and then began swimming tight circles around her.

When Arrick opened his mouth to speak, the small wake created by Akeila flooded in. After sputtering out a mouthful of frigid water, Arrick said, "At best we can tread water for two hours or so, but after that . . . and at this temperature, it won't be easy to fend off hypothermia for very long."

"I know," said Madora shivering, erratically sloshing about as she fought with her leather boots. Finally she succeeded in pulling them off, releasing them to sink to the bottom. "Problem is, there's no possible way for us to get out of this tin can. We're trapped like sardines."

* * *

"Where did you send them?" Harvey demanded.

"They're safe for the time being, but time is not on their side," said Gwen as she walked over to Sheef and knelt down next to his unconscious body. "Happily participate in the scene, and they'll be returned in short order. Now, once I awaken and heal Sheef, I want you to get him back into costume and over to the mansion set. We've been delayed long enough."

Gwen then reached over and lightly touched Sheef's head. He instantly gasped to life, and was immediately overwhelmed by the excruciating pain radiating from his shattered nose. The pain didn't have to be endured for very long. Seconds after waking him, Gwen placed her index finger upon Sheef's nose. Harvey heard the distinct sounds of rattling bones coalescing back to their original structure. The throbbing pain vanished.

Sheef reached up and felt a nose which was no longer bent to the side, but properly oriented with tip straight and pointed outward. He pulled a handkerchief out of the tuxedo pocket and wiped blood from his face.

Gwen smiled, stood, and walked over to the set. When she arrived, she was immediately surrounded by an entourage of actors, actresses, workers, gangsters, and a taxi driver.

Once she was out of earshot, Sheef said, "What was I thinking? I knew an outright attack against Gwen had little chance of success. My obliterated nose is more than ample evidence of that."

"You weren't," Harvey responded. "Thinking, I mean. If you'd been, you never would've charged her like that. It was done to rescue and protect a certain flapper in distress."

Sheef made no attempt to deny Harvey's words but only gave a slight nod in response. He then shook his head and asked, "Did you see what she did? Gwen somehow manipulated matter and reconstructed my nose with nothing more than a touch of her hand. It's like she's rewriting all the laws of physics and biology. And that invisible energy shield she created . . . There's no possible way anyone could break through something like that. It stopped me dead in my tracks, the impact nearly killing me. I hate to admit it, but this may be where our little adventure ends. I can't begin to fathom how in the world we can stop her now."

Harvey placed his hands under Sheef's arms, helped him to his feet, and gathered up his belly stuffing and skull cap. "You're right, Sheef, any outright attack is pointless, and there's absolutely no way she's going to let us anywhere near the Narciss Glass. And even if we were successful in stealing it, we would likely never see Arrick or Madora again."

Sheef, who had been unconscious when Gwen had sent Arrick and Madora away, was so preoccupied with his nose and reestablishing his bearings that he hadn't realized that Arrick and Madora were no longer hovering above.

Looking up, Sheef gasped, "Where are they?"

"I don't know. When you were out cold, Gwen sent them and Akeila flying out of the soundstage. She said that if we cooperate, they'll be returned, but apparently the clock's ticking."

"What does that mean?"

"That they don't have much time, and we've no other alternative."

"Then I was right," Sheef said despairingly. "This is it. She's won and the present situation is worse than when we started. Humanity, Ecclon, the Flurn . . . all lost."

"No," said Harvey calmly and with an otherworldly look in his eyes. "The Unseen wouldn't have brought us this far for us to fail now."

"Unless we missed His path somewhere along the way. Wouldn't surprise me if we made more than one bad decision and wrong turn at some point."

"Even if we did, I think the Unseen would've rerouted us so that his plan would still be accomplished. I don't know quite how or why, but I have confidence that he who began all of this will be faithful to bring about its conclusion."

"I sure hope you're right," Sheef replied, "but I personally have little to no hope right now. Sorry, but I just can't see any way of stopping her and the disaster that's certain to follow once she controls the minds of millions with her utopian propaganda and begins to build that egalitarian, kindergarten, every-body-share-and-just-play-nice world of hers."

"I might have an idea," said Harvey in the same calm and collected voice.

Sheef turned to Harvey, intending to give him his best dubious expression, but it failed to materialize because of the one Harvey was wearing. The young teenager looked years beyond his age. It was as if he had, within seconds, attained the wisdom and understanding of multiple lifetimes.

Harvey's expression had the effect of sparking a tiny light of hope in Sheef. "Yeah, okay then . . . don't suppose you'd like to share this idea you have with me," asked Sheef.

"Not yet. The details aren't clear. It's as if I'm on road and can only see twenty feet or so in front of me because of a sharp curve up ahead and a heavy fog clinging to the ground, but I'm confident that the Unseen's guiding us, one step at a time."

22

Grauncrock waited impatiently in the abandoned mine shaft for Rakkrid's return. He had sent him and the other Vapid Lords out to find Harvey, the Narciss Glass, and Akeila, and was seething with each passing minute that Rakkrid failed to show.

Flashes of yellow-green light illuminated and danced upon the walls of the dark cavern at Rakkrid's warping arrival. The long, skeletal Vapid tentatively slinked before Grauncrock.

"My Lord Grauncrock," began the toady, sallow-skinned Vapid, "I am pleased to report that—"

"Silence, you fool!" snapped Grauncrock. His booming command shaking the mine shaft, causing rock and dust to rattle loose and fall to the ground. "Pleasure is not yours to enjoy, Rakkrid. You were told to bring back three items, and unless my eyes are deceiving me, it appears that not even one of them is in your possession. I seem to recall that I warned you not to fail me again, for if you did, you would regret your existence."

Before Rakkrid could formulate a response, Grauncrock's leathery fingers were around his neck and squeezing unto death.

"But my Lord," Rakkrid squeaked, "the Narciss Glass, the boy, and even the Sadiki are all under the control of a very powerful enchantress, and I thought you should be informed before—"

"You thought!" shouted Grauncrock, shaking the cavern a second time. "You were explicitly ordered what to do, and thinking was not a part of that order!"

"But the enchantress is most formidable," gasped Rakkrid, making a perilous gamble by interrupting Grauncrock. "My Lord, she has the capability of altering matter and controlling minds. She is more powerful than the boy, and furthermore, has acquired additional protection. More than a dozen body-guards from the Phanatasian now guard her."

"Cowardice! Is that what I am hearing?" growled Grauncrock as he squeezed Rakkrid's neck tighter. "Shall I add that to your growing list of displeasing actions?"

Grauncrock's anger had reached a fevered pitch, and he was one notch away from snuffing out Rakkrid's life when the suffocating Vapid managed to gasp out, "They are all in one place for the taking."

Grauncrock stopped squeezing. He loosened his grip and asked, "What did you say?"

"They are all in one place, my Lord. The Narciss Glass, the boy, and the animal are presently in a large warehouse where humans make those entertaining distractions they are so fond of."

Grauncrock's eyes narrowed. His thin black lips twitched. "They had better be, Rakkrid, for the sake of your neck." Grauncrock then released Rakkrid to drop to the ground where he wheezed and choked for breath.

* * *

Back at the warehouse, Millud was all smugness as he sat in his director's chair, purring like a cat in the cozy comfort of his own self-importance. Though no one heeded any of his words or paid him the slightest bit of attention, every few minutes he lifted the megaphone to his lips and shouted out some random instruction. A burgundy beret was perched upon his head and his khaki pants were tucked into a brand new pair of leather riding boots. If ever there was a man trying to look the part of a Hollywood director, Millud would've won an Oscar for his attempt.

"People," began Gwen. Unlike Millud, when she uttered even one syllable, everyone's ears opened and attended. Harvey and Sheef inched closer to the front of the group so as not to miss a word. "We shall begin today filming a pivotal scene in the movie. If you recall from the original storyline of *The Tempests' Fury*, a paranoid, elderly uncle, who never married, but instead, spent his entire life amassing a fortune, has been invited to a celebration in honor of his one-hundredth birthday, organized and planned by one of his nieces, a Mrs. Susan Eleanor. The old man has outlived his twelve brothers and sisters, but dozens of nieces and nephews are in attendance for the event. As the story unfolds, the miserly uncle becomes convinced that everyone is conspiring to steal his money, circling like vultures for his death and inheritance, which is why he deals so ruthlessly with each of them. The second half of the script chronicles the disappearance of each of his relatives until only one is left.

"Not the most heart-warming and uplifting tale, and it's for this very reason that I've decided to change the story. To begin with, the role of Susan Eleanor will now be played by me, and in the scene we're about to shoot, my enraged uncle bursts into my bedroom as I am putting on makeup for the evening's planned festivities. This scene, incidentally, is in the original script, so at this point I have altered nothing. The uncle — who is delusional, paranoid, and raving mad — will accuse me of orchestrating the entire party so as to win him over and manipulate a larger share of the inheritance.

"In his rage, he will throw a vase of flowers at me, which will sail over my head and shatter the window behind my dressing table. The breaking glass will alert you, Harvey, who happen to be working in the garden just outside the window. You will peer through the broken window to check on my condition, while you, Sheef, will enter the room, alarmed by the sounds of shouting and shattering glass.

"Now in the original script," Gwen continued, "Susan Eleanor and the uncle have a raucous shouting match which is eventually broken up by the butler grabbing the raving uncle and forcibly escorting him from the room, but in this new, and I believe improved version, I will calmly reason with the uncle and invite him to have some refreshments with me. I will guide him over to the sitting area where I will show him a reflection of himself in a hand mirror from my dressing table, revealing to him what all the years of selfish living have done to his countenance. By the conclusion of the scene, the uncle will not only realize how deluded and erroneous his paranoia has been, but that his entire life of amassing wealth and power is the reason he hardened into such a lonely and miserable old man.

"In the subsequent scene, he will come to understand how his behavior has hurt and alienated others, and a heart transformation, not very different from that of Ebenezer Scrooge, will occur, resulting in his reconciliation with his estranged nieces and nephews. By the end of the film, he will announce his philanthropic plans to give away his entire fortune before he passes. It will be a heart-warming story, promoting the message of what can occur when we look out for the interest of our fellow humans, rather than just that of ourselves."

Loud applause erupted from every corner of the set. Even the umbrella man grinned and clapped. Millud, still seated in his director's chair, smiled, but not because of what Gwen had shared, but because, once again, he was lost in reverie, imagining that the clapping was for him, the most illustrious director in Hollywood's history.

After Gwen finished her explanation, she told everyone to look over their lines and to be ready to shoot the scene in ten minutes. Actors and actresses took the time to get into position and for makeup artists and costume designers to make last minute touch-ups and adjustments. Before moving to their designated staging positions, Harvey and Sheef had a quick conversation.

"She's definitely planning to use the film as a means of brainwashing people to support her vision for the world," said Sheef. That hand mirror she'll be using has to be the Narciss Glass, and I guarantee you that when she uses it to show the uncle his reflection, the camera, and ultimately the movie-going audience, will focus on it. Mix in her alluring beauty with a message about kindness and sharing, and it won't be long until people around the globe will follow her anywhere she wants to lead them."

"Remind me again what's wrong with her message of sharing, caring for others, being unselfish, and not living for material possessions?" asked Harvey.

"Nothing at all. In fact, it's a wonderful sentiment and something every human should aspire to. Lovingly caring for our fellow man and looking beyond our own selfish interests is what we should be about on a daily basis, and I sincerely believe it's one of the reasons the Unseen created us, but this is not the danger. The danger is that Gwen is manipulating the people into doing this. Very soon, millions of people won't be acting of their own volition or free will. They'll be forced to think and behave differently through trickery and deceit, and as Gwen has already stated and demonstrated, stronger methods of persuasion will be used if and when needed. And I fear that Gwen, like many well-intended leaders of the past who were corrupted by the power given to them to bring about a perfect society, is falling victim to the very same fate."

"There still might be a way to save and stop her," said Harvey.

"The idea you mentioned before?"

Harvey nodded.

"Got any more details?"

"Road's still foggy with a sharp turn up ahead."

"Well, I hope it clears and straightens out soon, because we're about out of time."

* * *

Madora and Arrick's teeth chattered like miniature jackhammers as their bodies did their best to generate heat in the cold water. Close to an hour had passed since they were deposited in the tower. Their legs and arms were becoming rubbery with fatigue. Akeila, who had not stopped dog paddling in circles, was breathing heavily. Madora understood all too well that they didn't have much longer. The only question that remained was what would kill them first, the cold or the fatigue?

When Arrick attempted to speak, Madora shook her head and whispered, "Save your strength. There's nothing you can do or say that will change the situation."

Arrick nodded in the darkness. He knew that she was right. It wasn't in either one of their natures to do nothing. They were both warriors, men and women of forward motion and action. But for the first time in their lives, doing absolutely nothing was their only option.

As Madora trod water, she thought of how ironic it was that she had lived to witness the rise and fall of so many civilizations and never once in all that time had she been ensnared by love. Then unexpectedly, she was captured by it. After so many years of waiting and then finally giving up, she had found the missing piece, but now it all seemed like nothing more than a cruel joke.

Arrick's thoughts weren't any better. He had just been reconciled with his son and had begun the process of building a relationship with him. And yet, the budding relationship would be cut short by his drowning in a dark water tower, while Harvey faced the greatest challenge of his young life, and once again, alone. The last flicker of hope they might have had when they were first dropped into the darkness was extinguished.

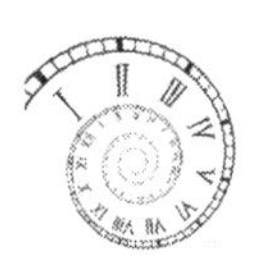

23

When Gwen reappeared from her changing room, she was wearing an elegant forest green dress and a string of pearls. Collective sighs rippled through those gathered before her. A makeup artist approached Gwen for a final touch-up but stopped short. It somehow felt wrong, or maybe even sacrilegious, for her to venture any closer and pollute perfection.

"It's quite alright," said Gwen sweetly to the makeup artist who stood paralyzed by her presence, not knowing which way to move. "I think my appearance is fine, but thank you all the same."

"Yes, of course," the woman said nervously. When she sheepishly backed away, a sense of relief washed over her to be excused from an awkward predicament.

Harvey was positioned just outside the bedroom window, while Sheef waited in the foyer, preparing to escort the irate uncle to Susan Eleanor's room. Gwen took a seat at her dressing table and signaled Millud to begin filming.

The only reason the self-absorbed director was paying any

attention to something other than himself and was ready for Gwen's signal is because this was the big moment that he had been waiting for all day. He raised the megaphone to his lips and yelled out in his high-pitched, oily voice, "Action!" The sound of celluloid spinning between wheels and sprockets was heard as the cameras began rolling.

At the word "action" the actor portraying the uncle breathed in deeply and then forced the air into his closed mouth, nose, and ears in order to redden his skin to the color of a ripe tomato, and when he began screaming at the butler, it looked as though the man's flushed face was the consequence of erupting anger. Though Sheef knew it was coming and that the raving uncle was only acting, he was nonetheless frightened by the explosive ranting.

The scene played out according to the original script until after the window was shattered. The vase went sailing at the window, only missing the head of Susan Eleanor because she ducked seconds before it arrived. The window broke as if on cue, and shortly thereafter, Harvey's floppy garden hat appeared above the windowsill. He then spoke his only line.

"Mrs. Eleanor, are you hurt? Should I get the doctor?"

"No, I'm quite alright, but you can inform your father that the window will need to be repaired."

Susan Eleanor then turned to the uncle and gracefully walked toward him, her hand held out in a gesture of friendship. The actor playing the uncle stared at the approaching woman and was so transfixed by her beauty that he not only forgot his affected emotion but also his next line.

Gwen could tell that the actor was stymied with no line.

Without missing a beat, she began adlibbing, mentally rewriting the script on the fly and then speaking the lines without the slightest pause, filler, or hesitation.

The character Susan Eleanor smiled warmly and said, "Cat suddenly got your tongue? No need to worry. I believe you've said plenty already. Why don't I take a turn at talking for a while? You can take a seat on the couch with me and listen to what needs to be said and heard." The dazed actor nodded and took a seat.

Susan Eleanor then took the actor's hand and began speaking to him about his life and the poor choices he had made along the way. As she spoke, the camera zoomed in on her face, so that when the scene was eventually shown on a giant movie screen, Gwen's beautifully mesmerizing face would stand fifteen feet in height — a divine goddess addressing her adoring worshipers.

Sheef observed the scene from the other side of the room, and he soon realized that whatever words were spoken by Gwen would slip easily through the minds of any future audience and lodge squarely in their hearts. Then they would return to see the movie and hear her speech again and again, becoming ardent followers and practitioners of her vision for a brave, new world.

Two minutes into her talk with the uncle, Susan Eleanor held up her hand mirror in order to show the uncle the unflattering physical effects of a life poorly lived. When she turned the mirror around and the cameraman began filming what should've been a close up of the uncle's reflection, he, instead, saw himself, as did the young man next to him who was holding a boom microphone above the actors seated on the couch.

The image — reflected in what only Gwen, Sheef, and Harvey knew was really the Narciss Glass — that the cameraman, soundman, and actor saw, was not remotely anywhere close to an accurate reflection of themselves, but a flawless depiction of the perfect version of each. The cameraman, for example, beheld a handsome and debonair man, exuding unbridled strength and vigor. In his eyes, he was a veritable Greek demigod, a spectacle of unparalleled achievement in all areas. The image was so absorbing and all-consuming that he failed to blink or draw breath for an entire minute.

Sheef's position in the room allowed him to observe the profiles of each of the three men. When Gwen turned the Narciss Glass upon them, their faces sunk inward, and with each passing second, they cratered more and more, until no defining facial features could be discerned. What had once been eyes, noses, foreheads, and lips, collapsed from view.

Sheef believed that if their exposure to the mirror had lasted much longer, each of the three men might've so imploded in upon themselves that they would've been lost to their own beguiling reflections forever.

Fortunately, Susan Eleanor placed the mirror face down in her lap and broke the connection. The faces of the men instantly snapped back to their original shape and size, but an addiction had already been irrevocably established, and all three would spend their subsequent days trying to figure out ways of obtaining additional looks into the bewitching object.

The soundman felt that he had finally found his life's

calling, that he had caught the elusive fulfillment he had been chasing for many years. The purpose, meaning, and goal of his life, in the end, he determined, was himself, but not in the manner that he had always viewed himself, but as he saw reflected in that simple handheld mirror of the actress. He decided, then and there, that when *The Tempest's Fury* was released, he would quit his job at Mammoth Pictures and work as a movie theater usher, escorting people to their seats and watching the mirror scene over and over to his heart's content.

"And that's a wrap," Millud smugly shouted through his bullhorn as the scene ended.

"Well, how does everyone feel the first take went?" asked Gwen as she rose from the couch and left the character of Susan Eleanor behind. Her question was answered with a rousing round of applause. Even Harvey and Sheef were caught up in the moment and found themselves joining in.

"Shall we film it again?" Gwen asked pleasantly. "This being my first movie, I'm not familiar with how these shoots typically go."

For a minute or two, no one uttered a single world. Those present had been so swept away by the current of Susan Eleanor's words that they were still swirling about in the eddies of her lovely rhetoric.

Her speech to her uncle was a plea for him to leave behind his old life of amassing wealth and exploiting people and to envision a brighter one in which he would transform the lives of his family, neighbors, and beyond by parting with his wealth and serving their needs. The message of a noble, selfless life was itself highly contagious, but when it was mixed with Gwen's unequaled beauty and warmly inviting tone, anyone listening was powerless to avoid being heavily infected.

Whether or not the scene warranted being filmed again, no one would ever know, for all who had viewed it were spellbound. When no one responded to Gwen's question of whether or not to reshoot the scene, she said, "Well then, if there are no objections to how it went, I suggest we move onto the next one that I have rewritten in which the uncle apologizes to his family for years of harsh treatment, vicious verbal attacks, and impugning wrong motives. Let's move to the dining room set and get the cast in their formal dinner attire. We'll shoot in an hour."

Gwen looked over to Millud who was startled back to reality and said, "Yes, yes, of course, whatever you say is just fine, Gwen"

Those gathered on the set broke away into pairs and trios, going about the tasks that needed to be completed within the hour, and conversing about what they had just witnessed. Harvey and Sheef overheard them speaking of Gwen's stunning performance and how her words had warmed their hearts and brightened their day. After only one scene, there were already murmurings of "Best Picture", "Best Actress", and "Academy Awards".

Sheef was leading Harvey off the set in search of a quiet nook where he could discuss with him what they had just witnessed, when Gwen called out to them.

"Before you scurry off, I would be very interested to hear your thoughts about the scene."

"It was . . . well . . . I guess very . . . I mean from what I saw," Harvey stammered. Unlike Sheef — who had had a direct view of the horrible effects of the Narciss Glass on the cameraman, soundman, and actor — Harvey, from his vantage point, was unable to see Gwen and what she was doing. He only heard her words, and thus, was completely captivated by them. When Gwen, in the role of Susan Eleanor, began speaking to her uncle, the effects were immediate. Harvey felt like he had fallen into a very thick and weighty sleep. Every one of Gwen's words had so induced a deep and rich sense of rest and rejuvenation, that when she asked Harvey and Sheef the question, Harvey felt like he was still below the surface of reality, drifting to the soothing movements of her dreamy words.

"Harvey! Come on, kid, snap out of it," Sheef said sternly as he shook Harvey by the shoulders.

"Sheef, is that really necessary? Harvey was about to share his thoughts with me about the scene," said Gwen approaching from behind.

Sheef spun around and said, "Leave him alone, Gwen, and for the good of this world of ours, stop this madness."

Gwen stopped walking and replied, "Why, Sheef, my dear father, stopping the madness of this world is precisely what I'm attempting to do."

"No you're not. I know that's what you think you're doing, but you're wrong. You twisted my words just like you're twisting everything else, including these people's minds."

"A little twisting, tweaking, and adjusting must be done in the minds of the less enlightened in order to get them onboard with what's best for them."

"Gwen," said Sheef pleadingly, "This world you hope to create, the one where everyone lovingly gets along and all their needs are met because of the vision and guidance of a talented, intelligent, and benevolent leader, is extremely dangerous, but you just can't see it. You're blinded by your own brilliance. What you're trying to do has been tried many times before but has always ended with the same devastating results."

"I'm well versed in your history, Sheef," Gwen said with impatience, "but the world has never had a leader like me. I am above the petty nature of humans and will not fall victim to their weaknesses. My intelligence will be the bright light that will finally lead humanity out of the darkness. And those you speak of who failed in the past, they failed because they were corrupted by their own frail natures. I am not corruptible."

"Are you kidding me? You're already succumbing to corruption. You've already used your power to manipulate people, or as you said 'tweak and adjust', which is just another shade of lying. Gwen, you're deceiving people around you, and deception, by the way, is one of the hallmarks of a corrupt leader. The rot in you has already begun and will only spread."

"A little lying here and there will not prove detrimental, and if I'm to make my vision a reality, a few dashes of deception are well worth it."

"A few dashes? Are you really that deluded?" Sheef asked with utter disbelief. "Everything you're doing, including this entire movie fiasco, is one gigantic lie! And if that wasn't bad enough, you've begun to physically harm those who opposes you, which is another trait of the despotic and oppressive rulers of the past."

"A few causalities along the way for the ultimate good of the many, Sheef."

"But a few has a way of growing exponentially. And you're using the Narciss Glass to get people addicted to seeing the movie over and over so that they will hear your little moving speech multiple times and support you no matter what you do. Can't you see that you're using the Narciss Glass as a weapon of propaganda."

"It's the quickest way to my intended end," she said with a broad smile.

"I have no doubt, but in the process, the Narciss Glass will destroy the minds and lives of everyone who sees it in the movie. That mirror is more addictive and destructive than any drug! What you're doing is immoral: exploiting human frailty, especially its propensity for self-love, to fulfill your dream. Gwen, you might very well change the structure of society to accommodate your vision, but along the way, you'll harm the very humans you say you're trying to help. Didn't you see what the Narciss Glass did to the actor playing the uncle? I guarantee you, right now the only thing he cares about is finding a way to get another look in the mirror so that he might adore and worship his own distorted image.

"I'm very sorry to hear that you're still so opposed to my plans, Sheef. The reason I wanted you and Harvey in this scene was for you to hear my speech, which was my last hope of winning you over, but alas, it appears that shall never be the case, at least for you that is. Therefore, I think it's time you joined your beloved, so that both of you may be together for whatever fate awaits you."

Before Harvey knew what was happening, Sheef was yanked backward off his feet. Seconds later he exited through the door and followed the path Arrick and Madora had flown earlier that day.

The darkness inside the water tower was briefly flooded with daylight as the roof tilted back for a second time, allowing Sheef to fall through.

24

Sheef splashed down only inches from Arrick's head. Landing partially on his side, the air was instantly knocked from his body. Unfortunately, he had no opportunity to catch another before he went under. His falling velocity plunged him deeply below the surface. His panicked, air-starved lungs cried for relief as he struggled upward through the icy waters, but with no light in the water tower, he was unable to determine the distance to the surface. Feeling that his lungs would burst at any moment, he reached upward and stroked with all his strength. Within a few seconds, his right hand broke through. He had made it, or so he thought, for as his head followed the lead of his hand, it was bumped, scratched, and pushed back down a half foot. He knew he was still close to the surface. Just one more stroke or two would take him to air and safety, but lack of oxygen was taking its toll: consciousness was slipping away.

A hand plunged down, grabbed his shirt, and yanked him to the surface. While sputtering and coughing up water, Sheef heard movement. He yelled out through the darkness, "Who's there?" and heard the sound of splashing in front of him. He reached out. His hand touched strands of wet hair. Madora was only inches away.

"Sheef!" Madora cried out. Is that you? Are you alright?"

"I am, now that I can breathe again, except for a nice scratch on my head."

"That was probably Akeila. You must've collided with her when you reached the surface."

"I assume that was your hand that saved me, but how did you know where to reach?"

"After I heard the splash, I was concerned when no one resurfaced, so I reached down, everywhere. It was just sheer luck that I grabbed you when I did."

"You're telling me. You saved my life! Another second and it would've been over for me. But what about you? Are you alright?" Madora could hear the concern, care, and relief in Sheef's voice.

"For the time being," Madora responded, as her teeth began chattering again. "But I don't know for how long. The hypothermia's already set in, and we've been treading water for over an hour."

"Arrick's here, too?"

"I am," said a deep voice.

"Where's Harvey?" asked Arrick. "I only heard one splash."

"He's still back at the soundstage."

"What? Why did Gwen only send you away?"

"She wanted us in the scene that was just shot so we could

hear the speech her character made. She thought that when we heard it, we might finally be won over to supporting her plan. When she asked Harvey and me our opinions once the scene ended, I let my unchanged feelings be known. As you can imagine, she wasn't too happy with me. Knowing that her last effort to persuade me had failed, she sent me flying out to join you three for a swim, but her speech had some effect on Harvey. To what degree I'm not sure, but I believe that's why she kept him there."

"So you think she's won him over?"

"Like I said, I'm not sure, but he shared something encouraging with me before filming began. He told me that there might be a way to stop her."

"Really?" asked Madora surprised. "Stop her how?"

"He didn't say, only that the Unseen was revealing something to him."

"Well, I hope the Unseen's with him and guiding him, because from here on out, he's on his own," said Arrick resignedly.

Though he couldn't see his hand in front of his face, Sheef looked around in the darkness. "So there's no way out of this tin can?" he asked.

"I don't think so," Arrick responded. "Madora and I have felt along the walls, trying to find a hatch or something, but we've found nothing. There has to be some type doorway in this thing, but it must be higher up, well out of reach."

"Then you're right," said Sheef despairingly, "Harvey's certainly on his own, and as it appears now, so are we."

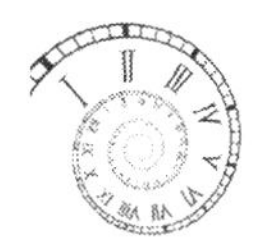

25

"Where did you send him?" asked Harvey, still stumbling about in a hazy stupor.

"Don't worry about him, Harvey," Gwen said tenderly as she approached him and lightly stroked his shoulder. "I've only set him aside, out of the way for the time being. I assure you that our dear father is safe, so there's absolutely no reason to fret over him, that is, as long as you cooperate with me. If you choose not to then you will join Sheef and the others, and well . . . that will be it then, won't it?

"The problem with Sheef, as I see it, is that he's simply too old and set in his ways, unable to grasp hold of the newness and better world which awaits us. You can't teach an old dog new tricks. Isn't that a popular saying of you humans?" Gwen asked rhetorically.

Harvey nodded, but not sure what he was agreeing to.

"Now that all the impediments have been removed, we can quickly move forward. Harvey, it would please me very much if you would agree to be in the next scene. The scene certainly doesn't call for a gardener's son, for it wouldn't make any sense to have a young man in overalls and a stained, floppy hat attending a formal dinner," Gwen laughed. "Which means you would need to be recast as one of the uncle's nephews. Why don't we get you out of that denim and into a tuxedo, and don't concern yourself with learning any lines. You're character only needs to smile and listen to what I and the uncle have to say."

Again, Harvey acquiesced. He felt he shouldn't agree to do what Gwen had asked of him, but he had no alternative if he had any hope of saving the others.

Gwen smiled and waved to a middle-aged man standing off to the side. "Jamison here will get you into proper attire for the scene. And let me tell you how wonderful it is to have my brother willingly participate and support his sister."

Gwen then hustled away and disappeared into a small office with Gundy, whispering something to him as the door closed. Harvey saw that she carried the mirror with her, and he felt certain that from this point on, she wouldn't let the Narciss Glass out of her physical possession, much less her sight.

"Shall we then," Jamison said to Harvey who followed him to the costume closet where the day's failed adventure had begun.

The acrid smell of something burning stopped Jamison. Harvey turned in response to the sharp, offensive odor. Wisps of black smoke were rising from thirteen spots along the wall.

Harvey initially thought that it was some type of electrical fire until he observed that in the center of each smoking spot, a circle of bright orange glowed. Within seconds, the circles turned yellow and grew ten times their original size. The super-heated metal melted away, leaving behind thirteen portals, and out of each emerged a Vapid Lord, with Grauncrock stepping out of the middle.

Gwen's gangsters responded immediately to the intruders, hustling over to the wall the Vapid had just entered through with guns and billy-clubs drawn. Grauncrock turned and grinned fiendishly. With lightning quick alacrity, he slammed his clawed hand into the concrete floor. Each of his talons easily pierced the cement. Cracks spread from his hand, rapidly growing wider and deeper as they sped toward the approaching gangsters.

The umbrella man tried to navigate around one of the approaching cracks but failed to accurately judge its speed. His left foot slipped, and as he attempted to shift his weight to save himself from falling in, the crack widened, removing any support for his other foot. He dropped in and away, snarling, his scar bulging bright red. The other thugs fared no better. Since their reaction time was slower than that of their boss, they were easily swallowed up by the yawing, deep abyss.

Cast and crew members initially thought the intruders were part of some sort of publicity stunt, possibly for an upcoming sci-fi movie. When the cracks appeared and widened into bottomless canyons, however, they quickly realized that this was anything but Hollywood fiction. Scattering about the sound stage to look for cover, some ducked into offices and changing rooms, while others were unable to avoid their falling fate.

The entire chain of events, from smoke first appearing to gangsters dropping away, took less than thirty seconds. Hearing the splitting concrete, Gwen raced out of the office to find that her hired muscle was gone. Rapidly assessing the situation, she focused her mind on the invading Vapid, preparing to send out bands of energy to subdue and bind them. However, as she lifted her hands to release the energy, she was hit by a sphere of white-hot fire launched from a Vapid just outside her peripheral vision.

A searing pain tore through her side as the sphere set ablaze her clothing and flesh. Her instinct was to turn in the direction from which the fireball had come, but as she did so, she was hit with several more. Each of the Vapid launched its own sphere, with every one of them slamming into Gwen, sticking to her flesh like colored fireballs launched from a Roman candle. If she had had a second or more to react, she would've been able to create an energy shield like she did against Sheef, but time, this time, was not on her side. The Narciss Glass in her hand dropped and clattered on the floor while Gwen screamed in agony and collapsed.

Harvey grabbed a quilt from the bedroom set and sprinted over to the smoldering mass on the ground, throwing the quilt and himself atop Gwen. Wildly patting every part of her burning body, he eventually succeeded in extinguishing the flames, but as he slowly pulled back the quilt, he was shocked by the unrecognizable form of a woman, who moments before, had stunned everyone with her unparalleled beauty.

Tear-mark stripes ran vertically down the cheeks of his smoky face, for as great as a threat she was to the world, Gwen was still close to his heart, and seeing her like this was emotionally jarring. He covered her body with the quilt and stood to his feet. Next to Gwen's motionless body was the Narciss Glass: the goal of their journey through the Phantasian and back to the 1930s. Now it was only feet away, but at that moment, it hardly seemed to matter anymore. He bent down and picked it up, careful not to look into it.

"The danger we faced, the close calls with death, and now losing Gwen, and all for just a hand mirror," Harvey thought to himself. His feelings of grief shifted to anger as he contemplated the amount of suffering that had already occurred because of the artifact he held in his hand.

Suddenly, his emotions again shifted. A shadow appeared, cast by something tall behind him. An icy, breath-snatching fear stole over him as he recognized the shadow's outline.

"Let me take that off your hands, young Harvey," hissed a threatening voice, "and alleviate a boy of the burden of saving Ecclon and Earth. That task, incidentally, was always too insurmountable, even for a full-grown adult warrior, much less a lanky teenager from a planet of weaklings.

More shadows appeared, and soon a ring of Vapid surrounded Harvey. He clutched the Narciss Glass tighter and turned around to face the source of his fear. He stood eyelevel with Grauncrock's broad chest.

"A dead end, so it seems, is the last chapter of your grand adventure." Grauncrock reached out touched Harvey's face with one of his razor-sharp talons, slowly dragging it down his cheek. The skin split apart, leaving behind a bleeding gash four inches long. Harvey winced at the pain but remained perfectly still.

"You should have never tangled with Lord Nezraut. You waded into waters much too deep and unfamiliar and are now in over your head, and by all appearances, completely alone. Where are your companions?"

Harvey shook his head slightly and shrugged his shoulders, still remaining silent.

Grauncrock bent down and peered into Harvey's eyes and said, "You are telling the truth. You have no idea what has happened to them, do you? How tragic to face your demise all by yourself," Grauncrock snickered to himself as he stood back up. "But please, do not overly concern yourself with your impending end, Harvey. Trust me when I tell you that it will by no means be quick or painless. The laceration on your cheek is but a foretaste of the pain you will endure before you experience the relief of death. Once I am finished torturing you, though, you will not be free to die, for I must deliver you to Lord Nezraut in order for him to tidy up unfinished business."

Grancrouck opened his right hand and said, "Now, place the Narciss Glass in my hand."

Harvey didn't move or say anything. He was too overwhelmed by questions pulling and tearing at his mind. "How, after everything he and his friends had endured, could it end like this, so cut and dry, such a sudden and easy defeat? Where were Sheef, Madora, and Arrick? And where was the Unseen? Had he abandoned him? What about His plan that had begun to take shape an hour ago? Wasn't the fog supposed to lift and the road to straighten by now?"

Harvey had never felt so alone and isolated as he did while

standing in the middle of a Hollywood soundstage encircled by a posse of leering Vapid. Even before he was tail-lassoed by Fromp and taken to Ecclon, when he had spent the majority of his days with no other companion than his own thoughts, he had never felt this alone.

Harvey had faced down towering opposition on multiple occasions, but it had always been with others and for others. Laying his life on the line for his friends and family had been, he now realized, the root of his courage. But now, with the possibility of everyone permanently gone, what would be his motivation to face and fight in this latest battle?

"Nothing," Harvey mumbled to himself. It seemed now that nothing was pushing him forward, nothing was watching over him, and nothing was calling him to fight. He suddenly felt extremely fatigued and only wanted to curl up on the floor and sleep. Hope of victory over the enemy, hope of saving Ecclon and the Flurn, and hope of saving his family and friends was cast into the air and carried off by a dry and empty wind. He absentmindedly released his grip on the Narciss Glass and let it fall into Grauncrock's outstretched hand.

"Not as foolish as I assumed," said Graucrock with a fiendish grin. A metallic ring chimed out as the Vapid's scaly fingers coiled tightly around the handle of the Narciss Glass. "Not that your compliance will lessen the torture I have in store for you."

Unexpectedly, Grauncrock's other hand shot out, its talons digging into the soft flesh under Harvey's chin. Harvey tried to cry out, but Grauncrock's thumb pressed down on his upper lip, preventing any sound from escaping.

HOPE

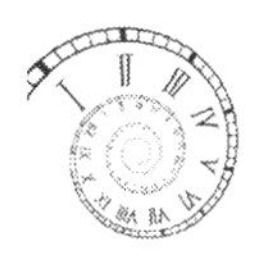

26

Grauncrock was about to lift Harvey up by the chin to begin the initial round of torture when he was distracted by something vibrating behind him. He released Harvey and turned around as did the other Vapid Lord. Dozens of dull yellow bands of light from all over the soundstage were moving along the floor, all headed to the same destination: the motionless body underneath the quilt.

The light bands were connected to the bodies of at least four dozen actors, actresses, and workers scattered about the concrete floor. They had all collectively fainted at exactly the same moment, just after Grauncrock began speaking with Harvey. After collapsing to the ground, they convulsed once and started to lightly vibrate, as if they were sitting atop an idling motorcycle. Out of their chests bands of light emerged. They slithered onto the floor and moved with quick serpentine movements to the quilt and the body it concealed.

When Harvey looked down at the quilt, he observed the first light bands arriving. They burrowed underneath. A weak inhalation of breath was heard. Harvey took a step back. Additional light bands arrived. The luminosity of each intensified. Soon, fifty or more bands were attached and feeding energy into the body beneath.

Muffled noises, a mixture of percolating coffee and crumbling paper, escaped from the edges of the quilt. Soon the tempo of the sounds increased, the bands of light brightening from yellow to white.

The entire quilt then began to move. Rounded mounds and troughs on its surface appeared and vanished like boiling water. Something was coming to life. Fear and curiosity pulled Harvey's mind in opposite directions. He desperately wanted to view what was occurring underneath but feared what he might find if he did.

Grauncrock, who was momentarily distracted by the light bands, turned his attention back to Harvey. Glancing down he hissed, "Her body is experiencing the last spasms of life. The death rattle rings loudly, a sound that you will soon hear for yourself."

Grauncrock again stretched out his hand for Harvey's neck, but before talon and flesh could make contact, the quilt covering Gwen flew up and wrapped itself strangling tight around Grauncrock's head and neck. The Vapid Lord clawed at the fabric, pulling with all his might to try and loosen its hold, but the more he fought, the tighter the constricting serpent squeezed.

The Narciss Glass fell to the floor, and as it did so, the quilt suddenly released its stranglehold on Grauncrock. He doubled over with mouth agape, desperately grasping and gasping for stolen breath. The other Vapid Lord stepped forward with swords drawn but quickly thought better of it.

A mass of blinding white light pulsated in the air above Gwen's body, its searing heat blackening and blistering the backs of Harvey's neck and arms. An invisible arm grabbed him and pulled him forty feet backward. The top and bottom of the mass rose and sunk, elongating into what looked like a vertical cocoon, its pulsing increasing to the rhythm of a rapidly beating heart. The skin of the cocoon stretched tight, becoming hard and shell-like. Cracks appeared from the strain of the expanding force.

When the internal pressure grew greater than the structural integrity of the cocoon, it exploded like a grenade, flinging out fiery shell shrapnel. The pieces weren't flung out randomly but flew along directed routes to their individual targets. Grauncrock was hit in the chest with a sizeable fragment, just as he recovered his breath and stood up. His armor and flesh provided no protection. A hole the size of a cantaloupe was burned clean through. Strands of seared flesh and wisps of black smoke were the only things impairing a clear view to the other side.

Shock was Grauncrock's last expression. Looking down at his wound, he keeled over dead. The other Vapid Lord had no time to react before they were hit with their own fragments and fell victim to the same fate as their leader, and with that, the threat of Nezraut gaining possession of the Narciss Glass came to an end.

Once the source of the Vapid's death was extinguished, Harvey's backward movement was reversed, and he was returned to his original position. A sharp and searing fire on his neck and arms throbbed more intensely with every passing second. The burns were easily third-degree, already inducing an incapacitating pain. Harvey bent forward, viciously gripping his knees. From his position, he could see through tear-filled eyes the Narciss Glass lying next to his foot, but because of the intense, all-encompassing pain, he had neither the ability nor the desire to reach down for it. All he wanted at that moment was relief from the agony.

"I would be more than happy to remove the pain and restore your skin. It would only require a thought," said a familiar voice from behind.

Harvey stood straight. Turning around, he looked directly into the eyes of Gwen, now standing only three feet away. Her skin, which had been burned and charred like campfire logs, was now radiantly flawless, textured and colored like exquisite porcelain. But it wasn't only her skin that was new, every one of her physical features seemed to have been remade with a superabundance of vibrant health. She glistened with more beauty than ever, but Harvey could sense that it was only a surface-level beauty, hardly penetrating below the skin.

"You only need but ask," Gwen said matter-of-factly.

Unable to enunciate even a simple "yes" because of the screaming pain, Harvey nodded. Gwen walked over and touched his body. The screaming was silenced, replaced by a soothing coolness.

"Better now?" Gwen asked in a tone that sounded kind but felt cold and threatening. Harvey nodded with relief but didn't smile. With the pain gone, the direness of the situation once again was front and center, and as he looked into Gwen's dazzling blue eyes, he knew that even though the Vapid had fallen and would no longer pose a threat, a more powerful and possibly dangerous one had taken its place.

"How did you . . . ?" asked Harvey, reaching out and touching Gwen's arm to verify that she was actually real. "You were . . . I mean I saw your skin and hair burn. You were covered in flames. I tried to put them out, but it was too late, and when I pulled back the quilt you were—"

"Dead?" Gwen interrupted and asked emotionlessly.

"Yes . . . dead," Harvey replied, becoming more astounded by the second.

"Not quite, but I was within a hair's width. If not for the aid of my colleagues, it would've certainly been my end."

Harvey turned around and took a quick inventory of those who had fallen to the floor. The dozens of bands, which minutes ago had crisscrossed the floor like electrical wiring, had all disappeared. Some of those who had been connected were slowly moving about.

Harvey knelt next to the nearest one — a young carpenter who was part of set design — and grabbed him under the shoulder to steady the man as he wobbly tried to stand to his feet. The man turned to Harvey, peering at him with vacant eyes, and though he was smiling broadly, Harvey could tell that whatever was occurring on the backside of his expression was just as hollow and desolate as his eyes. The color of his skin was muted and dull, no longer fleshly, tinged with warm shades of brown, pink, and gold, but faded cold and gray. Mumbling words heavily saturated with gibberish, the man eventually reached his feet and stood.

Harvey escorted the man for a few steps before letting him run under his own steam and stability. He took two shaky steps and then lost his balance, falling back to the floor. Leaving him there, Harvey checked on others who had also been connected to Gwen. They all wore the same vacant expressions and dull gray skin.

Walking back over to Gwen, he asked, "What did you do to those people? What's happened to them?"

"Only what needed to be done in order to preserve my life and the dream," she responded in a business-like tone.

"But why are they all so sickly and weak?"

"I absorbed a bit of energy and material from each of them. I couldn't very well generate new skin and muscle tissue without their contribution."

"You stole some of their life so that you could save yours?"

"I don't know if 'save' does the new me justice, Harvey, but yes, they did forfeit some of themselves for me, but whose life, and please be honest, was more important to save?"

"But look at what you've done to them," said Harvey as he pointed to two actors who were smiling idiotically and groaning as their tangled arms struggled to help them both stand up."

"Parts of average, no-account lives given for the health and wellbeing of the one who will save mankind. I ask you, could there be a more worthy sacrifice for them to offer?"

"But they didn't sacrifice for you. They didn't do anything willingly. You sacrificed them for your own personal ambition. You robbed them of their futures. Their lives are now ruined."

"Harvey, why can't you understand? There is no future

without me, not one worth living anyway. And a lesser life becoming less so, in order for a greater one to become more so, is well worth the cost and hardly what I would consider ruination."

"For you maybe, but certainly not for them. And who are you to determine what's a lesser and greater life?" asked Harvey angrily.

"The answer to that question is so self-evident that I'm surprised you even asked it. The greater life is the one which can do the most good, and since I'm positioned to do the most good that's ever been done for humanity, it follows that my life has far greater value."

Harvey starred directly into Gwen's eyes and said authoritatively, "There is no greatness in destroying another life simply to promote one's own selfish agenda."

Gwen shook her head and said condescendingly, "My intentions are anything but selfish, Harvey. It's distressing to hear you persist in your willful ignorance of what I'm trying to do for this corrupt world of yours. Everything I'm doing is for the good of others. How can you accuse my agenda as being selfish?"

Harvey's face softened as he looked at her with a curious sympathy. "You may not realize it, but you're using the pronoun 'I' more and more frequently, Gwen. This ambition of yours to usher in an earthly utopia is becoming increasingly about you, and what you just did — taking away people's energy and material, resulting in a diminished physical and mental state for the remainder of their lives — is the perfect description of selfishness. You robbed them of their freedom and futures. How is this not selfish? Gwen, I'm sorry to inform you, but there's only one who has the wisdom and power to save mankind, and it's not you."

Gwen's facial muscles contracted, her cheeks flushing red. Though Harvey was still many feet away from her, he could feel an angry heat radiating from her body.

"I assume," Gwen said cuttingly, "that you're referring to the great Unseen that you and the others have been desperately clinging to since your journey began."

Gwen smiled, spread her arms, and then continued tauntingly, "Then where is he, Harvey? If he really is guiding this quest of yours, then please, ask him to appear here and now. If he does, then I promise you that I will, without hesitation, relinquish my so-called selfish ambition."

"That's not how it works. The Unseen is not at our beck and call, ready to appear like some sort of magical genie."

"Oh, how very convenient for you. I suppose that if he did appear, he would have to change his name," she said with a cynical laugh. No, the real reason he won't appear is because he doesn't exist, and this mission of yours to acquire the Narciss Glass and somehow save Ecclon is nothing but a farce, a wild goose chase that has served to provide your lonely and meaningless little life with a temporary purpose. Harvey, my brother," she said in a calm and pleading tone, "The time has come for you to dispense with the fairy tale and embrace the world as it really is. Trust in nothing beyond your senses, for all else is naught but an illusion. Please understand that it's science and knowledge that will ultimately save this world. And it follows that since I'm the one with the most thorough understanding of science, I will be the one to bring it about."

Harvey shook his head and replied, "Gwen, I'll be the first to acknowledge the tremendous good that scientific and technological progress has done for humanity. Without question, it has improved the quality of life and eased the suffering of millions, but it can never be the answer to man's deepest needs."

"Is that so? It's frustratingly maddening to me that you refuse to grasp the truth that I can do far more to improve this world than any human brain could ever imagine. What you vainly hope for from this mythical Unseen of yours, I can actually deliver. Harvey, I'm offering you one last chance to join me. Why not let me be your god, so that together, we can bring heaven to earth?"

"He's not a myth and you're no god," Harvey said forcefully. "And as for bringing anything to earth, if you succeed, it will be more in line with a place far south of heaven."

"How very clever and profound are your words, Harvey," Gwen said bitingly, "but unfortunately profundities won't change the world for the better. And since you, like Sheef, remain stubbornly unmoved, I'm now compelled to send you to join him and the others. It really is a shame, though. I had high hopes for you. After hearing my speech to the uncle, I thought I was beginning to win you over, which is precisely why I healed your burns. But now, regretfully, I see that it was all a waste of time and energy."

Harvey knew he had no chance to win a fight with the pre-burned Gwen, much less the new and improved version standing before him, and since the specifics of the Unseen's plan were still shrouded in fog, he concluded that his only chance of hindering her efforts was to wedge the Narciss Glass still lying on the floor between his feet seconds before she sent him flying out of the soundstage. It would only work if his feet cooperated, and she failed to see the move.

Harvey whispered a short prayer to the Unseen and waited for Gwen to lift her arms or flick her fingers. As he prepped his feet for the adroit, soccer-like move, he was unexpectedly lifted four feet above the floor. Every muscle in his body was suddenly unable to contract. He was even incapable of blinking. A mass of golden energy materialized around his body like an ancient fossil encased in a glob of amber sap.

"Desperate are we?" asked Gwen rhetorically. "Surely you didn't think you had any real chance of snatching the mirror with nothing but your feet and then making it out of here without me noticing. And don't look surprised that I've learned how to read minds. Thought is nothing but energy in motion, and you know how skilled I've become manipulating energy in motion. Before you are sent on your way, there's one final thing I would like to—"

A booming thud rattled the metal roof. Gwen looked up, scrutinizing a large indentation in the metal. Gundy, who was separated from Gwen when Grauncrock created the crevices in the floor and was briefly knocked unconscious by a piece of flying debris, had regained consciousness and made his way back to Gwen.

"Miss Gwen, you alright? What was that sound?" Gundy asked excitedly. Not giving her any time to respond, Gundy began apologizing profusely. "I tried to get to you when you were attacked but couldn't. I swear I ain't no coward. I did the best—"

"It's quite alright," said Gwen as she reached out and lovingly touched Gundy's cheek. "It wasn't your fault, and your loyalty isn't in question."

"But, Miss Gwen, you was hurt and on fire, and I didn't do nothing to stop it. I should've—"

"Gundy, please stop and relax. As you can see, I'm fine and in very good health. Leave your regrets behind, and guard this for me while I investigate whatever has decided to drop in on us. I suspect that more of these Vapid creatures have arrived to try and secure my mirror."

Gundy nodded and nervously took the Narciss Glass from Gwen with a shaky hand.

"It's alright, Gundy. The object will pose no harm to you as long as you keep it face down. But under no circumstances are you to even glance in it, not even for a second. Do we understand each other?" she asked sternly, as if she was a parent explaining a prohibition to a young child about not playing anywhere near the street.

"Yes, yes . . . ma'am," he sputtered, "but what about the kid?"

"I will send him off to be with his friends soon enough," Gwen replied angrily, "but I am not quite finished with my conversation with him, so in the meantime, I'll just set him off to the side."

The energy bubble surrounding Harvey vanished, and though he was once again free to move his muscles, he was still suspended in the air. Before he had any time to figure out a way to reach solid ground again, Gwen, with a wave of her hand, sent Harvey flying across the soundstage and into the wall. The hard contact knocked the air from lungs. He slid down the wall and balled into a fetal position. When he attempted to draw a breath of air, he felt a sharp stab of pain on the left side of his torso. Touching the spot, he winced. Though he had never broken his ribs, he knew with certainty that he had done so now.

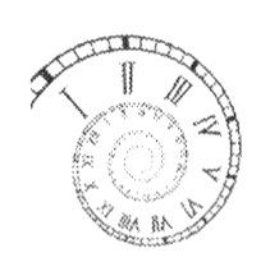

27

Fifteen minutes before the booming thud on the roof, Arrick and Madora were well beyond being physically spent from treading water for over two hours. Sheef, who entered and splashed down after the others and still had some strength left in him, grabbed Madora around the waist when he heard her beginning to cough water. She had exhausted much of her stamina holding Akeila in her arms. After twenty minutes, she could no longer support the Sadiki and released her to swim on her own. If Sheef hadn't grabbed hold of her when he did, she would've slipped under and away forever.

With his right arm around her waist, he trod water with his left while aggressively kicking his feet. Even so, the action barely kept the two afloat, his strength wanning much more quickly than if he was treading alone. He thought about asking Arrick for assistance but knew that he was probably no better off than Madora.

Instead, Sheef mumbled a watery prayer to the Unseen. Less than a minute later, he heard what sounded like scratching on the roof of the tower, but it stopped almost as soon as it started. When he didn't hear anything else for over a minute, he began to suspect that his mind was playing tricks on him in the dark. The scratching, however, soon resumed, accompanied by a very familiar growl.

Rays of light pierced the inky darkness, granted access by the metal hatchway having been violently bent back. A recognizable baritone bark reverberated off the sides of the metallic chamber. A shadow moved over the opening and blocked some of the sunlight pouring in through a three-foot gap. When Sheef looked up, he was never so happy to see the silhouetted head of a very large warp-hound.

Fromp whined pathetically for his people and his Akeila, who suddenly found a burst of energy and began swimming in agitated circles.

"I don't know how you ever found us and were able to bend open that hatch, you old warp-hound, but I'm so glad you did," Sheef yelled out, half crying and half laughing. "Good boy, Fromp! Good boy!"

Fromp's silhouetted head briefly disappeared. When it reappeared seconds later, something dropped from his mouth. Three consecutive splashes sounded around Sheef's head. Bobbbing in the water were three yellow balls.

"What in the world . . . ?" Sheef asked, reaching out for one. One touch was all it took for his question to be answered. "Kreen," he whispered to himself. "Three pieces of Ecclonian Kreen fruit . . . but how?"

Knowing that their lives were in the balance, Sheef realized that "the how" could wait. He bit one of the pieces in half and squeezed the nectar into Madora's mouth. In less than a minute, she was treading water with the strength of a hundred Olympic swimmers. Sheef then swam over to Arrick and gave him the other half before partaking of the nectar himself.

Madora grabbed hold of Akeila and shoved a chunk of Kreen into her mouth. Though not particularly fond of fruit, the Sadiki knew that whatever Madora was doing was for her own good and so swallowed the chunk whole. Before long, her fast paddling created a small wake, slapping loudly against the sides of the tower.

"Now we just need to figure out a way to get up and out of here," said Madora despairingly, "which, given the conditions, is easier said than done. Even with the benefits of Kreen rippling through our bodies, it's still impossible for us to make it up the fourteen feet or so to the top. It doesn't matter how much strength we have; the sides are just too slick to climb. So . . . anyone have an idea?"

The answer to their predicament wasn't long in coming. Metal groaned as Fromp widened the opening large enough for his bulky body to fit through. Encircling the hatch was a steel railing which Fromp securely wrapped the end of his long tail around. Once anchored, he dropped through the opening, snout and ears first. He fell about ten feet before his tail-rope halted his descent. His outstretched paws dangled only feet above the water.

Slobber dribbles drizzled on Sheef, who swam directly underneath the inverted dog that looked like a giant, mutated fruit bat. He laughed again as a single droplet of saliva landed on the middle of his forehead. He had never been so happy to make contact with Fromp's slobber.

"Not exactly the answer to prayer I had in mind, but beggars certainly can't be choosers," Sheef said smiling. "With the Kreen in our systems, we should have more than enough strength to climb up the rescue body and tail."

"But what about Akeila?" asked Madora.

"Oh, trust me, Fromp won't leave without her. You and Arrick go first. I bet I know what he has in mind to get your pup out of here, but it will require me going up last."

"But, Sheef, I can't leave her here."

"Just trust me. Your girl will be perfectly fine."

Madora reluctantly nodded and reached for Fromp's paws. Without the Kreen energy boost, she stood no chance of pulling herself up Fromp's legs, body, and tail, but in her supercharged state, Madora shimmed up Fromp like a circus acrobat and was soon sitting atop the water tower.

Arrick followed next, but before Sheef began his ascent, he transmitted a thought to Fromp. Taking Akeila into his arms, he kicked furiously to maintain buoyancy. He then lifted the Sadiki up to Fromp's opened mouth, which gently closed on the scruff of Akeila's neck. The bite was forceful enough to secure her without breaking the skin. When Sheef let go of her, Fromp's bite bore the full weight of the dog, causing Akeila to pitifully whimper.

Sheef yelled up to Arrick and Madora to pull Fromp up.

"But what about you and Akeila?" Arrick shouted back down.

"Fromp's got Akeila. That's why I need you to pull him up."

"Fromp's got Akeila? How? What do you mean?" asked Madora.

Having no desire to explain with shouting while still treading in freezing water, Sheef responded in a somewhat irritated toned, "You'll see soon enough. Just pull him up and then lower him back down!"

With their fruit-infused strength, Arrick and Madora roughly tugged Fromp and his passenger upward and out. Once Akeila was topside, Madora embraced her and went about inspecting the scruff of her neck.

"I don't know you did it, Fromp, but you didn't break her skin," said Madora as she reached out and wrapped her arms around the thick-necked warp-hound. "Thank you for saving all of us, including my baby girl. You're a good dog; no actually, you're a great one." Fromp responded to the praise by landing a very large wet one directly across Madora's lips.

"Sorry to interrupt whatever you doing up there," shouted Sheef from below, "but would you mind lowering Fromp back down. It's still freezing in here, and regardless of the Kreen, my arms aren't getting any younger"

Minutes later, Sheef joined the others atop the water tower. They all sat down with their backs against the circular railing, resting arms and legs and taking stock of the situation.

"I just don't get it," Arrick said while rubbing his shoulders. "How did Fromp ever find us, and where did that Kreen come from? Sheef, I thought you said your backpack with the Kreen went to the bottom of the ocean."

"I did. Not a single piece came with me."

"Then where did Fromp get it?"

"I think the answer to your queftion is his breed," said Madora as she bent over and rubbed Fromp behind his ears.

"You're not saying that he warped to Ecclon, are you?" asked Arrick

"Only planet that I know of where that particular fruit grows," interjected Sheef.

"Well, how about that," said Arrick, shaking his head. After a brief pause, he continued, "Okay then, one mystery solved, but how did he know where we were?"

"Can't say. Maybe he followed Akeila's scent or something," said Sheef.

"More like his heart," said Madora, pointing to Fromp who was licking the scruff of Akeila's neck.

"Well, whatever he followed, he saved our lives," said Arrick standing up. "But now that we've caught our breath, what do you say we get off this tower and do some saving ourselves, because if my son's still in that soundstage with Gwen, he'll likely need some saving of his own right about now. I just pray we're not too late."

At the word pray, Sheef recalled the simple and desperate prayer he had uttered to the Unseen moments before Fromp showed up. "Always faithful and always with us in unexpected ways," he thought to himself.

Madora picked up Akeila, but as she prepared to climb down the ladder that ran along the side of the water tower with only one hand, she asked" What about Fromp? He's far too heavy and bulky to carry down the ladder."

"I wouldn't worry about him," said Sheef with a chuckle. "He can take care of himself. I'm sure he'll get down the same way he got up, but we should probably get out of his way and give the mutt some room to do his thing."

Stepping down upon solid earth, the group briefly caught sight of a quick flash from above as Fromp warped away.

ILLUMINATION

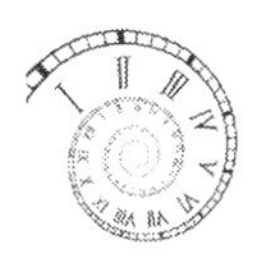

28

Harvey was still lying on the floor when Gwen left the soundstage to investigate the thump on the roof. His attempt to sit up was excruciating. The movement so riled up the pain in his rib cage that he was forced to retreat back into a fetal position. But as he lay there, the fog began to lift and the road to straighten. The Unseen unveiled the details, revealing to Harvey what he needed to do next.

The problem, though, was that there was no possible way he could come close to accomplishing the task in his present condition. And though he groaned out a prayer to the Unseen — not all that different from Sheef's back in the water tower — thoughts of hopelessness and despair wormed their way into his heart, eating away at his newfound hope.

While squeezing his eyes shut in response to the unabated pain radiating from his ribcage, something bumped against his cheek. He was no longer alone. The presence set his nerves on edge, and whatever it was, was peering down at him from above.

"Insips," Harvey thought. "They've finally found me. Likely drawn to my negative thoughts."

He feared opening his eyes and confirming his suspicion, for he was in no position, physically or mentally, to defend himself. True, he had the details of a plan to stop Gwen and retrieve the Narciss Glass, but it had been revealed too late. Regardless of how good the plan was, there was now no way for it to be executed. And as much as he tried to hold onto hope, it shriveled small and slipped from his grip. Such negative thinking, which he knew all too well, was an open invitation for Insips to attack and feast.

A droplet of liquid landed on the corner of Harvey's lips It seeped through to his tongue. The taste was strangely familiar, but for a hazy minute he struggled to identify it. Then the connection between taste and memory was made.

"Fromp!" Harvey shouted, grimacing in pain.

He opened his eyes to an enormous, boxy head bouncing about as if on a spring.

"Fromp, where did you . . . ? How . . . did you?" Harvey gutted out while wincing.

Fromp lowered his snout and rolled something at Harvey's head. When he turned and looked, he saw the last thing he expected but the first one he needed: a yellow piece of Ecclonian fruit.

Limiting movement as much as possible, Harvey grabbed the fruit and placed the entire piece into this mouth. He bit through the yellow rind, chewing the fruit until the pieces were small enough to swallow. The magic soon took effect.

He felt sharp pops of pain in his rib cage, the sound of plastic blocks being snapped together.

And then the pain was gone with no aftertaste. From debilitating to nonexistent, it vanished, replaced by an invigorating energy surge that electrified every muscle.

Springing to his feet, Harvey gave Fromp a peck on the head and said affectionately, "You are, without question, the most amazing animal in the universe."

Knowing that the plan could now be executed, Harvey looked over at the taxi driver standing in the middle of the soundstage and tightly gripping the Narciss Glass.

Looking up at the ceiling, Gundy was trying his best to figure out the stern warning Gwen had given to him about the mirror. Try as he might, it simply made no sense to him, for all he saw was an antique mirror, just one of any number of props lying around the soundstage. Tendrils of curiosity climbed the solid wall of loyalty and grateful obedience to Gwen, searching for any crack to enter through.

"I don't get it," Gundy mumbled to himself as he glanced down at the mirror. "I mean, what's all the fuss about? How dangerous could a mirror be, and what could possibly be the harm of taking a quick peek?"

As he lifted the Narciss Glass toward his face in order to cast a fleeting glance into it, he was violently blindsided. The blow knocked the mirror free from his hand. It spun and rattled on the concrete before coming to a stop ten feet from Gundy.

The attacker was Dexter Harris, the actor who Millud had

manipulated with the Narciss Glass to get him to star in *The Tempest's Fury*. Not only had Harris agreed, but had become so obsessed with the object that he lurked in the shadows of the soundstage all day, waiting for an opportunity to snatch it.

Harris, who was atop Gundy, tired to free himself from the taxi driver and grab the mirror before the Gwen woman returned from wherever she had gone. The problem was that Gundy had wrapped and locked his arms around the actor's waist and wouldn't let go. Whoever this man was, Gundy was certain that he desperately wanted the very thing that Gwen had told him to protect, and even though he had been seconds away from breaking her prohibition, there was no way now that he was going to fail her a second time and let the actor take it away.

"LET ME GO!" Harris screamed at the top of his lungs, his eyes bulging like a madman's. "YOU DON'T UNDERSTAND; IT NEEDS ME! I NEED ME! IT'S ALL ME, NOTHING BUT ME!"

Gundy squeezed harder. Even though he was determined not to let go until Gwen returned, he couldn't endure this lunatic screaming in his face for a second longer. Like the hollow-sounding collision of two coconuts, Gundy's head-butt against Dexter Harris's rendered the actor unconscious. The taxi driver released him, pushed him to the side, and stood to his feet. He began walking toward the mirror, confident that it would be back in his possession, with Gwen never being the wiser that it had been briefly knocked loose, when out of nowhere, a teenager bolted by and scooped it up. Before Gundy had a chance to process what had occurred, the teenager was standing before some type of swirling doorway.

Harvey looked at Gundy and shouted, "If she wants it back, tell her to come to the aisles where she first learned to read. She'll know what it means."

He then turned and stepped into the warp hole Fromp had opened and disappeared. Next to the portal sat a huge, panting dog. The animal barked once and jumped through.

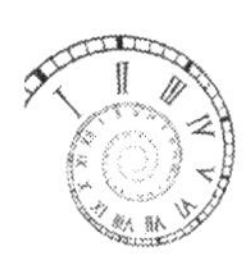

29

The portal opened next to the pond that a certain bus driver had landed in after falling from the top of a tree. Harvey and Fromp jumped down upon a blanket that a group of college students had laid out for a picnic lunch.

Harvey's right foot crushed a large basket of fried chicken, while Fromp's large paws struck and splattered a cherry pie, sending out fragments of crust and goo onto the bodies and astonished faces of the picnickers.

"Sorry about that," said Harvey sheepishly, looking down at the smashed basket and chicken breast bearing his shoe print. None of the students responded, each too baffled by the teenager and his enormous dog tumbling out of thin air and destroying their picnic.

"Physics experiment from over in the science department," Harvey said with a shrug, making up the story as he went. "Trans-dimensional teleportation experiment to be exact. As you can see, we're still working out the kinks. Once again, sorry about the food and everything. Come on, Fromp,"

Harvey said as he hurriedly walked to the library. Fromp followed, but not before latching onto a drumstick and swallowing it bone and all in a single gulp.

A sign outside the library informed students that the library was closed for repairs until further notice. The doors Gwen had blown from their hinges during her second visit to the library were still on the ground. Wooden sawhorse barriers blocked the entrance, behind which stood a skinny guard with thick black-rimmed glasses.

Harvey could see workers milling about inside, trying their best to get the academic lifeline of the university back up and running as soon as possible.

"Sorry, son," the skinny guard said to Harvey as he squinted through coke-bottle thick lenses, "like the sign says, the library's closed, unless you're a part of the repair crew, but since you hardly look old enough to be in high school, I assume that doesn't include you." The guard chuckled to himself, waving Harvey away. "Now, do me a favor: move on away from here. The last thing I need right now is some curious boy and his pony mucking things up worse than they already are."

Harvey nodded and called out to Fromp who was sitting a few feet behind him, "Come on, horsey, the man asked us nicely to move away from the entrance."

Fromp cocked his head in confusion and followed Harvey around the side of the library. Harvey stopped walking, turned around, and said, "Since going through the front door is no longer an option, I guess the easiest way in is through one of the windows that Gwen blew the glass out of. But it would probably be best for you to wait outside. Your presence might make it kind of tough for me to remain undetected. However, if things don't go according to plan, and you hear me yelling for help, don't hesitate to hop in and join the party."

Fromp sat down on his haunches and whined. Harvey scratched his ears and then climbed through the nearest window. Once in, he dashed behind a nearby bookshelf, hiding from a group of workers who were in the process of rebuilding the circulation desk.

Lying on the floor nearby was a stack of new library shelves to replace those damaged during Gwen's explosive reading session. Harvey picked up one and placed it on his shoulder, using it as a shield to hide his face and age from the workers as he searched for a particular section he hoped was still intact.

* * *

Minutes after Harvey warped from the warehouse, Gwen returned from her investigation of the roof. She saw no sign of what caused the large dent in the roof because the massive hound that made the distracting sound had just vanished with Harvey. Dexter Harris was still on the floor, weeping pitifully about his life's meaning being unfairly stolen from him. Gundy, meanwhile, was nervously straightening his shirt and coat when Gwen verbally lashed out at him.

"WHERE IS IT? WHY IS THE MIRROR NOT IN YOUR HAND WHERE I LEFT IT, GUNDY?" she demanded, eyes lit with fury.

"Miss Gwen," said Gundy falteringly, "it, it was that actor

there on the ground. He's a maniac. Came out of nowhere and slammed into me. Knocked the mirror clear out of my hand."

"I can clearly see that the actor's still here," Gwen replied a notch calmer but obviously still enraged, "but where's the mirror?"

"I was just about to tell you. During the attack, after the actor knocked me to the floor, that teenage kid you were talking to earlier ran by and scooped it up, and before I could do anything about it, he and this giant dog disappeared through a spinning doorway or somethin'. And just like that, they was gone."

"Gundy," Gwen said seething as she approached him and grabbed hold of his cheeks in a vice-like grip, "I asked you to do only one thing while I was gone. A very simple task, which was to safeguard the object that I gave you, and what did you do? You, my friend, let it be stolen right out of your hand by a skinny teenager half your size and strength."

"But, Miss Gwen," said a frightened Gundy, "it wasn't my fault. Like I said, that actor just hit me out of the blue."

"The time for excuses, my dear Gundy, has long passed," Gwen said with a cold stare that betrayed her calmer and pleasanter tone. "It seems that if I'm to ever right the wrongs of humanity, I will have to do it all by myself. Reliance on the inferior is fraught with folly so it seems.

"I regret to say that I will no longer require your services, for I need dependable workers, not excuse makers. All the pity, though, for I had such high hopes for you. But before you're dismissed from my service, I would like to know if the teenager said anything before he departed."

"He did, as a matter of fact. He said if you wanted the mirror back, you were to go to the um . . . I don't know . . . the island? No, that ain't it, but it was a place where you learned to read or somethin'. Does that mean anything to you?"

"Not your concern anymore, but thank you for the information." And with those words, Gwen released her grip on Gundy's cheeks and lightly flicked the bottom of his chin with her nails. His body responded by skyrocketing to the ceiling where it collided with one of the large lights, shattering the bulb into hundreds of showering sparks before he crashed back down to the floor. His broken body lay motionless, mere inches from death.

It was a violent and heartless action that the old Gwen would never have contemplated, and even the more recent Gwen would've shunned, for she had been quite fond of Gundy, but the attack by the Vapid and her near brush with death had taken its toll, resulting in a protective shell hardening around her heart, blocking any and all emotion from passing in or out. The ends were all that mattered now, and she was willing to use any means in order to achieve them.

"With a chauffeur no more, it seems that I must find another mode of conveyance," said Gwen brightly to herself, showing not even a modicum of remorse for Gundy who was moaning in pain.

Gwen pursed her lips, and as she did, two spheres of energy coalesced in the air before her. The floating spheres then elongated into oblong shapes, and before long, two large golden energy eagles hovered before her. With wingspans over six feet each, they alighted onto Gwen's outstretched arms. Their talons locked around her thin forearms, and as their massive wings paddled the air, the eagles lifted Gwen from the floor, gracefully carrying her across the soundstage.

Madora and the others had just arrived at the soundstage and were about to reach for the door handle when it was violently thrown open by two enormous golden eagles colliding with it.

Arrick caught a split-second glimpse of something large coming out of the doorway and instinctively ducked. Sheef, unfortunately, had turned around to check on Madora. When the door flung open, loudly banging against the metal siding of the building, he spun around, just in time for his eyes and nose to make boney contact with Gwen's knees. The blow knocked him backward onto the sidewalk. By the time he had rubbed enough pain out of his eyes to see what had hit him, Gwen was already hundreds of feet high, dangling like a hang glider pilot and soaring in the direction of the college campus.

"Is that . . . Gwen being carried by giant birds?" asked Sheef.

"It is. I think they're eagles, and based on the manner of her exit, I don't think she's in a very pleasant mood," Madora replied.

"Then she's probably after Harvey" said Arrick matter-of-factly.

"Let's hope you're right," said Madora, "because that would mean he's okay for the time being and likely in possession of the Narciss Glass. She wouldn't be after him for any other reason, and nothing but that would paint the scowl on her face that I observed when she flew past."

"That's the good news; the bad is that we've no idea where she's headed, and even if we did, there's no way we could get there in time to do anything about it," said Sheef, still staring at Gwen, who was now nothing more than a tiny black speck receding into a reddening sky.

"So once again my son's fighting alone," said Arrick despairingly.

"Hardly alone," said Madora. "Since I see no sign of Fromp, I think there's a good chance that he's with Harvey, and then there's always the Unseen, who's been with your boy since the very beginning."

Arrick looked down and nodded. A single teardrop fell to the ground.

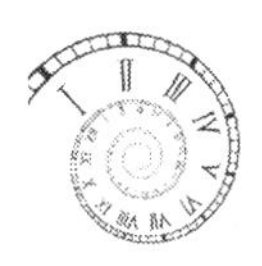

30

The group of students who had their picnic pawed and printed by Fromp and Harvey, had just recovered from the unexpected and unwelcomed disruption and settled down to try to salvage what was left of the day and their food, when a young man suddenly pointed to something gliding on the wind, rapidly approaching.

Twice stupefied in the span of an hour, the picnickers sat perplexedly paralyzed. With eyes affixed to the sky above, they tried their best to determine whether the thing gliding closer to them by the second was biological or mechanical. By the time they realized that it was a beautiful woman being held aloft by two shimmering eagles, they had only seconds to duck and flatten themselves on the blanket to avoid being hit, an action which destroyed what remained of their dinners and desserts.

The eagles carrying Gwen dimmed and then disappeared altogether, allowing their passenger to gently drop upon the grassy lawn on the other side of the picnickers. She took her first steps with determined purpose, with no hesitation or balance adjustment, and walked briskly to the library.

When she arrived at the blocked entrance, she gave no allowance for the guard to utter a single syllable of his spiel about there being no admittance due to ongoing repairs. Instead, she simply flicked her head to the left, which sent the guard cartwheeling multiple times in the same direction. With him out of the way, Gwen stared intensely at the barricades. The wood instantly disintegrated into minuscule fragments that were hurriedly ushered away by the afternoon breeze.

Only one of the workers attempted to stop Gwen to ask her why she was there. He, like the guard, was flipped aside, silencing him and everyone else who had any foolish notion of trying to interfere with the doings of the glamorous woman determinedly striding across the library.

Harvey peered through a gap between a row of books and the shelf above, providing him with an excellent view of Gwen's entrance. Even though she was eighty feet away, he could almost feel the heated scowl on her face, convincing him that it was probably best not to alert her to his location, but to let her find him in her own good time. He didn't have to wait long.

A halo of light surrounding her sent lurking aisle shadows scurrying away for nooks and crannies in which to hide. The halo suddenly stopped moving and turned in Harvey's direction. Gwen had arrived.

Harvey stood motionless at the end of an aisle that butted up against a wall. In order for the plan to have any chance of success, he needed to stay rooted where he was. If Gwen was determined to retrieve the Narciss Glass, she would have to come to him.

She stood motionless at the entrance to the aisle, leering at Harvey. The malicious glint in her eyes transitioned to one of scrutiny as she assessed the situation. Surveying the floor, shelves, and ceiling, she tried to figure out why Harvey had drawn her to this particular part of the library. She had the distinct feeling that she was walking into a trap, for it was all too easy: Harvey walled in at the end of a long aisle with no means of escape and holding the Narciss Glass in plain view.

Gwen attempted to again read Harvey's mind, but this time, her attempt to infiltrate his thoughts was blocked. After learning of her newfound ability, Harvey had erected a wall to keep out any mental intruders.

Using her newfound powers, it would be nothing for her to take the Narciss Glass from him, and this is precisely why she felt unnerved and suspected a trap. If she were to move down the aisle, it would be voluntarily placing her neck in the noose or knowingly biting the hook. Only a fool would take such obvious bait, and she of all people wasn't such a fool. Instead of moving toward Harvey, she held out her hand and folded back her fingers for him to come to her.

The golden energy eagles that had carried Gwen to the library reappeared, hovering just above Harvey. With sharp talons extended, they suddenly dropped down. Slices of fire laid open the flesh of his shoulders and back, but this was only one of the eagles, the other grabbed hold of the Narciss Glass and began flapping aggressively to tug it free from his hand.

Merely an hour ago, Harvey wouldn't have stood a chance against Gwen and her powers, but things had dramatically changed. For one, he was no longer bereft of hope. The Unseen had once again shared His thoughts, which to Harvey, was a reawakening of his awareness to the Unseen's presence and care, which had never left him, even when he was at his lowest and feeling alone and abandoned. For another, his body was crackling with Kreen nectar, infusing his muscles with rippling strength and enhancing his thought-connection with the Unseen.

Though still feeling the acute pain of his wounds, Harvey fired a thought at the eagles. The birds' wings immediately snapped backward and broke free from their bodies. Their heads both slumped forward, followed by their bodies disintegrating into tiny pinpoints of dancing light.

Gwen's brimming confidence momentarily waned. An expression of shock stole across her face. She assessed the situation again in light of what was clearly a more powerful adversary. Her eyes scanned the bookshelves all the way down to Harvey. She studied his blood-trickling wounds before letting her stare rest upon his face. She was again surprised, for it wasn't what she expected. Instead of a steely resolve to fight, she observed an expression of vulnerable compassion. Furthermore, she didn't detect any guile or deceit. She still suspected a trap, but whatever Harvey had devised, he apparently thought it was for her own good.

Gwen vacillated. She was prepared to do battle. A tenacious hostility had been aroused by the Vapid attack that nearly killed her, which was further fed by Harvey's resistance to her attempts at recruiting him and his taking of the Narciss Glass. The combined reactive effect had been a surging anger which she had never felt before, opening the door for her to commit the type of violence that heretofore she thought herself incapable of committing.

If Harvey was poised to fight, Gwen could've easily let her anger pour forth with a matter and energy onslaught, but he wasn't. Instead, he stood there in opposition, but not because he desired to battle a foe, but because he wanted to help a friend.

Gwen's hard edges softened. She sighed deeply before speaking. "I don't know what you're up to but . . . Harvey, I'd rather not hurt you. Please, just hand over the Narciss Glass and allow me to complete my work." As she said this, she reached out and opened her right hand.

"You know I can't do that, Gwen," Harvey replied, grimacing at the pain still radiating from his shoulders and back. "I know you mean well, but you're mistaken and deceived, and trust me when I tell you that I know what it is to be deceived. Your deception, though, isn't from invisible Insips implanting twisted thoughts in your mind. The source of your deception is your very own pride and overconfidence in your abilities. Gwen, you're lying to yourself, but you can't see it because you're the one who's spinning the lie."

"Am I now?" Gwen asked rhetorically, the lines and edges of her face once again hardening. "And what exactly, if I may ask, is the lie that I have spun and caught myself in?"

Harvey took a step forward. "Simply this, you believe that your abilities — your intellect and understanding of science, specifically how to manipulate its laws and principles to your advantage — are enough to solve mankind's deepest problems and meet his most profound needs. But, Gwen, these problems and needs go far beyond the reach of science and what any man or woman, regardless of intellect or skill, can fix, because they're unseen matters of the heart, which can only be solved by something unseen. As talented as you are, you cannot and should not attempt to solve and meet these needs. Such actions are only fit for one, and that one is not you. You simply don't qualify for such a role. Since the beginning of recorded history, humans have tried to play such a role, and it has always gone badly for the one attempting to play it, as well as those in close proximity to the attempt."

"I won't contradict what you said, Harvey," said Gwen. "History unequivocally confirms this, but there is one serious flaw in your reasoning. I, in fact, actually do meet the qualifications for being such a 'one' as you put it.

"Like I mentioned before, I'm not human. I began as nothing more than an idea in the mind of a screenwriter, and until recently remained as such, but as you witnessed, I emerged from the unseen world of the Phantasian, taking on flesh and entering into this world of yours. I'm not from here, Harvey. I came from an otherworldly magical and mythical realm, which is why I'm not bound by any human limitations."

Harvey slowly shook his head, letting the Narciss Glass fall to his side. "Gwen, you're human enough, more so than you realize. You were created by the mind of a human, and as such, cannot escape the frailty and flaws common to every man and woman who have ever drawn breath. And in a very short period of time, you've begun to display some of humanity's worst traits."

"Really?" Gwen replied with a facial twitch, that if it had been made by an animal would've qualified as a snarl. "Hoping for a better world for everyone in it is a bad trait?" With anger overshadowing her suspicion, she took two steps forward.

"Not at all," Harvey replied, "but the pride and your growing violent callousness towards innocent people is. I saw what you did to the guard and the worker."

"They were in my way, and I haven't the time nor the inclination to stop and explain how my vision for humanity will benefit them personally, and even if I did, they wouldn't have the intellectual capacity to grasp what I'm offering."

"You've just proven my point," Harvey said.

"ENOUGH OF THIS!" Gwen shouted, her voice rattling the bookshelves and dislodging bits of plaster from the ceiling. She then raised both of her arms, and as before, two energy spheres coalesced in front of her hands. This time, however, they were significantly larger, increasing in size by the second. Soon the spheres overlapped and merged into one, its poles kissing floor and ceiling.

Whereas her energy clouds and spheres had always been gold and transparent, this new one was opaque, composed of swirling oranges, reds, and yellows. The intensity of the light was impossible to look upon. As Harvey turned away, a memory flashed across his mind's eye. He had seen a photo of such an orb in his science textbook, though it was suspended in space. Gwen had somehow manipulated hydrogen into helium, generating a miniature sun in the middle of a university library.

Seconds after the sun's birth, a heat shield slowly radiated outward, its speed reduced by Gwen to a tiny fraction of its actual velocity in space. Just killing Harvey wasn't enough. Her flaring anger had obliterated any and all moral inhibitions. Before Harvey died, she would inflict terror upon him with the slowly moving, searing heat.

Ignition to flame was the fate of every combustible object the shield encountered. After thirty seconds, the books and shelving of the "A" and "B" authors were reduced to ashes, which meant that in about five minutes, the heat and flame would reach the "W's" and "Y's", and then, Harvey. He was searching his mind for any thought from the Unseen when he felt his body beginning to slide in Gwen's direction. It felt as if he had fallen into a stream, caught in a mild but persistent current. He dropped the Narciss Glass and reached out for the nearest bookshelf, but its varnished wood was too slick to keep his fingers from skidding off and away.

The miniature sun's gravity pulled Harvey closer. Once again, he grasped for anything to latch onto to, grabbing hold of dozens of books from the "R" section which tumbled onto the floor, having no effect on his backward slide.

There was one last hope. Harvey drew in a deep breath and calmed his nerves as much as possible given the situation, and then thought with every one of his brain neurons against the pull. With a face reddening like that of a powerlifter, he thought-fought ferociously with the sucking gravity.

The slide slowed momentarily, but as lungs need breath, so too does thinking. The break in his concentration lasted only a second or two, but it was enough, for in that thin sliver of time, the sucking current reasserted its dominance. With panic returning, Harvey knew there wasn't time to calm his nerves and refocus his thoughts, so he let go, allowing the current's will to have its way with him.

Death was now a certainty, and though he had failed to execute the Unseen's plan, he was at peace. He had accepted the terms of his demise and would make no attempt to fight them. He glanced over at the bookshelf and saw that he was moving past the "O's". The heat shield was inching ever closer, slowing consuming the alphabet.

Like a light switch turning off, the brightness and heat were suddenly gone. The current slowed and stopped. The smoke from the burning books was so thick that it was impossible for Harvey to see what was occurring on the other side, but he clearly heard two things: the shriveling snaps of burning wood and book, as well as someone moaning and gasping for air.

After a minute or two, the smoke cleared enough for Harvey to see the source of the second sound. Fromp was casually sitting on his haunches, his long tongue dangling out the side of his mouth. Twenty feet in front of him was Gwen, lying face down on the floor.

31

Alerted by the chaos and sounds of shouting, Fromp had jumped through the window and chased down the noise. When he saw Harvey trapped and about to be pulled into the encroaching flames, he rushed at Gwen, leaping at her back and breaking her concentration. She was sent flying down the aisle, finally landing in the middle of the "H's".

Though the bookshelves were still smoldering, the intense heat was gone. Harvey walked down the aisle, but then stopped, riveted in place by what he saw occurring around Gwen. His memory flashed back to when she first visited the library and absorbed the contents of hundreds of science books within minutes by lightly brushing her fingers across the books' spines. Touching each book caused a soft burst of colored light to emerge and snake its way into her head and mind.

This time, though, hundreds of light strands from both sides of the aisle emerged from the "G's" and "L's" and everything in between, but without her hands anywhere near the books.

Although it was Fromps' ramming collision that knocked her to the floor, it was now the weighty overload of multitudes of stories that kept her pinned down in the middle of the fiction aisle. Harvey couldn't determine if she was conscious but knew she was still alive by the slight jerking and shuddering of her arms and legs.

He still had no idea why he and Gwen were here. Harvey had simply obeyed the Unseen's thought to bring her to the stories, which was accompanied by an image of this exact aisle.

Harvey moved down the aisle and when he reached Gwen, he gently rolled her over. Her closed eyelids were vigorously vibrating as colored ribbons continued to weave through the air and into her head. He had absolutely no idea what to do. His natural instinct was to provide some type of aid, but not knowing if she was in distress or not, he had no idea if his actions might make things worse. After three minutes, the last ribbon emerged, drifted, and vanished.

Gwen's eyes flew open, and Harvey knew immediately that a significant change had occurred. The fierce, callous expression was gone, replaced by the curious and wondrous one she displayed when he first met her. She looked ten years younger, as if she had traveled back in time and recaptured the enthusiasm and hopeful innocence of youth.

She slowly stood to her feet, staring wide-eyed at Harvey, her lower lids full and threatening to spill over at any second. In a quavering voice, she said, "Harvey, I'm . . . I don't know what to say other than I'm so sorry for what I've done — how I treated you and . . . what I almost did just now. You were right all along, but I couldn't see it before . . . why I was doing what I was doing and where it would all lead. It's so clear now. I was . . . what did you say before? I think you called me blind, blind to what I was doing because of my pride. You were so right . . . but how did you know? And how did you know to bring me here?

Before Harvey had a chance to answer, Gwen answered her own question. "It was the Unseen, wasn't it? He told you to bring me here. Of course," she said to herself, "how would anyone else know that only stories could free me from my own deception and reveal the truth."

"Uh, Gwen," said Harvey gently, "Would you mind explaining what just happened and why the Unseen wanted me to lure you here?"

"You don't know?" she asked surprised. "Harvey, I apologize. I assumed that you knew, but then again how could you? How could anyone understand what I just went through without experiencing it? I'll try my best."

Harvey nodded.

"It was the stories," Gwen said with the same beaming excitement she had exhibited when first coming to the library and discovering the world of science. "They were the key, for in every one of them the main characters are all on the same quest or longing after the same things. They're all yearning for meaning and purpose, pining for perfect love, or trying to rectify a great injustice, and in almost all of them, the quest is accomplished, the meaning is revealed, the perfect is love found, the justice is done, concluding with some version of happily ever after. But the reality is, and this is what is so obvious to me now, is that such absolute and complete fulfillment only occurs in fiction, in made-up stories. Real life simply doesn't deliver the weighty meaning, the satisfying love, or the realized justice that all humans desperately search for their entire lives. The deepest and most profound desires can't be fully met in this world by any experience or relationship, no matter how good it proves to be.

"What humanity is crying out for is something transcendent, something that goes beyond and above physical existence, beyond anything humans can create. I suppose," she said with a smile, "that every man and woman is longing for an 'unseen' answer to the riddle of life, and I now realize that this unseen is not a mere abstract idea, but more like a person, who can be known and related to."

"You're telling me," asked Harvey, clearly astonished, "that all this was revealed to you by a bunch of stories?"

Gwen nodded like a little girl on Christmas morning and then burst out, "Harvey, the Unseen is real!"

"Yes He is," Harvey said warmly.

"But what I was attempting to do," said Gwen turning somber, "creating a paradise all by myself while completely ignoring the Unseen . . . It would've ended in tyranny and oppression. Mankind wouldn't have been liberated; it would've been enslaved. I was already hurting those who opposed me, including those who care most about me."

Harvey didn't respond, for what could he add to what Gwen had already said? Instead, he embraced her, and as he held her, he could feel the moisture of fallen tears seeping through his shirt.

Gwen abruptly broke free from the embrace and stepped back, a serious expression stealing over her. "The Narciss Glass must be removed from this world and destroyed. What it does to people . . . Harvey, that poor actor. It turned him inward to be consumed by his own selfish nature. He was already a prisoner to himself, and if he had continued to peer into that object he would have completely wasted away. I need to destroy it, take it somewhere where no one can ever find it.

Gwen reached out and gently touched Harvey's cheek and said softly, "Which means I must do it alone."

Harvey pulled away from her hand. "What do you mean you have to do it alone? Gwen, we came back here to keep Millud from using that mirror and hopefully destroy it, but we came back together. There's no way, especially now, that I'm letting you do whatever you have in mind by yourself."

"I appreciate the sentiment," Gwen said in the same soft tone, "but I know what needs to be done, and besides, you have a life waiting for—"

Gwen interrupted herself in mid-sentence, a look of panic washing over her face.

"What is it?" asked Harvey concernedly.

"The others! Harvey, I completely forgot. I sent them inside a water tower! By now they might be . . ." Her words trailed off as they were muffled by tears. Harvey made a move to embrace her again and try to console her, but saw that Fromp was already at her side, acting as if he had heard and understood what she said. He nuzzled her with his snout. Overwhelmed by the grief at what she had done, Gwen paid little attention to the first three snout nudges, but as they became more forceful, she finally withdrew her face from her hands and looked at the persistent warp-hound.

Fromp responded to her acknowledgment with a high-pitched whine. He then walked in front of her and reared up on his back legs, placing his massive paws on her shoulders. Gwen buckled under the weight but managed to remain standing. Following a second whine, he licked her from chin to hairline.

Harvey approached and stroked Fromp's head. "I believe he's letting you know that they're all okay, and I suspect he played a significant role in their welfare.

With a loud sniffle and eye wipe, Gwen asked, "Do you really think so? Harvey, I could never forgive myself if—"

"There's no need to worry; I just saw an image of them in Fromp's mind. Everyone's fine, other than their clothes being soaked.

Gwen smiled broadly and kissed Fromp on the top of his snout. He responded with a vigorous wag and a loud woof.

"Now that we no longer need to worry about their safety, why don't we get back to what you were saying about doing it alone. Gwen, whatever you're planning, I won't let you shoulder it all by yourself because—"

Cutting his words short, Gwen said, "You should know by now that you can't stop me. Harvey, I've made a terrible mistake, and that's why I must be the one to correct it."

With a soft smile that Harvey hadn't seen since they first arrived in 1930's Hollywood and with watery eyes, Gwen said brokenly, "Goodbye, Harvey, and thank you for never giving up on me. I need you to say goodbye to the others for me, and please tell Sheef and Madora, though our time was short, I felt like they had been my very own loving parents for years."

"But, Gwen, you can't—"

Those were the only words Harvey was able to utter before Gwen raised her hand and gently picked him and Fromp up, placing them upon two golden energy cushions. They were then sent gliding through the library's entrance, coming to rest upon the grass outside. Most of the workers in the library had fled when Gwen had created the miniature sun, but the few curious gawkers who still remained were ushered out in the same manner as Harvey and Fromp.

Once down, Harvey immediately turned back toward the library as the front doors slammed shut and locked. Fromp, who had jumped down from his floating cushion before it touched down, was already at one of the windows, peering in with front paws resting on the window sill. Harvey soon joined him, looking at Gwen through the glass panes of a newly installed window.

She had once again conjured up a sun, but unlike the first time, it quickly aged, turning red and multiplying in size, and though the red giant completely filled the room and engulfed Gwen, she wasn't harmed by the heat. This couldn't, however, be said about the interior of the building which burst into flame. The panes of the new window buckled and then melted, their transparent molten flow dripping down the library's walls. Before jumping back from the expanding wave of heat, Harvey witnessed the sun collapse in upon itself, contracting into an infinitesimally small point of incredible density.

A tearing sound was heard by everyone outside as the dense pinpoint ripped a hole in the fabric of space. The gravitational pull of the newly formed black hole sucked the air from the room, extinguishing the fires and drawing what was left of the charred furniture and clouds of black ashes into it. Using her powers to momentarily resist the pull, Gwen looked over at Harvey, who had stumbled back to the glassless window, and smiled.

She stopped contending with the gravitational pull and let herself and the Narciss Glass in her hand to be taken by it. The last thing Harvey saw was Gwen rapidly compressed smaller and smaller until she was invisible to the naked eye.

Once she was gone, the black hole snapped shut and everything in the library stopped moving. Harvey continued to stare at the place where Gwen had been standing only seconds before. After a few minutes, he wiped his nose with the back of his hand and said to Fromp, "What do you say we go and get the others and warp back to our own time. I've had enough adventure to last a lifetime and just want to get back home where everything's boring and predictable."

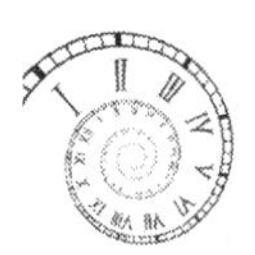

32

Sheef, Madora, and Arrick entered the soundstage, which now resembled a cratered battlefield. Their entrance caught the attention of all but two. Completely oblivious to what had occurred around him, Dexter Harris was curled up in a fetal position in the middle of the soundstage, moaning and crying out for just one more look into the mirror, while Millud, who was still perched in his director's chair, was grinning and dreaming of his life as a famous Hollywood director, totally unaware that that particular ship had already sailed and sunk, and that the only thing he would be directing in the future was a mop and bucket.

Madora and the others were worriedly speculating about the fate of Harvey and discussing a plan for what to do next, when a warp hole popped open to their right. Harvey and Fromp hopped out, directly into relieved embraces.

Sheef was the first to speak and asked concernedly, "But what about Gwen? Where is she?"

"Gone," Harvey said solemnly, "to a place we can't follow.

Though you'll be happy to know, she turned back in the end and single-handedly destroyed the Narciss Glass, but I think she also destroyed herself in the process." Staring unblinkingly across the soundstage, he added, "No one could've survived that."

Fifteen minutes later, Sheef stood speechless in the wake of Harvey's narration of what had transpired at the library. "I agree," said Arrick. "It would be impossible for anyone to survive that, but then again, we don't really know what she was capable of."

"Even so," Madora responded, clearly moved by the actions of Gwen, "as gifted as she was, I just can't imagine . . . You know her sacrifice wasn't just for us. She did it for everyone on this planet and beyond."

They were quiet for many minutes, processing what Gwen had done and beginning to grieve her absence. Arrick was the first to break the silent tension by saying, "It seems the time has come for us to warp back to the present."

"Mission accomplished," Sheef added with a nod. "Though I can't believe that we actually did it. I mean, I always knew there was a chance, but it was looking pretty bleak there for a while, especially when we were treading frigid water in that tower."

"Truth is," said Harvey, "there was a whole lot more than just 'we' involved in this crazy journey, from the beginning to what now appears to be the end."

"You're right there, kid," Sheef replied with a playful tussle of Harvey's hair."

"So . . ." said Arrick, beaming with fatherly pride at his son's words, "how should we proceed in getting out of here and back to our own time and place?"

"Same way we came," Madora answered. "Back through the Phantasian. There should still be enough remnants of our trail for Akeila to detect and follow, and it won't take very long to get back, seeing as this time you'll have no reason to linger in any of the three movie worlds."

Harvey blinked and stared questioningly at Madora. "What do you mean by 'you'll'? Madora, you're coming with us, aren't you?"

"Not this time," Sheef said in broken and crumbling words. "It seems that our little adventure together has finally reached its conclusion. You should've known that the fun couldn't go on forever," he added with a chuckle to hold back the tears. "Besides, you've got yourself a whole new life just waiting for you in the future."

Harvey looked over at Madora and then back at Sheef, clearly perplexed. "Sheef, I . . . I don't understand. Why would you want to stay here?"

"Because I've waited my whole life for that special someone to come along, and I had all but given up on finding her, but then it happened, hit me out of the blue, and in Egypt of all places."

Madora stepped up beside Sheef, taking his hand in hers. And I've waited a bit longer. No comment, smart guy," Madora said as she squeezed his hand.

"Okay. I get it. It's been pretty obvious from day one that there were sparks between you two, but what does that have to do with not going back?" asked Harvey.

"It has everything to do with it," Sheef replied. "Harvey, what we've done here in the 1930s has already rewritten the future. Since the Narciss Glass is no longer a threat, it will never be used in Millud's movie, which means millions of people won't be manipulated by it and turn away from the thoughts of the Unseen. And Ecclon's—"

"Clouds won't dim and die," Harvey finished. Harvey thought about the implications of Sheef's words and asked, "We won't ever meet in the future, will we, Sheef?"

Sheef shook his head and said softly, "No, kid, we won't. Arrick will never warp to Earth, and I'll never travel in the opposite direction to Ecclon and meet Bellock and the other Flurn Elders, who, incidentally, should be alive and well now.

"But that would also mean that you and Madora would never meet."

"And now you understand why we can't go with you," Sheef replied. "Once you've found real love, you'd be a fool not to do everything in your power to keep it. If I were to warp back to the future, not only would I never meet Madora, but even worse, I wouldn't have any memory of ever having met her."

"Does that mean my memories . . . Are you saying that I won't remember any of this?"

Sheef nodded. "It will be like when Gwen left the Phantasian. This life of yours will be completely erased, a clean slate for a new one to be written upon."

"But, I don't want—"

"I know," interrupted Sheef with tears in his eyes, "neither do I, but all stories, even the really good ones, must eventually come to end, but it doesn't mean that there aren't new ones to be told, and I have a feeling you're going to really like the next one."

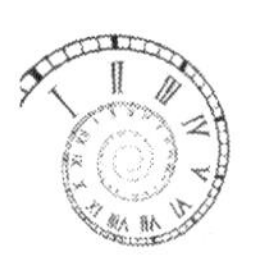

33

Harvey awoke in a large canopied bed in the middle of an ornately decorated room. He was trying to get his bearings and connect his last memory with his present reality when a beautiful, resplendent woman walked in and threw open the curtains.

Bright light tumbled in, rolling up the walls and across the ceiling. Harvey squinted until his eyes adjusted and then glanced out the window. Billowing, luminescent clouds were drifting southward on the breeze, pulsating vibrant yellow and white light as they moved.

"Time to get up, sleepy head," said the woman smiling. "You don't want to sleep away this day. You only turn thirteen once, and it's your first day as an Ecclonian prince in training. Now that you are of age, you'll be allowed to travel with your father to Council Gorge, which I don't need to remind you is exactly where you two are going this evening for the first gathering of the year. Isn't it exciting? You'll finally get to meet Bellock and the other Flurn Elders we've talked so much about. Remember, your father promised to take you to see Gnarl the Petrified, whose proverbs you've been memorizing since you were in diapers."

Harvey stared at the woman. For a moment his thoughts were muddied. Wisps of memories lingered briefly before dissipating and vanishing altogether. Everything was suddenly clear and Harvey smiled broadly.

"Mother. . . you're. . ."

"I'm what?" she said laughing. I don't think somebody's woken up quite yet."

Harvey rubbed his face with his hands and said. "It's my birthday, isn't it? So, what'd you get me?" he asked grinning.

"Oh, now you're awake. Well, I was actually hoping you would ask."

Harvey's mother opened the door and spoke to one of the palace servants.

"Yes, but of course, your Majesty," Harvey heard from the hallway.

A few minutes later, Arrick opened the door. An indigo blur shot across the floor and onto the bed, where it buried Harvey under a barrage of slobbery licks.

"It's a warp-hound puppy," said his father entering the bedroom. You've been asking for one forever."

"Harvey giggled wildly as the puppy attacked his exposed toes.

"So, have any ideas for a name?" asked his mother.

Harvey thought for a moment and then replied with the first word that popped into his head. “Fromp. I don’t know why, but it just seems like a good name for him. What do you think of that, Fromp?”

The warp-hound puppy reared up on his back legs and barked.

ACKNOWLEDGEMENTS

Once again, I would like to thank the gang of encouragers, influencers, teachers, contributors, editors, and friends. There are too many to list here, but you know who you are. And a special thanks to my lovely wife, Terri Michelle. I am forever grateful to all of you. Without your involvement, the journey to Ecclon would have never begun.

ABOUT THE AUTHOR

R Duncan Williams has been in the education field for over twenty-five years as a speaker, trainer, writer, and teacher. Along the way, he has crafted numerous stories for use in and out of the classroom. Williams currently resides in Austin, Texas, with his wife and two sons. Be sure to read the first two books in the Thinkwave series.

To learn more about R Duncan Williams, visit his website at www.rduncanwilliams.com

Made in the USA
Lexington, KY
24 October 2019

56001704R00184